One Perfect Dance

A TWIST UPON A REGENCY TALE
BOOK 2

BY JUDE KNIGHT

DRAGONBLADE PUBLISHING, INC.

ARE YOU SIGNED UP FOR DRAGONBLADE'S BLOG?

You'll get the latest news and information on exclusive giveaways, exclusive excerpts, coming releases, sales, free books, cover reveals and more.

Check out our complete list of authors, too!

No spam, no junk. That's a promise!

Sign Up Here

www.dragonbladepublishing.com

Dearest Reader;

Thank you for your support of a small press. At Dragonblade Publishing, we strive to bring you the highest quality Historical Romance from some of the best authors in the business. Without your support, there is no 'us', so we sincerely hope you adore these stories and find some new favorite authors along the way.

Happy Reading!

CEO, Dragonblade Publishing

ADDITIONAL DRAGONBLADE BOOKS BY
AUTHOR JUDE KNIGHT

A Twist Upon a Regency Tale, The Series
Lady Beast's Bridegroom (Book 1)
One Perfect Dance (Book 2)

ABOUT THE BOOK

Regina Paddimore puts her dreams of love away with other girlish things when she weds her father's friend to escape a vile suitor who tries to force a marriage. Sixteen years later, and two years a widow, she seeks a husband who might help her fulfill another dream—to have her own child.

Elijah Ashby escapes his abusive stepfamily as soon as he comes of age, off to see the world. Letters from his childhood friend Regina are all that connects him to England. Sixteen years later, now a famous travel writer, the news she is a widow brings him home.

Sparks fly between them when they meet again. Regina begins to hope for love as well as babies. Elijah will be happy just to have her at his side. However, Elijah's stepbrothers are determined to do everything they can—lie, cheat, kidnap, even murder—so that one of them can marry Regina and take her wealth for themselves.

Love and friendship must conquer hatred and spite before Elijah and Regina can be together.

Chapter One

London, April 1802

ELIJAH ASHBY WAS polishing his stepbrother's boots. Choosing this task first was a calculated risk. Dilly was more likely to find a sneaky way to cause him pain if the boots did not shine to his exacting standards. Compared to his older stepbrother, who would just clout Elijah if he was late cleaning the grate in his room.

While Elijah polished, he entertained himself with visions of their reaction the day of his birthday, when he would tell them their skivvy and whipping boy was leaving.

Elijah had started as valet to his stepbrothers when he was fifteen, not long after his mother married Major Deffew. "Good training for the boy," the major told Elijah's mother. "You know he will have to earn his own living one day, my dear. Not as a valet, perhaps, but hard work will be the making of him. If you will excuse my saying so, Mrs. Deffew, if his father had not lived the wastrel life of a younger son, you and he would be much better off."

Elijah's mother could have pointed out that the major's sons, both older than Elijah, had never done a day's work in their lives. However, she said nothing, a habit that came from years of not criticizing Elijah's father, who was inclined to be nasty in his cups, which was most of the time.

Elijah became valet to his stepbrothers.

From the day he cleaned out his first grate, the Deffew men had mangled his surname to Ash Boy, though not when his mother was around to hear. Elijah retaliated by silently renaming them, in his turn.

Matthew was the older of the two, ten years Elijah's senior, with pretensions to excellence in all gentlemanly sports. He was happy to give his opinion on any topic and expected Elijah to take his frequently erroneous facts as gospel truth. Elijah's private name for him, Mouth Almighty, fitted him perfectly.

David was two years younger than Matthew, and fancied himself as a connoisseur of fashion, a veritable Tulip. Nothing was more important to him than his clothes, many of which he had designed himself, but none of his creations quite hit the mark. Elijah thought of him as Daffadowndilly, the country name for a daffodil.

The work had not been so bad at first. Many of the tasks were obvious, which was just as well, for he was offered no training. He had been punished for every mistake, but Elijah had always learned quickly. He was also not too proud to take advice from his stepfather's valet and others in the neighboring houses.

Mouth and Dilly were careful not to give their stepmother cause to complain to their father. Whatever his faults, the major—Major Defect, as Elijah thought of him—demanded that his sons show respect to his wife.

Elijah examined the shine on the leather. *Yes. Good enough.* He placed the boots carefully back on their custom-made stand and left the dressing room by the door into the servants' passage to complete another couple of tasks before Dilly rang for him again when he was ready to dress for his ride. The man had his coats and boots made so tight he could not get into them without help. In any case, Dilly was of the opinion that being dressed by a valet added to his consequence.

Elijah went down the narrow servant stairs slowly, pausing on each step. Long ago, Dilly had tripped him on these very stairs. His own clumsiness, the brothers had claimed, giving each other an alibi for being elsewhere at the time.

Elijah's head injury and badly broken leg lost them a valet for several months and annoyed their father by distracting their stepmother's attention from the man. After that, they confined themselves to the occasional buffet, sly trip, and near-constant disparaging remarks.

The leg healed shorter than the other and ached when Elijah was on his feet for too long or when he hurried up or down stairs. Far too often, these days. As if being valet for two men was not enough, he took over the work of managing the house and maids when his mother fell ill and Matthew Deffew's wife ran home to her father, a wealthy merchant who refused to hand her back.

Not that Mouth tried over much to retrieve her. He had been forced into the marriage after being caught with the girl in his bed, and he now had the benefit of her dowry without the inconvenience of her tears and sulks. He occasionally made noises about seeking custody of the boy child she produced a few months later. *No chance of that. Her father can afford better lawyers.*

Elijah had been forced to give up his studies. He was doing lessons with the local vicar to prepare him to pass the entrance exam for Oxford, but the extra work left him no time.

When his mother died, a little over a year ago, things got worse, so much so that he'd run away. But Major Defect set the constables on him, and he was dragged back to the Deffew house and beaten for his attempt at freedom.

After that, they'd heaped more tasks on him, until he was doing the work of three servants. For six more days.

Elijah reached the bottom of the stairs and hurried to Major Defect's study. He had just time enough to clean the fireplace and reset the fire before the major finished his second coffee of the morning and moved to his desk to read the newspaper and his correspondence.

Elijah slipped the ash into the bucket and laid a new fire. He carried the bucket over to draw one of the curtains. Then he stood by the desk to catch up with the headlines on the front page of the newspaper. If the major came in, Elijah would pull back the other curtain, as if that had been his purpose on this side of the room.

The *Morning Chronicle* was on top, which was disappointing. The front page was mostly given over to advertisements. He preferred the *Morning Herald*, which generally gave news from the European newspapers on its front page.

He did not dare pick the newspaper up. It would be hard to touch the freshly ironed paper without leaving marks that would alert Major Defect to his visual larceny. He scanned quickly down the page. No point in reading the theater news. He had never been—though he had read and enjoyed *The School for Scandal*, which was on at the Theater Royal. Someone was offering a reward for the recovery of a lost watch. They must really want it back, for the reward was more money than Elijah had ever seen at once. He wished he had found it. He could do with five guineas.

Nothing of interest. He might as well move on and do the fireplace in the parlor.

The morning correspondence also sat on the desk, and as Elijah was about to leave, his eye was caught by his own name on an envelope. *Mr. Elijah Ashby.*

He snatched it up and put it inside his coat. He did not recognize the hand—neat, almost delicate, writing. He had no idea who might send him a letter. But he was confident that, if he left it for Major Defect, he would never hear of it again.

He managed to snatch a moment to hide it in his little attic room before the three Deffew men left the breakfast room.

Dilly called him to wrestle the popinjay into jacket and boots. Mouth came in while Elijah was buffing the left toe, which Dilly was certain had been dimmed by Elijah's hand on it during the struggle.

"You should have worn gloves, you fool," Dilly was complaining.

It was useless to point out that Elijah's gloves no longer fit his hands, any more than his other clothes had stretched to cover his growing body. They were all hand-me-downs from his stepbrothers, and Elijah had grown bigger than them a full two years ago. The major and his sons didn't care to spend anything on Elijah. Asking for clothing, even a pair of gloves, would only fetch him a lecture about gratitude, if not a beating.

At least he had a roof over his head, and the food was plentiful. And he could last six more days.

"Never mind, Ash Boy." Mouth waved a newspaper. "Regina Kingsley is making her come out at a ball next Tuesday. Remember Miss Kingsley?"

Elijah remembered Regina Kingsley. She was the daughter of the manor in the village where he'd lived with his mother when his father was alive, and after until his mother married Major Defect. Four years younger than Elijah, Regina had looked like a delicate fairy, as if at any moment she would spread wings and fly. But she was as bold and as brave as any boy, and well able to hold her own as one of the youngest of a tribe of village children who swarmed across the countryside when free from their lessons and chores, looking for fun and adventure.

Ginny Kingsley. Somehow, as one of the older lads, it had fallen to Elijah to make sure that the viscount's daughter was returned home each day in one piece, not visibly battered. Despite the four-year difference in their age, they'd had a lot in common. They'd both loved to read, especially books of adventure. They both wanted to travel and see the world. They were both lonely children with fond, if ineffectual, mothers and largely absent fathers.

Then, when Ginny was ten, her mother suddenly noticed her daughter was *socializing with urchins*, as the viscountess put it. Suddenly, she was confined to the manor, able only to leave under strict escort, and dressed in expensive silks even when accompanying her mother on a visit to the tenants.

Elijah wished he could see her again. She must have grown into a lovely young woman.

"Why would you want to see Regina Kingsley again?" Dilly's question was so in-tune with Elijah's thoughts that he nearly answered it. But Dilly was, of course, talking to Mouth, and he hadn't finished. "She was a stuck-up brat when we were in that village. Thought she was better than everyone else just because her father was a viscount. I don't imagine she has improved any in the past six years."

Mouth grinned, as he propped himself on the corner of Dilly's dressing table. "Now that is where you would be wrong. I saw her yesterday, riding with her parents in Hyde Park. She is not bad. I think we should try to get an invitation to the ball. After all, Father does know the viscount."

Dilly snorted. "The viscount hired Father to gather investors for a canal project and fired him when Father tried to blackmail him. I can't see the viscount doing Father any favors. Anyway. I cannot think of a single reason why I should want to go to a ball for a chit like Regina Kingsley." He gave Elijah a kick to push him away from the boot. "That's good enough, Ash Boy. Leave them alone."

Elijah wanted to hear what else they had to say. Instead of taking his dismissal, he began picking up Dilly's discarded cravats and the other items of clothing strewn around the bed chamber. His stepbrothers went on talking as if he was not there.

"It was a waste of six months," Dilly continued grumbling. "Worse than wasted. We left that village with a heap of debt, our landlady as father's new wife, and Ash Boy."

"I can give you a reason to go to Miss Kingsley's ball," Mouth said, ignoring the rest of Dilly's grumbling. "I'll give you ten thousand good reasons. Well, perhaps not quite that much since I only want to talk the chit into loving me and be paid off. Even if I didn't already have a wife, curse her, I wouldn't want to marry a baby out of the schoolroom, especially a spoiled aristocrat."

He suddenly noticed Elijah. "Get out, Ash Boy. I am going riding. Make sure my horse is at the door in five minutes."

Elijah left, though he would have liked to hear what else they had to say.

He heard Dilly tell Mouth, "I have better address than you."

Mouth replied, "I don't care which one of us does it, as long as we share the money. Once I can get some funds behind me to pay better lawyers than my father-in-law, I'm taking my son back." One of them closed the door, and Elijah had to go downstairs.

He remembered the viscount as a smart man. Surely, he would see straight through the Deffew brothers, and keep them a mile from his only daughter?

Even so, Elijah fretted about the brothers' plans as he carried on with the day's tasks. It put his own letter right out of his head, and he didn't remember it until early afternoon when all the Deffew men were out, the cook and butler were both having their naps, and Elijah was taking ten minutes to himself in his little room, where he had been making a pair of pantaloons that actually fitted him. He had managed to get the cloth for a few pennies because it was soiled, had laundered it himself, and had managed to cut three pairs from it. Pantaloons were the last item he needed for his new job.

He had the new position thanks to his old friend and teacher, the vicar. On the day after his twenty-first birthday, he was boarding a ship with his new employer, to leave on a world tour. By nightfall that day, he would have sailed down the Thames and out to sea, but not before giving himself the pleasure of saying goodbye to his persecutors.

He'd learned to sew and make alterations as part of his work as a valet, and he thought the fit of his new pantaloons, waistcoat, and coat was not too bad. Not fashionably tight, of course, because he was going to be a working man, after all. But neat and tidy.

He knotted the thread and there, he was finished. Three pairs of pantaloons, a single coat (bought second-hand from a barrow and refurbished with new buttons and some deft sewing for a better fit), two waistcoats remade from some Mouth had thrown out, and half a dozen shirts.

He went to put his sewing kit away in his drawer and saw the letter.

He glanced at the door. He probably still had a few minutes. He slipped his scissors under the seal—the wax had been stamped with a circle containing a delicate drawing of a crown.

The folded paper contained a piece of glossy card. The same crown was embossed on the top as part of an elegant frame, touched with gilt. He read the words inside the frame twice.

Viscount and Viscountess Kingsley seek the pleasure of the company of... Then, on a line all its own and in a different hand and slightly different ink: *Elijah Ashby...* There was a return to the first writing, *...at the coming out ball for their daughter Regina on the occasion of her birthday, at ten of the clock, in the evening of Tuesday, April ninth.*

There was an address to reply to the invitation, and then there was the actual letter, for the folded paper was covered with the same neat handwriting as his name on the invitation.

Dear Elijah

You may not remember me, though I hope you do. I was the little girl who made such a pest of herself when I used to follow you around the village.

I never had the chance to tell you goodbye when your mother married Major Deffew, and you went off to London with them. I was sad when you left.

I am all grown up now and having my very first ball. Papa and Mama said I could invite anyone I liked, and I would be so pleased if my very first friend could attend, especially since it is your birthday, too. Remember you told me we were twins born four years apart to different parents?

When I asked Papa whether you were still in London, he said you were, but that your Mama had died. I am very sorry,

Elijah. I liked your Mama a lot.

Papa got me your address. He told me that he did not mind if I invited you, but he didn't want to invite Major Deffew or his sons. I hope you do not think that is rude, but after all, I do not know them. They were all too old to take any notice of me when I was a little girl. And it is my ball.

Please do come. I know you can dance, for we learned together.

Yours sincerely
The Honorable Miss Regina Kingsley

Under her full formal name, she had signed again, this time simply as *Ginny*.

Elijah looked at the letter for a full minute after he had read it several times, smiling. It sounded just like Ginny. He was tempted—after all, he was twenty-one that day, so Major Defect and the two louts could not stop him.

But he had nothing to wear. Finally, he sighed and hid the letter away again.

Then Cook sent for him. Her assistant had burned the onions she was meant to caramelize, and she needed more onions, urgently. Elijah returned to his room for his coat and the pair of trousers he had just finished. He would seize the opportunity to call past the vicarage and add them to the trunk the vicar was storing for him until his transformation from skivvy to secretary.

Partway down the servant stairs, he turned back for the letter and invitation. He'd add those to the trunk, too. Perhaps, when he was far away, he could write Ginny a letter.

Or he could leave a message with the vicar. That might be better. Gentlemen did not write letters to young ladies who were not their relatives.

So, when he had his bag of onions, he called on the vicar, and showed him the invitation.

"You should go, Elijah."

"How can I?" Elijah asked. "Even in my new clothing, I

would be an embarrassment to her."

"Now as to that," said the vicar, "I was not going to mention this until your birthday, but I have a present for you that will help."

When the vicar pulled out a full dinner costume, complete with dancing pumps and several pairs of silk stockings, Elijah protested. "It is too much!"

"Nonsense," the vicar told him. "It is not new, Elijah, so you need not let cost worry you. My brother is about your size and has more clothes than he knows what to do with. He gave me these in a box of items for the poor box."

Elijah touched the silk stockings, which he was certain had not come from any poor box. The vicar cleared his throat. "Most of it, in any case. I knew you would need to dress for dinner when Lord Arthur asks you to accompany him, as he often will. And I believe I might justifiably claim to be a substitute for your godfather, young Elijah, given that I am both your minister *and* your mentor. You must allow me to give you a small token to mark the day of your majority and the start of your great adventure.

Which left Elijah with nothing to say but "thank you."

Chapter Two

R EGINA KINGSLEY HELD her ball gown up in front of herself
and admired her reflection in the mirror. Her ball had just
become even more exciting to her.

Of course, she was delighted to be making her debut to Polite
Society, even if she was a little nervous about, as her mother put
it, *establishing herself creditably.*

That was, after all, the whole goal of the Season. Her mother
expected her to choose a husband, someone well-born, with
connections that would be useful to her father, and after him, to
her brother. Someone with sufficient wealth to keep her in
comfort for the rest of her days.

Regina had every intention of pleasing her mother. And if she
hoped to find a handsome young man who fell in love with her at
first sight, was that too much to ask?

"You will look just like a fairy princess," said her maid. Annie
was a niece to Mama's dresser. Her promotion from parlor maid
to lady's maid had made her a devoted slave to Lady Kingsley,
and she was determined to do everything she could to ensure
Regina's success.

Regina's mother had already mapped out her daughter's
entire evening. She would be escorted into dinner by Mr.
Paddimore, her father's closest friend. That must have been by

her father's decree, for Mama would have selected anyone except Mr. Paddimore, whom she disliked.

Regina would also be led out in the first dance by Mr. Paddimore. It should have been Papa or Regina's brother. But the doctor had forbidden Papa to dance, and William was only fifteen and away at school.

Mother had chosen partners for all of Regina's dances that evening. Mostly the sons or younger brothers of people that Papa knew. They were all men Mama deemed suitable as suitors for Regina, though Regina had so far met very few of them.

The one person Regina had invited to her ball was not on Mama's list. She'd coaxed her parents into permitting the invitation. When she was a child, Elijah Ashby was the only boy close to her social status in the village near her home, but he had gone down in the world since then.

"No." Her mother's refusal to add Elijah to the guest list was immediate and firm. "He is not of our class."

"We played together when I was a child, Mama. You thought him acceptable then."

"That was before his mother stooped to taking in boarders after her husband died. Ashby would have turned over in his grave, Regina. He may have been the younger son of a younger son, and estranged from his family, but at least he did not shame his cousin, the earl, by working for a living."

Regina privately thought that, if Mr. Ashby had worked for a living, his widow might not have had to take in boarders, but there was no point in saying that to her mother.

"You told me I could choose five people to invite," she pointed out. "Mr. Ashby is the only person I know in London who is not already invited."

"Quite apart from his mother's behavior in taking in lodgers and then compounding the error by marrying one of them—and him the fiend who spread rumors about... Well, enough about that. The Ashby boy's bloodlines are no more than respectable, and he has no influential friends at all, let only money or family connections."

"Not every gentleman at the ball will be a marriage prospect, Mama. Some of the guests are already married. And some are far too young to consider marriage."

"The little princess has you there." Papa had been ignoring the conversation in favor of his dinner, but both ladies shut their mouths when he spoke, to listen to whatever wisdom he had to offer. "I will tell you what, Lady Kingsley, Regina. I will find out Ashby's current circumstances and address, and I will let you know what I find. If he is respectable... *If*, I say, Regina. Then you may send him an invitation. You may not, however, encourage any attention from him unless he has come into the possession of a fortune since we last met." He laughed at his own joke.

He was, however, as good as his word, telling his ladies at dinner the following night, "Ashby is working as a servant to his stepfather."

"That is the end of that, then," said Mama, with some satisfaction, although she added, "Though it is sad to see an earl's great-grandson come to such a pass. Just what I would have expected from that horrible Deffew person."

"Not so fast, Lady Kingsley," said Papa, before Regina could begin to be disappointed. "I am happy for the boy to be invited. It will please Regina, and she is too good a daughter, and has too much wit, to allow her head to be turned."

Mama, of course, subsided. "As you wish, Lord Kingsley."

Regina was certain this was not her mother's last word, and sure enough, she heard the rest of the discussion later that evening, when she came back downstairs on the pretext of fetching the book she had deliberately left in the drawing room.

Waiting outside the door, she heard her mother say, "... anyone associated with that dreadful man."

Her father chuckled. "Actually, Lady Kingsley, from what I understand, no one will be more upset about Elijah receiving an invitation than Major Deffew. Can you believe that the man had the unmitigated gall to approach me at my club, and ask if his sons could be invited? To show there were no hard feelings over what he called some *unfortunate suggestions on his part that were taken the wrong way*? I'll give him hard feelings."

Mama was not satisfied. "But, Lord Kingsley, you agreed with my decision to restrict Regina's activities when she was ten, so she no longer met that boy. And from what you were told, he has fallen even further."

"Young Ashby is about to rise again, Lady Kingsley. What if I were to tell you I have it on good authority he has taken a position as secretary to the fourth son of the Duke of Dellborough? And since they plan to leave England for several years the day after the ball, you need have no fear he is a threat to your hopes for our little princess. I see no harm in letting her have her way in this invitation business."

Regina crept away. She would write the invitation tonight. Yes, and a letter to go with it. It would give her something to do between now and when her parents went to bed, and she could go down again to fetch her book.

That had been four days ago. Today, she received a note in reply. Elijah was coming to her ball. She could hardly wait.

ON THE DAY of his emancipation, Elijah rose before dawn, as usual, washed in cold water, dressed, and went downstairs. That was the end of similarities between this day and every other day for the past four years.

In a satchel over his shoulder, he carried every possession he counted as his own, except for those that he had already transferred to his trunk at the vicarage. For the last time, he used the servant stairs to descend to the basement. When he walked through the kitchen, only the kitchen maid was awake. The girl was stoking the fire to have it ready for Cook when she came downstairs.

"Tell Cook I will not be eating here this morning," Elijah told her, and let himself out the back door.

A brisk fifteen-minute walk brought him to the vicarage, where he joined the vicar for a hearty breakfast, but only after he had changed into his new clothes.

He had a great deal to accomplish today. This afternoon, he was meeting his new employer at the ship that would take them abroad. They were sleeping on the ship overnight, for it would depart on the tide first thing tomorrow morning.

"I'll do my shopping first, then meet you back here," he told the vicar.

Elijah had a few things to purchase from the list Lord Arthur had sent a couple of days ago, and he intended to get a professional haircut. He had been cutting his own hair since his mother grew too weak to wield the scissors. Those errands would take half the morning.

He also wanted to tell his stepfather to his face that he was leaving. He had thought about leaving a note, or simply walking out with no word. However, he could not resist the chance to see Major Defect's face, and, better still, the faces of Dilly and Mouth. If they had failed to make Elijah's life miserable for the past six years, it was not for want of trying.

The vicar insisted on going with him to the Deffew household, which was probably a good idea. Major Defect had no grounds on which to stop Elijah from leaving, but that did not necessarily mean he would not try.

Elijah was both nervous and exultant when he and the vicar knocked on the Deffew front door. Elijah had not used this entry to the house since his mother died, and rarely while she was still alive.

The butler began a tirade as soon as he saw Elijah on the doorstep. "Where have you been? The house is at sixes and sevens! The major is beside himself. And what are you thinking coming to the front door? Have you gone mad? You had better come inside. The major said you were to present yourself to him as soon as you turned up." His rant had not prevented him from looking Elijah up and down, taking in Elijah's much-improved appearance. The crease between his eyebrows deepened, and he said, "About time you spent something on your appearance. It has been a disgrace to this house. But you know better than to do that sort of thing on the master's time. Save it for your day off."

Elijah, who had not had a day off in years, made no comment, but just led the vicar in the direction of the major's study. The butler opened his mouth, perhaps to object to the vicar's appearance, but caught the man's glare and closed his mouth again.

All three Deffew men were in the study.

"You are in trouble, Ash Boy," gloated Dilly, from the chair across which he was elegantly draped.

Mouth had propped himself by the elbows against another chair. He said nothing, but grinned, as if he was looking forward to the show.

Major Defect surged out of the seat behind the desk, his voice at a roar. "Where the hell have you been? How dare you disappear for more than half a day?"

He glanced behind Elijah to where the butler stood smirking in the doorway. "The butler tells me this is the third time in the last month you have disappeared for hours." Which was true. Elijah had met the duke's secretary for an interview, and then last week spent half an hour with Lord Arthur, his new employer.

"Yes," he replied provocatively. "I had things to do."

Major Defect's brows beetled together in a ferocious frown as he took in Elijah's appearance. "New clothes? Where did you get the money for new clothes? Have you been stealing from me?"

He rounded the desk, catching up a riding crop from its surface.

The vicar said, "That's enough!"

The major ignored him, slashing at Elijah's shoulders with the crop.

Elijah moved smoothly out of the way, grabbed his stepfather's hand, and squeezed it. He took the crop with his other hand and broke it over his knee, tossing the pieces into the fire.

The two brothers started forward but stopped uncertainly when the vicar stepped between them and Elijah.

The major, however, continued to ignore the extra person in the room. "How dare you! I'll have you arrested for assault, as well as theft."

"Actually," Elijah commented, "the vicar will bear witness that you assaulted me, and I defended myself."

Major Defect, who was already red in the face, turned a brighter scarlet. "I have a right to discipline my ward," he said to the vicar, his first acknowledgment of the man's existence.

"It is questionable whether that right extends to beating your ward with a riding crop," the vicar replied, calmly. "But since Mr. Ashby is no longer your ward, the point is moot."

Elijah had been right. His enemies had no idea today was his twenty-first birthday. The look of astonishment on all three faces was a delight to behold.

"It is my birthday," Elijah explained. "Since I am no longer under your guardianship, I am leaving your household. In fact, I have already left it. I returned only because I thought it courteous to let you know my intentions." A shading of the truth that made his motives sound more virtuous than they were.

The brothers both spoke at the same time.

"But what will I do for a valet?" Dilly asked.

"You will have to serve out the period of your notice," claimed Mouth.

Elijah laughed. This was even more amusing than he had expected. "You have never paid me," he pointed out. "Therefore, you do not employ me. So, no notice is required."

Major Defect seized on one of Elijah's points. "You admitted it then. You stole the money to buy those clothes."

"I earned a few pennies here and there doing chores for less-miserly households," Elijah told him, calmly. "I have taken nothing from this house I did not have from my parents. Even the clothes your sons handed down to me, which I outgrew more than a year ago, are still in the room where I slept when I lived here. Apart from the ones I wore out of the house, which are now in a flour sack in your front hall."

Major Defect glared at him with his mouth open, then turned to the vicar. "You can't let him leave us like this. Tell him. Tell him he has obligations to me for all I've done for him since I married his mother."

"On the contrary," said the vicar. "It is you who have failed in your obligations—to educate this fine young man, to clothe him respectably, to give him opportunities commensurate with his abilities. I was already of the opinion that you and your sons have behaved disgracefully, and what I have witnessed today has only solidified that point of view."

The major made some blustery noises, and both brothers burst out with entirely false claims about the favorable treatment that an ungrateful Elijah had received.

The vicar ignored them, turning to Elijah and saying, "I think we are done here."

They walked out past the butler, who had been standing in the open door listening. Undoubtedly, the story would be all over Town before the day was out.

Chapter Three

M R. PADDIMORE THOUGHT that Regina looked beautiful. So
did Mama and Papa, but Mr. Paddimore was not a
member of her family, and so did not have to say such nice things
to her.

However, he made several favorable comments about Regina's appearance. Her favorites were that her lovely gown was
almost a fit setting for her own beauty, and a flattering remark
about her hair.

"How delightful that you wear my flowers in your hair, Miss
Kingsley," he said. He had sent her flowers, a small bouquet of
delicate hothouse orchids, blushed with a pink that almost
precisely matched her gown. "I would not have thought of using
them to adorn your dark curls," he said, "but they are a perfect
setting for them."

Was that not a sweet thing to say?

Regina did not know Mr. Paddimore very well since he seldom came to the Kingsley house. He was a handsome man for his
age—not as old as Papa, but at least thirty, and probably older.
She had not realized how charming he was. Regina was delighted
to have him take her into dinner and lead her out in the first
dance.

Regina had thought that the dinner party would drag, given

how excited she was about the ball, and how eager for the dancing to begin. Mr. Paddimore, however, proved to be an entertaining dinner companion. He told Regina several stories about funny things that happened at balls he attended and assured her he was happy to fight off any suitors she would prefer not to entertain.

Before she knew it, dinner was over, and Mama was saying it was time to form the receiving line. That, too, was exciting. All of these people had come to celebrate Regina!

She received many compliments. Mama and Papa, too, for having such a beautiful and charming daughter. Even so, she was glad when the stream of new arrivals dwindled to a trickle, and Mama announced it was time for the first dance.

Her one disappointment was that Elijah had not arrived. She had gone to such trouble, too. Yesterday afternoon, at the dancing class that one of Mama's friends had got up for young ladies and young gentlemen who were new to the Season, Regina had managed to speak to several of the young men to whom mother had given one of her dances.

One of them—a youth she had known from the cradle—was more than happy to forego his dance with her in return for an introduction to another of the debutantes who had caught his eye.

If Elijah arrived, she would be able to dance with him. She had always wanted to, since she had seen him dancing with his mother at a village festival more than six years ago.

However, if he could not be bothered to come to her ball, she was certainly not going to spare him another thought. She smiled at Mr. Paddimore and allowed him to lead her out onto the dance floor. He was a very graceful dancer. She supposed that, at his age, he had had a lot of practice.

She enjoyed every minute of the next two hours. She did not enjoy some of her partners, especially the clumsy ones who trod on her feet or tried to lead her the wrong way. Then there were gentlemen who talked the entire time, yet never had a single interesting thing to say. Worst of all were those who served ridiculous and overblown flattery with a helping of questions about how rich her father really was.

But Regina loved to dance, and was happy to imagine the clumsy, boring, or calculating partner of the moment replaced with the perfect gentleman of her imagination. The perfect gentleman who would partner her in one perfect dance.

It was for that imaginary person she danced gracefully to the music, smiling, and glowing with pleasure.

At supper, her partner was tongue-tied, so she carried on with her daydream, imagining that her perfect gentleman had selected morsels to tempt her appetite from the best of the dishes set out for the guests.

Her escort managed to break his silence long enough to stammer, "Are you enjoying the evening, Miss Kingsley?"

Regina heard the question in her perfect gentleman's thrilling tones, and it was to him that she answered, "I am having such a wonderful time. Everything is so exciting, so beautiful, and the people have been so kind."

The enthusiastic response loosened her escort's tongue a little. "It is very easy to be kind to one as lovely as you, Miss Kingsley."

He might not be her perfect gentleman, but he was a very nice person.

As they left the supper room, the butler announced two late arrivals. "Lord Arthur Versey. Mr. Elijah Ashby."

Elijah had come! Her mother was hurrying to greet the new guests. Or, rather, Lord Arthur. Regina examined the man who was receiving all of her mother's attention. She had been well-enough schooled in the peerage to know Versey was the family name of the Dukes of Dellborough, so Lord Arthur must be the younger son who had hired Elijah to travel with him. Lord Arthur had not been invited, but duke's sons could expect to be welcomed whether invited or not.

He was now introducing his companion. They were both tall

men, though—unlike Elijah—Lord Arthur had not yet put on width to match his height. He was a long, thin string of a youth, immaculately dressed for the evening. Elijah was also beautifully dressed, though without the extravagant embroidery and extra touches of lace. The well-fitting black coat stretched over broad shoulders, and his fawn breeches clung to muscular thighs.

He was in time for their dance, and Regina needed to let him know he had been so favored.

"I enjoyed our supper," she told her escort. "I am returning to my mother now. I do hope you enjoy the rest of the evening."

The boy said something about calling on her tomorrow, and Regina managed a polite bob of a curtsy before hurrying away.

Her mother's eyes lit up as Regina approached. "There you are, dear. There is someone I want you to meet." She grabbed Regina by the arm, as if afraid her daughter might escape.

Regina smiled at Elijah. "I am already acquainted with Mr. Ashby, Mama."

Mama looked at Elijah as if he had suddenly popped out of nowhere. "Oh, yes. Good evening, Mr. Ashby. But Regina, allow me to present Lord Arthur Versey. Lord Arthur, my daughter." She beamed, as if Lord Arthur's presence was all her own doing.

Regina held out her hand to the young aristocrat, and he bowed over it and mimed a kiss some inches over her glove. "Do you say that you have a dance free, Miss Kingsley," he begged. "My friend Ashby is hoping for the opportunity to renew his acquaintance with an old friend."

Mama interpolated a long sentence, the gist of which was that Regina's dances were all taken but that, if she had any, Lord Arthur would be her preferred partner.

Regina waited politely for her to stop, her eyes on Elijah's the whole time. What would he say if she told him she had saved him the next dance? What would her mother say?

Elijah spoke when Mama at last made her way to a full stop. "I am delighted to see you again, Miss Kingsley," he said. "Thank you for inviting me tonight."

Regina made up her mind. After all, this might be her only chance. "As it happens, Lord Arthur, Mr. Ashby is my partner for the next dance." She took a step from her mother and slipped her free hand into Elijah's bent elbow, smiling up at him.

Mama said, "Oh, but—"

Lord Arthur interrupted. "Lady Kingsley, would you be kind enough to present me to your husband?" He offered her his elbow, and Mama was presented with the dilemma of releasing Regina's arm and letting her go with Elijah or insulting the younger son of a duke and neglecting her duties as a hostess.

She went off with Lord Arthur.

"Nicely accomplished, Miss Kingsley," said Elijah. "I see you are still a minx."

"I prefer to think of it as defending myself from my mother's matchmaking," Regina replied. "After all, I am only just turned seventeen. I do not need to be a bride tomorrow." She gave a light tug on his elbow. "Come, let us walk before Mama comes back with a very good reason why we should not have our dance."

He obliged, setting off around the ballroom at a slow stroll. "Happy birthday, Regina."

"Happy birthday to you, too, Elijah." He was limping. He did not use to limp when he was a boy.

"Have you injured your leg?" she asked him. Mama would say personal questions were rude, but how was one to find things out if one never asked questions?

He looked down on her with a somewhat twisted smile. "An old injury. I'm afraid I cannot accept the privilege of a dance with you, Regina. I would not wish to embarrass you on the floor. Even if my leg was whole, I have never learned these dances." He took a breath and puffed it out again. "I expect Lord Arthur—"

Regina reacted to the regret in his eyes as the musicians took up their instruments, and the caller announced the longways dance Allemande Swiss. "Then we shall continue to walk," she proposed. "Or perhaps find a seat. That will give us an opportunity to chat, a much better idea than dancing."

Elijah looked around them. A number of people were watching, but Regina didn't care. It was her ball, her birthday, and her childhood friend. But perhaps he did not feel the same? "Only if you want to," she said.

"Oh, I want to." His fervent tone thrilled her, as did the sincerity in his eyes. He gave a single decisive nod. "Very well, Miss Kingsley. Let us find somewhere we can sit and talk."

It was the finest dance of the evening. The music became a background to sharing of their plans and hopes for the future.

Elijah told Regina that he was heading off overseas with Lord Arthur the very next morning. "I'm meant to be his secretary, but the man who interviewed me for the job made it clear that the duke wanted someone young enough for his son to see as a friend and ally, and level-headed enough to keep him out of trouble. He has been much protected, I gather."

"He seems nice," Regina offered.

"He does, doesn't he? This afternoon was only the second time I met him. We are meant to be leaving on the next tide, which is at dawn tomorrow. We had so much to do aboard that I thought I would have to forego the ball. When I said as much to Lord Arthur, he insisted I go off and get dressed, and when I came out, he had changed into his own evening dress, and ordered a carriage for us both."

Regina asked about their destination, and Elijah explained they were heading for Paris first, and after that, wherever Lord Arthur's whims took them.

Regina's surge of longing would do her no good. If she wanted to travel, she would first have to find a husband willing to take her. Single young ladies did not undertake grand tours.

When Elijah asked about her own plans, she explained she had every intention of thoroughly enjoying her Season without committing herself to a betrothal. "I am only seventeen," she said again. "Mama thinks I should marry this year, but Papa will not make me choose a husband before I am ready. Perhaps next year,

I will want to settle down. Or the year after. One day, of course, I would like a home of my own and family. But first, I intend to have fun." It all sounded very boring and trivial compared to what Elijah was about to do.

Chapter Four

B EFORE THEY LEFT the Firth of Thames, Elijah concluded that the most senior of the men in Lord Arthur's retinue intended to keep the Duke of Dellborough's youngest child wrapped in the kind of protective custody poor Lord Arthur was attempting to escape.

Albert Smith, a middle-aged man who had previously served as under valet to the duke before accepting a job as valet to Lord Arthur, did his best to convince his master that he should go below deck and take a nostrum against sea sickness.

"Your lordship knows that you are subject to stomach up-sets," he pointed out.

Lord Arthur's tutor, Frederick Beckham, assured all present that he well knew how delicate the young lord was, but pre-scribed remaining on deck. "Downstairs is close and smelly, my lord. You'll be better up here where the air is fresh."

Pierre Mitterrand, who had been employed as guide and translator for the French leg of the tour, claimed that he never suffered from *mal de mer* and he was convinced no one of character needed to do so.

Beckham and Mitterrand were also middle-aged men, and all three seemed to think that their age advantage allowed them to treat their employer as if he was a willful schoolboy and they his fond uncles.

Three hefty individuals had been sent along to act as guards, drivers, footmen, porters, and whatever else was needed. They did not express an opinion.

Nor did Elijah, who had already decided that his dual roles as secretary and friend did not include telling Lord Arthur what he should and should not do.

His lordship listened politely, smiled sweetly, and suggested that the three gentlemen need not worry about him, as he was very well, and enjoying watching the coastline of England as they sailed by.

The three men-of-all-work went below. The other three stayed, hovering in the vicinity of the duke's son, and occasionally rephrasing and re-presenting their advice. Elijah, who had no wish to trade the views and the sea air for the cramped quarters below deck, took a seat a short distance away, but stayed out of the conversation.

As his advisers continued to try to persuade Lord Arthur, he dismissed them all politely, but with a thread of steel in his tone and expression. "Thank you, gentlemen, for your concern. If you prove to be right, I give you free license to say that you told me so. Meanwhile, I wish to have private conversation with my secretary. Please, go below or stay above, as you wish, but go away. If I need anyone of you, I will send for you."

Perhaps the fractious waters the ship had reached aided Lord Arthur's exercise of authority. Certainly, Beckham and Mitterrand showed the slight green cast to their skin that hinted at an uncomfortable digestive system. They retreated, Smith and Mitterrand to go below, and Beckham to apply his own prescription and move as far forward along the ship's rails as he could.

Elijah moved closer to his new employer. "You wish to speak with me, my lord?"

"I wished to be free of my nannies, at least for a few minutes." Lord Arthur grinned. "I'm surprised it worked. If I had tried that in England, they would have threatened me with my mother or His Grace. I suppose they could do so by post, but the sanction loses some of its effect when the appealed-to authority cannot thunder into the room within the half-hour."

"They appear protective," Elijah observed.

Lord Arthur sighed. "I cannot even be annoyed at them. They are merely carrying out my parents' wishes. And what of you, Mr. Ashby? Are you going to remind me to wrap up warm, warn me against staying out after midnight, object when I want to stroll through the streets of a strange town?"

Elijah shrugged. "I have been employed to be your secretary, my lord, not your minder."

Lord Arthur waved a dismissive hand. "I am not sure I need a secretary. And from what I heard about you last night, I don't know if you can give me what I do need. I have moved a little in Society since I recovered from a long illness a year ago, but I know almost nothing of the rest of the world, and you have spent your last few years in London and before that in a village no one has heard of. And I certainly do not need another minder."

Elijah wondered how to reply. Even the little he'd seen of Lord Arthur's domestic tyrants had engaged his sympathy for the man. Besides, his lordship was correct. Their Graces were not close at hand and were getting further away by the minute. In the months to come, when Lord Arthur won his battle for independence, Elijah would like to still have a job. "The gentleman who interviewed me implied that your parents had kept you close, my lord. He said you needed an ally of your own age. A friend, if it so pleases you." Inveterate honesty prompted him to add, "He also suggested you might benefit from what he was pleased to call my *common sense.*"

"My father's secretary. It's thanks to him and the doctor I've been able to make this trip. My parents can't quite believe in my good health. But Fitz told His Grace that I had to be allowed to grow up somewhere my mother did not fuss about each little thing, and the doctor said travel would be good for me." He shifted over slightly on his bench and patted the place beside him.

"Sit down, man. Tell me about yourself."

Elijah obeyed the first injunction but wasn't quite sure what to say to the next. "There is not much to tell, my lord."

Lord Arthur's sigh was impatient. "You cannot go my lording me all the time, Ashby. You've been hired to be my friend, have you not? Friends call one another by nicknames, or so I have observed. Let me see. I shall call you... Ash. A useful tree. Unassuming but strong, flexible, and durable. It is excellent for cricket bats." He cocked an eyebrow, a smile lurking around one corner of his mouth, and waited for Elijah to react.

"Am I to give you a nickname?" Elijah asked. "Artie, then." It should be Artful, for the young lord was as artful as could be, manipulating those around him to get what he wanted. Elijah didn't blame Artie for it when he had been so hedged about. Time would tell if he'd continue to try to bend Elijah to his will. Elijah would back himself, if his lordship made the attempt.

"Not Artie," the young aristocrat objected. "My family calls me Artie. Makes me feel five years old."

Elijah thought for a moment. "Rex then. *Rex quondam, Rexque Futurus.*"

He met his employer's gaze, dead pan.

Lord Arthur gave a crack of laughter. "The once and future king. Perfect." He gave a nod. "Rex and Ash.

"Very well, then. Are you up for some food? I could eat a horse! All this sea air."

ALL THROUGH THE morning the day after the ball, the butler was kept busy receiving bouquet after bouquet of flowers from those who had danced with Regina, and even some who asked too late to secure a place, but who declared their hopes of winning that privilege next time.

None from Elijah, but, as Regina checked each card, she

assured herself he had no opportunity.

Where would he be now? Free of the Thames, she supposed, somewhere out to sea. Gone, probably for years. Once again, for perhaps the tenth time that morning, she consigned Elijah to her past. It was not, after all, as if he could ever have been a suitor.

Regina did not have time to think about Elijah more than two or three times an hour for the rest of the day. First, her mother was anxious to re-examine every moment of the previous evening. Regina waited for the scold over walking with Elijah rather than dancing with Lord Arthur, but Mama was inclined to be philosophical. "No one knew who he was, but he was with Lord Arthur, so I daresay they will assume he is someone of consequence who, like the poor young lord, has been kept out of public sight."

She paused to think about that, and added, "I must say Lord Arthur did not look like an invalid. But everyone says the doctors despaired of his life, and that he is being sent overseas for his health. Either that, or the illness left him a half-wit, and he is being exiled to hide that fact from Society. But I must say he did not seem a half-wit to me."

She insisted on supervising as Regina changed to receive afternoon visits. From the quantity of bouquets, they could expect the drawing room to be crowded, and she was determined Regina would be perfectly turned out.

The gown she chose was one of Regina's favorites. Mama might be silly in some ways, but she had wonderful taste. It was pale, of course, in a tone of pink the modiste called *fairy blushes*. Mama insisted that pastel colors were the only appropriate option for a girl of seventeen. But the cerise embroidery on every edge, the ribbons that trimmed the sleeves and the matching sash added the color that Regina craved.

Certainly, when Mama finally pronounced her ready and they went downstairs, Papa pronounced her the loveliest young lady in London. Mr. Paddimore was there, too, with a huge bunch of purple irises and golden narcissus.

As the clock chimed three, the first gentlemen callers arrived, and after that, the door knocker banged every few minutes to announce another visitor. By the time five o'clock signaled the end of her calling hours, Regina had accepted a ride in his curricle the following day with Viscount Waterman, a walk before visiting hours the day after with the Honorable George Palmer, afternoon tea later in the week at Fourniers with the Markham sisters and a party of other young people, and an excursion to watch a balloon ascension. She had also promised dances to more than a dozen gentlemen at three different engagements.

Papa and Mr. Paddimore, who had withdrawn to Papa's study at the first knock, came through to the drawing room to vicariously enjoy Regina's triumph, as Mama once again dissected every action, conversation, and especially invitation. "Our little girl is going to make a magnificent marriage, Lord Kingsley. You wait and see."

Papa patted Regina's hand. "No hurry, Lady Kingsley. The princess has plenty of time to look around and make up her mind. If not this year, next year, right, Gideon?"

Mr. Paddimore, with a cautious glance at Mama, murmured diplomatically, "Miss Kingsley is sure to be a huge success."

Over the next few weeks, Regina became accustomed to going asleep after midnight, and sometimes so late the under-maids were already cleaning grates and setting fires. She learned to sleep late in the morning, and to catch a brief rest after visiting hours if she was not otherwise engaged.

It was good she had a memory for faces and names, for every outing introduced her to new acquaintances, and she soon gathered a bevy of regular admirers. Mama was over the moon, but Regina did not believe any of the gentlemen were serious in their pursuit. Somehow, admiring Miss Kingsley had become the fashion.

Making friends with the other ladies proved to be more diffi-cult. Here, her looks and her wealth apparently counted against her. The other reigning beauties treated her like an interloper, and less-favored ladies kept her at the same cautious distance they applied to the beauties.

That changed one day when she overheard a particularly obnoxious beauty, a Miss Wharton. She and her two bosom friends were in the ladies' retiring room one evening, attempting to cow another girl. Regina was behind the screen when they entered, three of them clearly on the heels of the one they wanted to harass.

"Please, leave me alone."

Regina didn't know the voice, but she did recognize Miss Fairchild's falsely sweet coo in the answer. "Oh, girls, Miss Millgirl wants us to leave her alone."

Regina had not met Miss Milton, but she recognized the name, even skewed to be an insult. The pretty girl's mother came from a middle-class family whose considerable fortune was founded on mill ownership. Mrs. Milton had won one of the marital prizes of twenty years ago, the second son of a wealthy viscount, and some in Society had not forgiven the trespass.

Miss Wharton hissed. "Go home and we shall leave you alone. You stink of the shop, and we do not plan to put up with you. These are our ballrooms, our suitors. Just because your mother was lucky enough to trap a gentleman doesn't mean we are going to let you do so."

The horrid cow.

"Is this because I danced with Lord Spenhurst?" asked Miss Milton, shrewdly. Lord Spenhurst was heir to a marquis and was showing considerable interest in Miss Milton.

Miss Plumfield screeched, "You will not do so again." The sound of fabric ripping brought Regina hurrying out from behind the privacy screen.

All three of them were tearing at Miss Milton's clothing and hair, while she batted at them, begging them to leave her alone.

Regina caught Miss Plumfield's raised hand. "I cannot abide bullies," she announced.

"This is none of your business, Miss Kingsley," Miss Wharton insisted. "If you interfere, you'll get the same treatment."

"Yes," Miss Fairchild agreed. "Get out of here while you still can."

"What has happened to the maid?" Regina wondered aloud.

A smug twitch of Miss Wharton's lips gave her the answer.

"You bribed her to leave, did you not? You did not want a witness. Unfortunate for you that I was already here. Come, Miss Milton. Let us go and find our hostess. I am sure she will be interested to know how her guests behave when not under the eyes of their chaperones."

Miss Wharton swung her hand to slap Regina's face. Regina blocked the blow with one forearm and clenched both fists. "I would not do that if I were you." Regina's mother would have stopped her excursions with the village children much earlier had she known they had taught her to swim, to climb trees, and—most relevant in this situation—to fight.

Slapping would have been regarded by her tutors as a girlie thing to do. If Miss Wharton tried it again, Regina would let her, Regina decided. A red mark on her cheek would be her defense after she punched Miss Wharton in the belly.

Some of this calculation must have shown in her eyes, for Miss Wharton did not repeat the attempt.

"Who do you suppose will be believed if you tell tales on us?" Miss Fairchild demanded. "We are the diamonds of this year's debutantes. Everyone says so."

Did she really believe that?

Miss Milton didn't. "Miss Kingsley is the daughter of a viscount," she pointed out. "Her mother is acquainted with most of the great ladies of Society. And my grandmother, who is also a viscountess, knows the rest."

The three bullies exchanged glances. Miss Wharton tossed her head. "If you mention this to anyone, I will make you pay," she promised.

A threat with very few teeth. Regina ignored it. "Go away, ladies. And send the maid back. We need her to help Miss Milton make repairs."

"You haven't heard the last of this," Miss Plumfield growled.

Regina, who was examining the damage to Miss Milton's sleeve, turned around at that. "What on earth is wrong with you? Do you want to be treated as a pariah by the whole of Society? For I promise you, that is what will happen if I tell my mother what happened here, and she passes it on to her friends. Now apologize to Miss Milton and get you gone."

Miss Wharton opened her mouth, but Miss Fairchild tugged on her arm, and Miss Plumfield said, "Come on, Estelle. The silly bitch is not worth it."

As the door closed behind them, Miss Milton commented, "Though you be but little, Miss Kingsley, you are fierce."

"I think that is a compliment," Regina suggested.

"It is. Very much so. Also, a quote from Shakespeare. Thank you for coming to my rescue. Will they really make trouble?"

"I expect they will try," Regina said. "Do you want me to talk to my mother? It is just that, if I do, they will almost certainly be exiled, at least for the rest of the year. But their friends will not. And Miss Fairchild's mother—Miss Plumfield's aunt, too—will hold a grudge."

"And Miss Wharton's mother?" Miss Milton asked.

"Her aunt," Regina corrected. "According to my mother, Miss Wharton senior does not care for her niece, and has few connections within the *Ton*."

While she was speaking, Regina had used the card of pins she carried in her reticule to pin up the torn sleeve and the lace that had been ripped off the bodice. "Sit down, Miss Milton, and I will put your hair back up."

"You are being very kind," Miss Milton commented. "We hardly know one another."

"I hate bullies," Regina repeated. "Besides, I have seen you at several entertainments and thought you had a kind face. But I did not know anyone to introduce us."

Miss Milton smiled. "I have seen you, too, and thought you

were too beautiful and popular to be nice. I do apologize for that." She held out her hand. "How do you do, Miss Kingsley. I am Cordelia Milton, and I am pleased to make your acquaintance."

"Please," Regina said. "Call me Regina."

She had made enemies this evening. But perhaps she had also found a friend.

Chapter Five

Paris, May 1802

A SH NUDGED REX in the side. "She's looking at you, Rex."
Rex, who had been peering at the boxes on the other
side of the theater, turned his attention to the line of dancers
performing the part of Greek maidens in *Iphigénie en Aulide*. He
waggled his fingers at the third girl from the end. Rex had hired a
box at the *Théâtre de la République et des Arts* for their stay in Paris.
It was close enough to the stage that Ash could see the girl wink
in their direction.

Ash was touched by the emotion and the music, though—
after two months in France—he was still having trouble following
French in everyday speech. Declaimed or sung from the stage, it
was largely impenetrable. Although, this particular opera might
be in Italian or German, since Ash was finding it more difficult to
follow than usual.

"I will send Monsieur Mitterrand at the interval, with my
invitation to supper," Rex decided. He had been courting this
dancer for the past three weeks, taking flowers to her in the
dressing room set aside for the dancers and the chorus, sending
her little presents, joining her and others of the company when
they gathered after a performance for food and drink.

In Ash's opinion, Mademoiselle Giselle Tremblay had long since made up her mind to accept the English milord as a protector, but Rex had told Ash that it was not wise to hurry the pursuit. "There is more to choosing a mistress than looks," he lectured Ash. "My father says that many a young man has come to grief by allowing his whiffles to negotiate for him."

Apparently, the duke, as protective as ever, had given his convalescent son detailed instructions on how to be a customer for commercial sex, including bringing in a tutoress to provide practical experience in the physical aspects of the practice. Ash, who had not so much as stolen a kiss from a girl, was not sure whether to be appalled or envious.

The duke's wisdom, as passed on by his son, said the disposition and habits of a mistress contributed greatly to a protector's happiness during the term of the arrangement. "Within obvious limits," Rex quoted, "one should treat a fashionable impure with the same respect as a lady. They don't expect it, so are all the more grateful."

Ash found the duke's self-serving cynicism chilling but didn't say so. Rex regarded his father with an uncomfortable combination of worship and resentment, and any implied criticism was unlikely to be well received.

Rex went back to examining the audience. He was looking for people he knew. While he had not participated in the London Season or been away to school, he had grown up attending house parties with his parents and had made a spare at his mother's dinner parties whenever he was well enough since he was seventeen.

"I swear, a good third of the audience are British," he told Ash.

That might be an exaggeration, something Rex was prone to, but Ash had to agree they had met many English people in recent weeks. The wealthy had flocked to Paris as soon as the Treaty of Amiens had been signed. Those with business interests or family in France had come too, trying to find out what had happened to their assets or their loved ones during the war.

After sending Mitterrand on his errand, Rex waved to yet another acquaintance. "It is definitely time to sign the contracts with Mademoiselle Tremblay. I see Richport in the audience."

Ash raised his eyebrows in question.

"The Duke of Richport. He's richer than I am and better looking. He is also several years older and has an actual title rather than a courtesy one. And he doesn't waste time. If he sets his mind on Giselle, he'll have a contract under her nose before we could blink. He does not care about her character or comportment. If he decides a mistress is too much trouble, he gives her a present and find a new one."

Ash took a good look at the young duke. He was probably in his mid-twenties, and Ash had to admit that he was handsome, with his dark, perfectly symmetrical good looks. The cynical cast of his expression, however, made him far less appealing than Rex. At least in Ash's opinion.

Mitterand's errand was successful. Rex was to meet mademoiselle at a local restaurant. "Thank you, Monsieur," Rex said, and sat impatiently through the rest of the performance.

Afterwards, he dismissed everyone except Ash, his carriage driver, and one guard. Ash protested that he would be out of place at a supper for two. "I asked her to bring a friend for you," Rex explained. "If things go poorly, that will give her someone to go home with. And if they go well, you can keep the friend entertained while Giselle and I come to terms."

Mademoiselle Tremblay, having cleaned off most of her paint and dressed for the evening rather than the stage, was a very pretty young woman. Ash couldn't tell her age. Her eyes seemed older than the rest of her, but her skin was still firm and unlined. She wore her dark curly hair half up and half down, so a long lock curled strategically just above one of her breasts.

She introduced her friend, another attractive young woman, Mademoiselle Vivienne Cadieux. Ash could only assume that Mademoiselle Cadieux had been given similar instructions to his own: *Keep the English milord's secretary busy so the milord and Giselle could reach agreement.*

Mademoiselle Cadieux accomplished her task by flirting, in French, in broken English, and in the unspoken language of eyelashes, smiles, coy glances, and increasingly bold touches. Meanwhile, the waiters kept filling their glasses with a light, bubbly white wine far more potent than it appeared.

The women were also intoxicating, from their appearance and behavior, designed to seduce, to the perfume they wore—something rich and musky. When Mademoiselle Cadieux leaned close, Ash found himself drowned in tones of vanilla, nutmeg, sandalwood, and something floral and exotic. Ash preferred the light English florals that Ginny wore.

No. He would not think of Ginny tonight.

By the time Rex called for his carriage, Ash was in a high state of physical arousal, and Vivienne, as she insisted Ash call her, did not help by seating herself astride his lap as soon as the carriage began to move.

Rex was not going to be of any assistance. He and Giselle had clearly reached sufficient accord to begin the preliminaries to the evening's main purpose. Ash could only hope they would not move beyond the initial stages until they put a closed door between themselves and Ash.

Meanwhile, he surrendered sufficiently to Vivienne and the demands of his own body to accept her mouth on his.

His first kiss. He had nothing to compare it with, but in his uninformed opinion, Vivienne knew exactly what she was about, and the kiss had been a mistake. He had not known he could grow to such proportions, and Vivienne's roaming hands made things even harder—in both senses of the word. Clearly, she misunderstood his situation. She would reject him as soon as he could persuade Rex to explain in French that he was a poverty-stricken secretary. He would only increase her irritation with him if he took advantage of her belief that he had the money to afford the luxury of his own *chère-amie.*

Nevertheless, short of dumping her on the carriage floor, he could not quench her enthusiasm. Nor could he resist it.

By the time the carriage paused outside a large *maison*, he had his hands full of Vivienne's breasts and his placket half-opened. Vivienne briskly did up the buttons she had just undone, popped her breasts back into her bodice and patted Ash's cheek. She made a remark in French to her friend, who was also putting herself to rights.

Rex, looking nearly as tidy as when they started, descended to the street, and assisted Giselle down the carriage steps. Ash hastened to perform the same courtesy for Vivienne, and then found himself with the opera dancer clinging to his arm, following his friend into the building.

Rex had the keys to a delightful apartment, with two bedrooms, each with its own small dressing room and two reception rooms. The girls dragged their escorts from room to room, expounding on its virtues in French far too rapid for Ash to pick up more than a word here and there.

He understood, however, when Vivienne laid claim to the bedroom decorated in purple, with bunches of violets on the wallpaper and violets painted as accents on the delicate, white-painted furniture.

Giselle declared for the rose room, and then suddenly discovered one of the reception rooms had a balcony. She and Vivienne hurried out to examine the view, leaving Rex and Ash inside.

"They like it," Rex announced with great satisfaction.

"You are not..." Ash trailed off and rephrased his statement as a question. "Are you planning to take them both into your keeping, Rex?"

"Technically, I suppose. But Vivienne is not for me, Ash. She's for you." He put up a hand to stop Ash from speaking.

"It's the perfect solution," Ash insisted. "Giselle will have company when I can't be with her, and you'll have company when I'm with Giselle. You don't have to share Vivienne's bed if your sense of morality is offended at the thought, but I need you.

You know the nannies are not going to let me spend time here with just Giselle. They'll insist on you or one of them staying in the apartment, too. I prefer you, Ash."

Ash wanted to argue, but he didn't want to sound Puritan. And then Rex delivered the *coup de grace*. "Vivienne would prefer you, as well. I don't think she would nearly as happy with one of the nannies."

Still Ash hesitated.

"Is it Miss Kingsley?" Rex asked.

"No," Ash protested. "She is far above me, and by the time we return to England she will be married, probably with a tribe of little children."

In the end, he stayed the night with Vivienne. In the weeks that followed, his French improved beyond his expectations. In bed, Vivienne was skilled, and happy to tutor him in how to please her.

Out of bed, things were not so pleasant. They really had very little in common, even when he had learned enough French to hold a conversation with her. Her world revolved around the Opera and the petty rivalries within the ballet.

Perhaps Vivienne's greatest contribution to Ash's life was a temper tantrum one evening, when he accompanied her to a costume ball and refused to dance with her.

"Explain to her, Rex," Ash begged, unable to understand more than one word in three of the torrent she hurled at him.

Vivienne stopped long enough to listen to Rex, as he rattled away in quick-fire French, pointing to Ash's leg. She spat a few more words at him, turned on her heel and went off with one of the male dancers from the Opera.

Rex was staring after her with his mouth open.

"What did she say?" Ash asked.

"She asked why you don't have your shoe built up so both legs are the same length," Rex replied. "Would that work, do you think?"

He dragged Ash off to a cobbler the very next day, and within a week, the constant ache was largely gone from Ash's hip and lower spine. Furthermore, at the next opportunity, he took Vivienne dancing.

When he told her she'd always have his gratitude for the suggestion, Vivienne said she'd rather have a present. He changed the subject and later bought her a bonnet she admired.

Chapter Six

London, June 1802

B Y THE MIDDLE of June, London was getting hotter and hotter, and Papa began to make noises about going home for the summer.

Regina was happy at the thought. For the most part, she had enjoyed her first Season. Cordelia's friendship was a great blessing, and over the weeks, other young ladies had joined their circle, forming a loose group in opposition to those who hovered around the edges of the Wharton flock.

On the other hand, Regina was tired of being constantly on show, constantly aware of the lurking gossipmongers waiting for a misstep.

The risk of nasty gossip had grown worse since the open declaration of war with Miss Wharton and her two friends—or *the three harpies*, as Cordelia called them.

Already, several rumors had been nipped in the bud when one of Regina's friends heard about it before it could blossom into full-fledged poison. Each time, she had been able to prove she was somewhere else, and not the lady one of the harpies claimed to have seen in a compromising situation.

As for suitors, most of Regina's court had no interest in settling down any time soon, which suited Regina very well. Regina's father had had several applications for her hand, two from known fortune hunters and none from anyone to whom Regina could imagine herself married.

She had been inclined to regard one of the fortune hunters with favor when she learned he was stepbrother to Elijah Ashby, but one mention of Elijah was enough to change her mind. Mr. David Deffew's opinion of Elijah was scathing and nasty. When he followed up by gleefully repeating some of the tricks he and his brother had played to get poor Elijah into trouble, Regina asked him to leave, and assured him she would not be at home if he called again.

She was grateful her father was prepared to let her take her time, though Mama was another matter, and inclined to regard Regina's unwed status after three months on the marriage market as a personal affront.

In a desperate last attempt to see her daughter "settled," as she called it, she persuaded Papa to stay until the end of the third week in June and began accepting every possible invitation that came into the house. Regina found herself rushing to as many as five events a night—perhaps a formal dinner, followed by a short visit to a rout-party, then an hour at a ball, then another rout, and afterwards another ball.

The afternoons were just as busy. More than once, Regina came home in one gentleman's curricle, only to be assisted down and then immediately passed over to the next gentleman to be helped up into his.

A quiet outing, or even a talk, with her friends was impossible to organize, and Regina began counting down the days until her family's return to the country. One evening, in the second week of June, Cordelia approached her where she stood with her mother and asked if the two of them might be allowed to stroll on the terrace.

One set had just finished, and the musicians were refreshing themselves. "Please, Mama," Regina begged. "I shall be back for the next dance."

Mama hesitated. She looked around as if for a potential suitor who might be substituted for Cordelia as a walking companion. Her initial objections to Cordelia had diminished in recent weeks since Lord Spenhurst's attentions to Regina's friend had become obvious enough to signal Cordelia's potential change in status. Lord Spenhurst was the son and heir of the Marquess of Deerhaven, and if he proposed to Cordelia, she would instantly become the highest-ranking lady in this Season's crop of debutantes.

Mama gave her consent.

Regina did not allow her any time to change her mind. She slipped a hand through her friend's arm and tugged her in the direction of the French doors that let out onto the terrace.

"My mother!"

Cordelia giggled. Regina, whose thoughts had been on her own miseries, took a good look at her friend. Cordelia was glowing, so happy about something that she was unable to cease smiling. "Something has happened," Regina guessed. "Something delightful."

"My aunt and I have been invited to a house party by Lady Deerhaven," Cordelia confided. "I am terrified, Regina. What if his parents don't like me?"

Regina snorted. "They will love you. Just be yourself, Cordelia."

"Surely, I am not the marriage they planned for their son? You know my mother was a mill owner's daughter. Perhaps they just want to meet me so they can tell me in person that I am reaching above myself. Perhaps I shall make a stupid mistake and show everyone how unsuited I am to being a marchioness."

Regina took her friend by both hands. "Listen to me, Cordelia. You are as good as anyone else." She indicated the ballroom with the tip of her head. "Better than most of those empty-headed idiots who can trace their ancestry back on both sides to some villainous robber who came over with the Conqueror. Your father was born a gentleman, and you were born a lady. You've been raised to it, too. You have had the same training as the rest of us in proper etiquette and in managing a house and servants. And you are clever enough to work out what you don't know and learn it."

Cordelia still looked doubtful.

Regina took another tack. "You need to think about what will make you happy. Do you want to be a marchioness?"

The glow returned. "I want Paul. Lord Spenhurst, that is. I would prefer he was not in line to become a marquess, but I would rather learn to fit in his world than live in mine without him." Her eyes turned dreamy, and her smile broadened. "And Regina? He feels the same way."

Regina pressed down her surge of envy. "That's your answer, then. You can do this, Cordelia. Remember you are every bit as good as they are. And I suppose your uncle has already advised you that your dowry will be very much appreciated."

"Paul says he doesn't care about my dowry," Cordelia insisted.

Regina, having seen Lord Spenhurst watching Cordelia, thought this was probably true. "Which is excellent," she said. "You don't want his title but will get the advantage of passing it on to your children anyway. He doesn't want your money but will be able to spend it on his estate which, if rumor is true, would benefit from the infusion of cash."

Cordelia laughed. "Dear Regina, so practical. Thank you, my darling friend. I will write to you to tell you how I get on."

The following afternoon, Mama and Regina had a garden party to attend. Papa had initially accepted the invitation, but he said he was feeling unwell, and they should go without him.

He looked pale and was mopping sweat from his forehead. "Should we call a doctor, Papa?" Regina asked.

"No, no," he insisted. "I shall be perfectly well. Something I have eaten disagreed with me." He put a hand to his chest as if to ease the pain. "You ladies go and enjoy yourselves and be sure to tell me all about it when you return."

Regina said that she would prefer to stay home, but Mama refused to consider it.

"I'm certain Mr. Paddimore will stay with Lord Kingsley," she huffed. Regina had no idea why Mama disliked Mr. Paddimore so, but her antipathy was clear. Papa preferred Mr. Paddimore's company to Mama's, so perhaps that was the explanation, but Regina could not imagine Mama enjoying the quiet evenings that Papa preferred, and why should he not spend time with his friend when she was out at one social event after another?

According to the gossipmongers, Mr. Paddimore had taken his illegitimate son into his house to raise as his ward. While mildly scandalous, this did not prevent Mr. Paddimore from being received everywhere. However, perhaps Mama's dislike was rooted in the existence of the little boy and Mr. Paddimore's refusal to ignore him. Regina thought it was rather admirable of him to give the child his name and his protection.

None of her particular friends were at the garden party, but Miss Wharton's allies were out in force. Regina wished even more that she had been permitted to stay home with her father.

She wondered where Cordelia was. Had she already left London? How would Lord and Lady Deerhaven receive her?

"Go for a walk, Regina," Mama said. "I have seen someone I wish to talk to."

Mama had relaxed a little over the Season, accepting that Regina was not going to run wild when out of sight for a minute or two. Usually, Regina was happy to go off with friends, but with none of them in sight, she asked, "May I not stay with you, Mama?"

"No, dear," Mama said, firmly. "Run along."

Regina put up her parasol and strolled down through the garden, nodding to acquaintances. She crossed the lawn at the bottom and strolled back up the path on the other side. She was approaching the house when a footman hurried up to her. "Miss Kingsley?"

"Yes, that is I," she said.

"A note for you, miss." He handed over a folded piece of paper and hurried away before she could question him.

It was from Cordelia, her friend's usual neat copperplate an untidy scrawl that hinted at a perturbed mind.

Regina, I don't know what to do! It is dreadful. I need your advice, dear friend. I am waiting in a little parlor by the front door—I cannot bear for all those horrid gossipers to see me. Please do not fail me. Cordelia.

Regina didn't hesitate. She hurried through the house, too anxious to find her mother and let her know where she was going. To the left of the front entrance, a door stood a little ajar. Regina could see a couple of chairs and low table through the gap. This must be it.

She pushed the door wider and was three steps into the room before she realized that Cordelia was not there.

Behind her, the door slammed shut. Regina spun around.

Mr. David Deffew stood there, grinning. "Hello, Miss Kingsley. How good of you to join me."

"Please get out of my way," Regina demanded. "I am looking for my friend."

"I would like to be your friend," Mr. Deffew crooned. "But if you mean Miss Milton, she has, or so I understand, left Town."

"It was a trick," Regina realized.

Mr. Deffew's smirk confirmed her suspicion.

"Get out of my way, Mr. Deffew. Whatever you think you are up to, I am not interested."

"Such fire," Mr. Deffew crooned.

At that moment, someone spoke on the other side of the door. Suddenly, Mr. Deffew leapt on Regina, crushed her in his arms, tore at her dress, and pressed sloppy kisses to whatever part of her face he could reach as she struggled.

The door burst open, and people crowded into the room. Miss Wharton, exchanging triumphant glances with Mr. Deffew. Regina's mother, looking outraged. Lady Beddlesnirt, one of the most notable gossips of the ton. Others, too, all expressing gleeful horror.

Regina broke free of Mr. Deffew and ran to her mother. "It is not what it looks, Mama. Mr. Deffew tricked me. I got this note!" She held it up and Miss Wharton snatched it out of her hand and threw it in the fire.

Mama turned to Mr. Deffew. "Shame on you, sir."

Mr. Deffew bowed. "I was overcome by love, Lady Kingsley. I will make it right, of course."

"A betrothal," Mama announced to the room.

"No!" Regina exclaimed. "Mama, he tricked me. I don't want to marry him."

"Nonsense, Regina," Mama insisted. "You have no choice. You must marry. Everyone has seen..." She indicated Regina's bodice, torn right down the front so that her corset cover showed.

Before Regina could respond, the crowd stirred and then parted as Mr. Paddimore excused his way to the front. He took in Regina's tattered state, Mama's expression, Mr. Deffew's triumphant mien.

Regina saw the moment when he decided to set it all aside. He addressed Mama. "Lady Kingsley, Lord Kingsley is very ill. The doctor says you must come at once."

"My poor darling!" Mr. Deffew pronounced, loudly. "I will, of course, come with you. As your betrothed, my place is by your side."

The softening of the censorious faces around her loosened Regina's tongue. "I am not betrothed to you, Mr. Deffew. I did not come here to meet you. I did not ask to be assaulted by you. I will not marry you. I do not want you in my house."

"Lady Kingsley," Mr. Paddimore said, his voice harsher and more commanding than Regina had ever heard it. "Your shawl, if you please."

Mama looked as if she would argue but thought better of it in the face of Mr. Paddimore's expression. He took the shawl from her and tucked it around Regina, covering her torn gown. "We have no time to discuss this," he said. "Deffew, call on me at my club tomorrow. Lord Kingsley will not be able to receive you."

"You go too far, Mr. Paddimore," Lady Kingsley said. "It is not for you to make decisions for Lord Kingsley."

Mr. Paddimore still had a comforting hand on Regina's shoulder. He gave it a brief squeeze. "Miss Kingsley, we must hurry. I can take you in my coach if your mother is not prepared to leave yet."

"If the gel doesn't marry the Deffew boy, she is ruined," Lady Beddlesnirt announced.

Mr. Paddimore turned his glare on her. "As we speak, her father is struggling for his life, madam, and you are in my way."

He conducted Regina through the gap that opened under the influence of his commanding presence, and Mama scurried behind.

He came with them in Mama's carriage, and for the first time, Mama asked what was wrong with Papa. "The doctor says it is his heart," Mr. Paddimore explained, his voice strained, as if he had to force the words. "He had a bad attack perhaps an hour ago. I didn't realize how bad—he kept saying it was something he had eaten. And then he clutched his arm and fell unconscious."

He blinked a couple of times, as if to clear his eyes. "He is still unconscious, Elizabeth. He might not wake again."

Regina must have made a sound, for Mr. Paddimore put his hand over hers and pressed, gently. "I am sorry, Miss Kingsley. I know this is hard."

Mama's snort was her only comment, and nothing further was said until they were in the Kingsley front hall.

"How is he?" Mr. Paddimore asked the butler.

"Much the same, sir. The doctor is still with him."

"I will go to him," Mama announced, and Regina was about to follow when Mr. Paddimore put a hand on her arm. "Run upstairs and change, Miss Kingsley," he advised. "If he awakens and sees you so disheveled…"

Regina almost dropped her mother's shawl at the reminder.

She had forgotten how she must look, and when she got up to her bedchamber and was able to see herself in the mirror, she realized it was even worse than she'd thought.

Her maid entered the room and gasped. "Miss! What happened to you!" There was no chance that she would keep Regina's state to herself. It would be all around the house in ten minutes, and across London with the breakfast cups.

Regina sighed. If the servants didn't gossip, the *Ton* would. "I was attacked, but that doesn't matter now. Find me something I can get into quickly and help me tidy my hair so I can go and sit with my father."

Papa was nearly as white as his sheets and was so still Regina thought he had died until she saw his chest rise and fall. She waited, holding her breath. It seemed a very long time until the next rise and fall. Mama was sitting at his bedside, holding his hand. Like Regina, she had taken the time to change into undress and have her hair taken down from its ornate style.

Mr. Paddimore was in the corner with the doctor. They were speaking in undertones, with frequent glances towards the bed.

Regina took the chair on the other side of her father.

Her mother's lips were moving. Was she praying? It was a good idea. Regina tried to pray, too, but all she could think was, *please, God. Please, God.*

Mr. Paddimore and the doctor parted. The doctor walked to the door, and Mr. Paddimore came over to the bed. "Lady Kingsley, the doctor would like to have a word with you." He put out a hand to help her rise, but she ignored him and stood up on her own. "Would you like me to come with you?" he asked.

Mama treated him to a scathing glance—a comprehensive rejection, and all without a word.

She left the bedroom with the doctor, and Mr. Paddimore took the seat she had been using, and fixed bleak eyes on his friend's face.

"What did he say?" Regina asked.

He seemed to come from a very long way away, needing to

refocus his eyes so they could see her. "I had better let your mother tell you," he said. "Regina, about Deffew. You will not be made to marry him," he promised. "Your father wouldn't hear of it."

Regina took another look at the still figure in the bed and caught back her fear that her father would not be alive to stop it.

Mr. Paddimore must have read her face. "Regina, if your father is too unwell to protect you, he has declared me your guardian and trustee of your wealth. I promise you, neither Lord Kingsley nor I will give our consent to a match with Deffew."

"How dare you, Gideon!" The shocked and angry words came from the doorway, where Mama stood, her fists clenched. "The girl has been ruined, I tell you. Marriage to Deffew is her only chance of marriage. Do you hate me so much you would destroy Regina to get your revenge?"

"I will not discuss this in front of Geoffrey and Regina," Mr. Paddimore said. "Pull yourself together, Elizabeth. We can argue tomorrow, and in another room. At the moment, your husband needs you and so does your daughter."

Mama opened her mouth and then closed it again, clearly having second thoughts about whatever had sprung to her lips.

"You have not eaten," Mr. Paddimore said. "I will order something light. Elizabeth, Regina asked me what the doctor said. I told her she should ask you."

Mama stepped to one side to allow Mr. Paddimore to leave the room, suddenly looking much older. She sank into her chair and took up her husband's hand again. "I am sorry, Regina. The doctor says his heart is struggling. He is unlikely to survive more than a few days, and if he does, another attack like this one could carry him off at any time."

"Mama!" Regina protested.

Mama sighed deeply. "It is best you know the truth without the bark on it. Your Papa will not be there to lend his protection against the consequences of today's mischief, and Gideon, for all he thinks so much of himself, does not have any influence on the

Ton." She shook her head.

"I expect that Deffew will make a poor husband, but at least your money will mean you will not have to live with his horrid father, and soon enough you will have children to console you. If Lady Beddlesnirt and that nasty creature Miss Wharton had not seen—but it is of no use to repine. Your choice is between Deffew and ruin. You will live the rest of your life in the country as a spinster. And, if you choose ruin, you take me and your brother William down with you. Think of that while you are deciding what suits yourself."

Regina sat back in her chair, stunned that her mother would promote this heinous marriage over the body of her dying father. The room remained silent until Mr. Paddimore returned, carrying another chair, and leading a short procession of maids with food and drink.

Chapter Seven

Paris

ASH WRESTLED WITH guilt. He had it all. Amazing accommodation. Gourmet food. A high-fashion wardrobe. Servants to
do the cleaning and cooking and all the hard physical labor.
Access to libraries, museums, entertainments, even a mistress.
And on top of that, a quarterly salary that gave him more money
than he had ever seen in his life.

And all Rex asked in return was for Ash to manage every
aspect of Rex's correspondence. Answering invitations and
requests for donations. Replying to letters and notes. Even
personal letters from his mother. Ash was required to read
everything to Rex, and then write the answer that Rex dictated—
or, more often, outlined, for Ash to fill in and make courteous.

Ash wondered why. Certainly, secretaries expected to deal
with business matters and importunate beggars. But wouldn't it
be easier for Rex to read his personal correspondence? Wouldn't
any normal person write to their own mother?

Until one day, towards the end of their stay in Paris.

Beckham, the tutor, was sulking. That morning, he had complained again about Rex's plans to continue to explore the
museums and art galleries of Paris without him. Today, they

planned to visit the Louvre Museum, in the old royal palace. Rex had talked the official in charge of the restoration of the Louvre Museum into a special tour, ahead of the reopening in July, and Beckham wanted to go, too. "This is part of your education, Lord Arthur," he insisted. "You will not read, so you must experience."

At that, Rex lost his usually endless patience and told Beckham that he didn't know nearly as much as he thought he did, bored his pupils to sleep before he taught them, and was, whatever he said, not coming.

Beckham seethed for the rest of the morning. Rex ignored him, and Ash took his cue from that and continued with his usual morning tasks.

One of the letters in the morning pile was a hand-folded billet on pale lavender scented paper, sealed with purple wax. The stamp was a simple four-petalled rose. Ash opened it, then closed it and said to Rex, "You might not want me to read this one. It is from one of your admirers and is very... shall we say... specific."

Rex grinned. "I have no secrets from you, Ash, but perhaps we might save it until later."

"He has no secrets, he says," Beckham sneered. "So, Mr. Ashby, personal secretary and partner in depravity, has his lordship told you that he does not read because he *cannot* read?"

"Enough," said Rex, but Beckham talked right over the top of him.

"He is the shame of the Verseys. Twenty generations of scholars and men of letters, and now this. Is he stupid or just lazy? Even his parents cannot tell, and yet I am meant to tutor him? How, I ask you? He ignores everything I say, and he won't even try to read the simplest documents. As for writing, his copybook was a disgrace, back when he was young enough to be beaten for it. All they could do was send the dunce overseas so no one at home could find out that he was a buffoon; an ape masquerading as a lord."

Rex took a step towards Beckham then sat down, gasping for breath, his face white and his eyes wide and anguished.

This had happened once before, and Smith had leapt into action, with a warm flannel on his master's chest, a bowl of steam, and a glass of hot water and honey. Ash called for him. "Smith! Lord Arthur needs you."

Beckham ran out of words, staring at the suffering young man. Smith hurried into the room, took one look at his master, and ran to hover over him, rubbing his back and muttering about calming down.

"Get out," Ash said to Beckham. "Go to your room. Go for a walk. Pack your bag and go back to England. I don't care but get out. Lord Arthur doesn't need to see you until he is ready to deal with your insolence and your treachery."

"You can't..." Beckham began, but when Ash took several steps towards him, fists clenched, he broke and ran, out of the room and down the passage to his bedchamber.

At Smith's command, Ash ordered one of the men to fetch a bowl and a jug of boiling water, and soon Rex was breathing in steam, sipping honeyed water, and breathing a lot more easily.

"So, there you have it," he said to Ash after Smith packed up all the paraphernalia and returned to whatever the crisis had interrupted. "Your employer is an illiterate buffoon."

Ash shrugged. "Not a buffoon," he objected. "You're one of the smartest men I know. Your memory is amazing. You notice things I would never see without you. And you have an incredible ability to work out what other people are thinking so you can talk them into doing what you want them to."

"Then why can't I read and write, Ash? Every other child can write their name before they leave the nursery. I could not make anything but a capital A when I was six, and half the time, I got that upside down or on its side, or so they said. It looked fine to me." He shrugged.

"Once I was in the schoolroom, my governess tried, my sisters tried, everyone tried to teach me my letters. But even after I had mostly mastered them, they wouldn't form into words. They just wouldn't. They still don't. No matter how hard I try, they wriggle away from me, or dance around on the page until my brain hurts. And now you are going to think I am crazy." He slumped in his chair, staring at his second glass of hot water and honey, which his valet had abjured him to sip, slowly.

Ash shook his head. "I don't understand it at all. But if you say it is so, I believe you. So, do you want me to read you the Comtesse's letter?"

Rex straightened and shifted his stare to Ash. "Is that all you have to say? Don't you mind?"

"For your sake," Ash said. "Not for mine. I hope you don't object, but I like knowing there is something I can do for you, when there is so much you do for me. I was feeling quite unnecessary, Rex."

Rex looked stunned. "Right." He took a sip from his glass. "Right. Well, then." Another sip, as he continued to absorb Ash's reaction. "Go ahead. What does the Comtesse want?"

"You, you gorgeous specimen of English aristocracy, you," Ash drawled, managing to look disgusted in a suitably envious way. He read the letter, a mix of flowery phrases and earthy suggestions, some of them a real challenge to his growing French vocabulary.

"Is that actually possible?" he asked a couple of times, and Rex suggested he ask Vivienne to demonstrate.

Rex dictated a stiff and proper reply, all polite nothings. "His Grace says that titled women with the morals of barn cats are more trouble than they are worth," he told Ash. His Grace, Ash was learning, was the fount of all wisdom in the eyes of his youngest son. Poor Rex, to be considered a disappointment by his greatest hero.

They made their tour of the Louvre, Ash watching Rex closely. He was a bit breathless by the end of the tour but recovered quickly in the carriage home. "You don't have to hover, Ash," he said. "I usually know my limits, except when I'm ambushed, like this morning."

"What are you going to do with him?" Ash asked.

Rex gave his most wicked grin. "Send him back to England, and you are going to write a letter to my father telling him exactly what Beckham said. Word for word. His Grace will not be amused."

Beckham departed as soon as Mitterrand was able to organize his travel. He would arrive several days after the letter to the duke. "If he is wise," said Rex, "he won't present himself to my father."

Ash didn't ask Vivienne about the suggestions the Comtesse made. He was increasingly uncomfortable with the relationship. It was impossible to ignore the fact that he and Vivienne had nothing in common apart from the obvious fact that their breeding parts were complementary.

Out of bed, she bored him. And to be fair, he bored her. Ash didn't think he was cut out for shallow dalliances that satisfied nothing except his physical arousal. It wasn't enough—for him, at least. If he ever took another mistress, he was going to look for one who was able to converse about something other than dance movements, the politics of the dance troupe, and ladies' fashion. Not one, though, who smelled like an English garden. And there he was, thinking of Ginny again.

When it was time to leave Paris to see something of the rest of France, he was relieved the two dancers refused Rex's invitation to come with them. He accompanied Rex to the jewelers to help choose their parting presents.

As Rex haggled over the cost of a necklace and earrings each—pearls with rubies for Giselle and pearls with emeralds for Vivienne—Ash roamed around the store looking at the displays. His eye was caught by a little enamel brooch in the shape of a dancing shoe dangling from a matching bow.

Rex, having finalized the deal to his satisfaction, came to see what Ash was admiring. "It's a pretty little trinket, but I don't think Vivienne will appreciate it. She'll expect something she can sell if times get tough."

Ash agreed. "A practical soul is our Vivienne. I wasn't thinking of her." In his mind's eye, he saw Ginny, her eyes shining as she watched the dancers and talked to him about her hopes and dreams. "How much?" he asked the jeweler.

He refused Rex's offer of adding it to his own purchase. He had money in his pocket—money he'd earned by answering Rex's correspondence and even writing Rex's letters to his parents and sisters.

This was to be a gift from him, if he could think of a way to send it without offending.

Chapter Eight

REGINA'S FATHER NEVER recovered consciousness and breathed his last not long before sunrise. Mama, once the doctor pronounced him dead, sent Regina and Mr. Paddimore from the room, saying that Regina was too young for what came next, and Mr. Paddimore was not family.

In the parlor, Regina cried on Mr. Paddimore's shoulder. Papa was gone. She couldn't believe it. "I didn't even know he had a bad heart," she sobbed.

"He did not want you to know," Mr. Paddimore soothed. "He did not want you to worry. The doctor said, if he was lucky, he could have a few more years. And Geoffrey was always lucky."

Regina heard the strain in his voice and looked up to see tears sliding silently down his face. "You will miss him, too."

Mr. Paddimore nodded. "I will. He has been my dearest friend for ten years. There was no one else like him."

Regina nodded her agreement. "At least he did not know I had ruined myself. He would have been so disappointed."

Mr. Paddimore patted her back. "From what little I heard, it was not your doing. Here. Come and sit down. I shall send for tea, and you shall tell me all about it. Miss Kingsley, you are not to worry. I will sort out this problem with David Deffew, I promise you. But I need to hear from you what really happened."

He left the room to order the tea and came back to say he had also sent a traveling coach to fetch Regina's brother William, now Lord Kingsley, from school. "He will be here before noon, Miss Kingsley, and you can be a comfort to one another."

William would at least be a comfort to Mama. He had always been closer to her, just as Regina had been closer to Papa. She caught back another sob.

The servants brought food as well as tea—a selection of pastries and bread rolls. Regina wanted nothing, but she sipped the tea Mr. Paddimore poured her.

"Tell me about last night," he said.

She did, haltingly at first, and then it all poured out. The note she thought was from Cordelia. Mr. Deffew's attack. All the people crowding into the room. Miss Wharton burning the note, which was Regina's only concrete evidence she had been lured there by a lie.

She didn't tell him about Mama's insistence that she marry Mr. Deffew. Mr. Paddimore and Mama's relationship was hostile enough, without her adding fuel to the fire.

After he reassured her again, she went up to get dressed for the day. Mr. Paddimore was going back to his townhouse to do the same, and would go on to his club to have a word with Mr. Deffew. "Then you can put this behind you, Miss Kingsley," he said.

Regina thought he was overly optimistic. The gossip would already be all over town.

By the time Regina went back to her father's bed chamber, Mama had left. Papa lay on the bed dressed in his Parliamentary robes, looking like a wax effigy of himself. His valet was tidying the room, stopping from time to time to wipe his eyes.

"I came to sit with Papa," Regina told him.

"Of course, Miss." The chairs that had been beside the bed had all been put back in their places, but he fetched one for her, then left her alone. She could hear him moving around in her father's dressing room.

Regina sat and took her father's hand, then put it back. It felt horrid. Cold and stiff.

She found herself pouring out all her worries to him as she always had.

"I do not want to bury myself in the country for the rest of my life, Papa," she concluded. "Yet I will not marry Mr. Deffew, and I cannot imagine anyone else will have me after Miss Wharton and the other scandal mongers finish shredding my character. You would be so disappointed in me."

"Miss Kingsley?" It was her father's valet, returning into the room.

"Yes, Medhurst?"

"I am sorry, Miss. Your mother is downstairs with Mr. Deffew, and he has a traveling coach outside."

For a moment, Regina froze, torn between disbelief and anger. *She wouldn't. Would she? How could she!*

"Medhurst, could you get a message to Mr. Paddimore? He might still be at his home, or he might have gone to his club, Westruthers."

Medhurst nodded. "I will take it myself, Miss. What am I to tell him? Or will you write a note?"

She thought for a moment. "What you told me about Mr. Deffew and the coach. And please ask him to come quickly."

She was just in time. The door opened and her mother swept into the room. "Ah. Here you are, Regina. You have a journey to make, child. Come along. You shall need to change into a carriage dress."

"Why, Mama? What is happening? Can I not sit with Papa?" She did not have to feign tears. They rose unbidden.

"I know. You are upset, of course. But this is more important. I will not let you be ruined, Regina. Mr. Deffew is willing to marry you and save your reputation."

"I cannot marry Mr. Deffew, Mama," Regina explained. "Mr. Paddimore said he is my guardian now, and he will not give his consent. I will not be of age for another four years, Mama."

Mama ignored what she did not want to hear. "Hurry and get dressed, child. I have told your maid to pack for you, so you need only to get yourself ready. Medhurst? Bother the man. Where has he gone?"

She bustled away, certain her commands would be followed.

Regina gave her father's cold cheek a kiss. She hated leaving him alone, but she had a better chance of delaying her mother if she pretended to comply.

Her maid expressed her sympathies but otherwise said very little. She was packing a large trunk. How long did Mama expect the trip to be? They were headed to Scotland, Regina supposed.

She saw gowns of every color going into the trunk. They gave her a possible way to delay being forced to leave with Deffew.

"I cannot wear those, Annie. I am in mourning. Find me a black carriage dress, please, then unpack everything colored from the trunk and repack it."

As her maid repacked the trunk, Regina took her time, changing everything from the skin out, and calling her maid from the packing every few minutes to help with a tape or a button. Then, when she was fully dressed, she waited a few moments, turning this way and that in the mirror before saying, "I have changed my mind. This one does not feel at all comfortable, and I cannot imagine what it will be like after hours in a carriage. I'll have the dark grey one with the black ribbon trim."

"But, Miss," her maid protested. "That was the first one I packed." Poor Annie. Regina felt bad for using her this way, but it had to be done to stop her mother's plans from succeeding. So Regina insisted, and the whole trunk had to be unpacked. Her maid was part way through the repacking and Regina was all but dressed again when her mother came to see what was taking so long, spoiling Regina's plan to insist on a third gown, one that she knew was now nearly at the bottom of the trunk.

"Why are you still dressing? You and Mr. Deffew must be away from here quickly. Already, I have told them to move the traveling carriage around to the mews, so the neighbors don't know what is going on. Hurry, Regina, hurry. Here. Let me."

She batted Regina's hands away from the buttons on the redingote she was studiously misbuttoning, and quickly set them to rights.

"Have you not finished packing that trunk yet, girl?"

"It is my fault, Mama," Regina volunteered, guilt washing over her again. She hadn't wanted to get the girl into trouble. "I wanted something she had already packed, so she had to start again. I will finish, Annie. You had better go and pack a bag for yourself."

"No need for that," Mama said. "Annie will not be going with you, Regina."

"But I cannot travel with Mr. Deffew alone, in a closed carriage, Mama. Even with my maid, it is improper."

"You are already compromised beyond repair, silly child. And he will be your husband within days. Any impropriety will be forgiven once you have his ring on your finger."

Regina searched her mind for any other way to delay, but Mama grabbed her arm and began hauling her towards the door. "Hurry," she said again.

Mr. Deffew was pacing in the parlor. He looked harried. "Are you sure this is a good idea?" He said to Mama, as they entered.

Regina looked at him and something her father had told her surfaced in her mind. She heard his words so clearly it was as if he was in the room with her and as if his voice was not only in her memory. *You don't have to worry about a fortune hunter, princess. Just tell them I've tied your dowry and your wealth up so tightly they'll never get their hands on it.*

"Mr. Deffew, a word, if you please."

Mama gave her a glare. "We don't have time for that now, Regina. Go out through the back to the mews, Mr. Deffew. The carriage is there."

"I don't have any money, Mr. Deffew," Regina said.

"Don't be ridiculous, Regina," her mother said, at the same

time as Mr. Deffew objected, "Five thousand pounds, and whatever you inherit from your father."

Regina spoke over her mother's insistence that none of this mattered and they must hurry. "The dowry, if I marry with the consent of my guardian. My inheritance from my father goes into a trust, and I cannot touch it—again, unless I have the consent of my guardian."

Mama protested again, but Mr. Deffew narrowed his eyes and told Regina, "Your mother said her brother has been appointed your guardian and will approve our marriage."

"Mr. Paddimore is my guardian, Mr. Deffew. You should have met with him this morning, as he asked. It would have saved you the expense of a traveling carriage."

Mr. Paddimore spoke from the doorway. "Miss Kingsley is correct, Deffew. So, consider this. If you had forced an elopement—one that Miss Kingsley does not want, by the way—I would have put the dowry back into Miss Kingsley's trust. You and your father would never have seen a penny of it."

A gleam in Mr. Deffew's eye hinted he had seen a way out. "If she doesn't marry me, she will be ruined," he warned. "And if she does, and you don't release her dowry—and make us a substantial allowance from her trust—I will tell the whole world your dirty little secret. I know about you and Lord Kingsley, and I know who the true father of the boy is that you have claimed as your own. *And* the identity of his mother."

Mr. Paddimore sighed. "Well, Elizabeth? Is this what you wanted? A son-in-law who attempted to ravish your daughter, will marry her although she loathes him, and threatens to drag your husband's name through the mud in order to get his hands on her money?"

Regina's mother had turned white, with two hectic spots of color on her cheeks. She pressed her lips together and said nothing.

Mr. Paddimore turned back to Mr. Deffew. "Publish whatever lies you can create, you cur. Make your attempt to tarnish the name of a highly respected peer. And I will use every penny I have to destroy you. Yes, and your brother and father, too. But! Mark my words! You. Will. Not. Marry. Miss. Kingsley. Now get out of here before I chase you out with a riding crop."

He took a step towards Mr. Deffew, who broke and ran.

Regina's mother broke the silence he left behind him. "Now what, Gideon? He will destroy Geoffrey's reputation as he has ruined Regina's. And you are going to let him."

"He can try, Elizabeth. But you and I will treat his accusations with scorn, as we did last time. And it will all be speculation and hearsay, as it was last time. As to Regina, we have several courses of action."

He smiled at Regina. "Do not worry, Miss Kingsley. We shall contrive to brush through."

Chapter Nine

Sardinia, February 1807

ASH'S BROOCH AND the covering letter had been returned, with no comment. He tucked them both into a trunk and decided to forget both them and Ginny. Despite his best intention, the sylph stayed in his mind, as did the dance that they never had.

He did nothing about it until one day several years later when he came across an ornament—a delicate pair of slippers in Venetian glass—in a street market in Sardinia after they left the Kingdom of Naples ahead of the French armies.

He couldn't resist buying it.

Elaine, Lady Barker, was the sister closest to Rex in age, and Rex's most regular correspondent. She had found Regina's address at Ash's request, and with it sent a chatty letter full of all the gossip she could find, which was not much:

People remember that she married in haste shortly after her father's death. There was some talk that she had been compromised, but I remember her husband, Gideon Paddimore, and I must say it seems unlikely. No one seems to know any more. Mr. Paddimore was badly injured some three years after their marriage. Highwaymen, it is said. The villains were never caught, despite the efforts of the authorities. You might be interested to know that Ash's stepfather, Major Deffew, was shot dead by the same reprobates.

As to the Paddimores, since the incident, Mr. Paddimore has been an invalid, and the family has lived retired in the country."

So, she was married. Of course, she was. She probably had several children by now, though Elaine didn't mention them. All the more reason why Mr. Paddimore might allow her to receive a couple of presents from a childhood friend. Meaningless tokens. Nothing threatening.

He packed them with great care and wrote a covering letter. A reminder of who he was. His compliments to her husband. His discovery that a built-up heel allowed him to dance, and his wish that he'd known in time for them to dance. And the story of his discovery of the little glass dancing slippers, and the fierce little street peddler who had eventually consented to sell them to him. For three or four times their value, but he would not tell her that.

Rex wandered into their living room with a glass of Sardinian wine in each hand and gave one of them to Ash. "Is that a reply to Elaine? Read what you've said."

"It is a letter to Mrs. Paddimore," Ash told him.

"Private, then. I beg your pardon." Rex turned away, but Ash stopped him.

"Not at all." He read it out loud, and Rex offered to draw the peddler in the margins.

Ash handed over the letter, and sipped his wine while Rex worked. It was a local *Vernaccia*, dry and full-bodied. Another skill that the duke had conveyed to his son and that Rex had shared with Ash—the ability to enjoy the subtleties of wine.

He laughed when Rex handed him back the letter. The pen and ink sketch had certainly captured the essence of the wizened little man.

"You should send the little sylph a copy of our book," Rex

suggested. "She and her husband might enjoy it."

Ash added a note about the book to the letter.

I hope you and Mr. Paddimore enjoy the little stories that Lord Arthur and I tell of our travels. They began as letters to Rex's sisters, and it was one of them, Lady Barker, who said that they might give pleasure beyond the family circle.

Rex and I wish to send you both our kindest regards.

Your humble servant
Elijah Ashby.

"I need you to sign the flyleaf," he told his friend.

Rex took the pen Ash held out to him and made his usual illegible scrawl in the place Ash pointed to. In the past five years, he'd managed to improve both his reading and his writing, but it was still not something he enjoyed.

They were rightly on the books as co-authors, though. Rex had a near-perfect memory, and the knack of picking the perfect word to describe sights, smells, sounds, and other details to bring a description alive.

Ash could string Rex's ideas together into a coherent story and add his own observations.

And both of them contributed to the illustrations, Rex focusing on people and animals, and Ash on buildings and landscapes.

He put the letter inside the flyleaf to the book and began to wrap it.

Little sylph was a good description. *Was she still a sylph after nearly seven years?*

The package went down to the British envoy the next day, to be included in the diplomatic post, and thus began a correspondence that would last for more than a decade.

Three Gables, Chelmsford, July 1809

REGINA HAD FINISHED her reply to Elijah's latest letter. His letters arrived at random intervals, always with a present tucked inside. They had become a highlight of her quiet life in the country. He claimed to appreciate her replies, and the little items she sent in return—an embroidered handkerchief, a card of pressed wildflowers, a jar of marmalade sent when one of his letters described Lord Arthur searching an oriental market for the delicacy.

She put down her pen. With her other hand on the little shoe brooch she wore, she read out loud to her husband what she had written.

Dear Mr. Ashby

I am writing to thank you for the package of shawls that arrived a few days ago. How beautiful they are, and so warm! The pretty hair ornament, too! I am amassing quite a collection of shoes!

Your accompanying letter made me feel as if I were with you in the marketplace in Acre, smelling the crisp, desert air and the wonderful spices, and hearing the bellows of camels and the shouts of hawkers. Please thank Lord Arthur for the wonderful painting of a camel and rider, which our son Geoffrey loves. We had it framed by the estate carpenter, and it now hangs in pride of place over his desk in the schoolroom.

I also wanted to let you know how much my husband and I enjoyed the most recent volume of Adventures Around the World, *by* Two Gentlemen. *Much though Gideon and I appreciate your signed copies, we could not wait for the next installment, so put in an order with the publisher as soon as we received your letter saying the manuscript was on its way to England.*

Please give my kindest regards to Lord Arthur.

I remain,

Sincerely, your friend

Regina Paddimore.

"What do you think, Gideon?" she asked, when she had finished.

He smiled, and nodded, a short single jerk of the head. During the attack three years ago, he had been shot in the spine defending Regina from abduction and worse. It had given her time to pull out the little muff pistol he had taught her to use and prevent the assailant from taking a second shot which would surely have killed him.

He was having a bad day today, though he never complained. Regina knew, however, when the pain was close to unbearable. He would sink into himself and find even the briefest speech a strain. On such days, she would spend hours by his bed reading to him, because he had once told her that her voice helped to keep him anchored in the world.

He seldom took laudanum, or even alcohol unlaced by opium, telling Regina, "Once I start taking it regularly, Regina, it will affect my mind. I've seen it happen to others. When I've taught you and William all you need to know, then perhaps."

He was determined that she and her brother would be well-prepared to manage the businesses and other investments that grew their wealth. Indeed, since the attack that had nearly killed him and had left him permanently disabled, Regina and her brother had taken over much of the work—Regina for the Paddimore holdings, and William for the Kingsleys.

Gideon was still the final authority, as William's trustee until he turned twenty-five and as Regina's husband. More and more, he was expressing any disagreement with their decisions as a point of view to be considered rather than a correction. Twice, after vigorous discussion, they had changed his mind.

William and Regina had been thrilled, and Gideon said he had never been prouder.

Cairo, January 1811

THE SOUNDS OF the city dropped away as the three men entered the house in Cairo, with its thick walls. Ash and Rex stopped to take off the European clothing they had donned for the funeral to do honor to one of their two remaining men-of-all-work, a companion in travel for seven years, who had died of a fever.

In the more comfortable robes of Ottoman gentlemen, they went out to sit in the inner courtyard, where a large jug of freshly squeezed juices waited.

Rex lifted a finger to attract one of the silent servants who squatted on his heels in the shade. "Ask Mr. Fullaby to join us, please." Fullaby was the last man-of-all work, and the only other English person in the house. He should be here, grieving with them.

Of the seven who had set out from England, only three were left. After Beckham, Mitterrand had been next to go. He'd tried to sell Rex to the French authorities when the Peace of Amiens collapsed, but Ash overheard his plotting with the innkeeper and the officer in charge of the town where they were staying. The rest of Rex's party escaped and fled up into the mountains and across the border into Spain.

One of the men-of-all-work had fallen in love with a local woman in Greece and stayed behind. Rex had pensioned his valet off a year ago, paying his passage back to England with a letter for Rex's bankers that would leave him comfortably situated for the remainder of his days.

Rex and Ash could afford to be generous. Over the years, they'd sniffed out business opportunities and political information. Their investments and their travel stories earned both of them a nice income. They were not rich, but they could afford to travel as they pleased and to live well while they did so.

They were also on the payroll of the Foreign Office, though

that money was being held for them in England and went back into their investments. Ash had long since ceased drawing a salary as secretary, but Rex continued to insist on taking their travel and living expenses out of his allowance from the duchy. He called it, with no small bitterness, "the money the duke pays me to stay away from England."

Fullaby arrived to argue about whether he should be sitting with the gentlemen, but gave into Rex's persuasions, and they sat in the cool of the courtyard next to the splashing fountain. At first, they talked about their deceased friend, but that led to discussion of their travels so far and where they might go next.

It was not until later that Ash found the local British representative had sent over the mail while they were out. Two of Rex's sisters had written, as had their publisher. And Ginny Paddimore, whose occasional letters were like a breath of home. Much though he loved seeing new places and learning new things, there were times he ached for England's changing seasons, verdant pastures, leafy trees, and all the dear, familiar things of his birthplace.

He began a reply immediately.

Dear Regina,

I was so pleased to receive your letter and delighted that you and Mr. Paddimore enjoy the little stories that Rex and I tell of our travels. Thank you for the slippers. Rex and I are in awe at your talent with a needle and will wear them with great pride.

Your letter arrived at a sad time. You may remember me mentioning Melling, who came with us from England. I am sorry to report that he caught a fever here in Alexandria, and the local physicians were not able to save him. We will miss him, Rex, Fullaby, and I. The four of us have become very close during our travels, and we did not expect to leave him behind in this strange if beautiful and fascinating land.

I enclose several sketches that Rex and I have made of the wonderful sights we have seen here in Egypt.

These were the originals of illustrations they had made for the third volume of their travels. The pyramids, rising out of the desert. The sphinx, with its head of a human and body of lion, broken nose and all. A row of camels silhouetted against the sky as they traversed a sand dune, *dhows*, river cruisers, and *feluccas* on the mighty Nile.

He wondered if young Geoffrey would take some of them to decorate the walls of his chambers.

Rex wandered into his room, already talking. "Muhammed Ali has come through at last, Ash."

Muhammed Ali was the *Wāli*, the Ottoman viceroy of Egypt. Rex had been attempting for weeks to charm the man into allowing their party to leave Egypt and cross the Levant and Syria for Persia. The *Wāli* had taken some convincing that the English travelers could not be co-

opted to help educate his military and bureaucrats in European ways. An ambitious man, Muhammed Ali.

"We leave in two days," Rex said. "Is that a letter from *the sylph?*"

"We have several letters," Ash told him. "I'll read them to you." He handed over the slippers intended for Rex. "Mrs. Paddimore made you these."

They spent a pleasant half hour over the letters from England, and then returned to the topic of their departure. "If Ali had let us go a month ago, perhaps Melling would still be alive," Ash said, though agues and fevers could happen to anyone, anywhere.

Given some of the places they had been, it was surprising it had not happened earlier.

Three Gables, Chelmsford, July 1812

REGINA'S FRIENDSHIP WITH Cordelia had survived her retirement to the country. She had married her earl and was now his marchioness, and the mother of a growing tribe of daughters.

She wrote most weeks, chatty letters mostly full of the doings of her girls, two of whom were Regina's goddaughters. Regina wrote back with stories of her village and her household, and snippets of Elijah's letters. While the village gentry were most impressed that Regina was close friends with a marchioness, Cordelia was awed that Regina knew the famous travel writers.

Several times a year, Regina traveled to spend a week with Cordelia at Deercroft, the seat of the Marquesses of Deerhaven, leaving Geoffrey and Gideon to the care of the servants.

Gideon, who had finally given up arguing she should divorce him and find herself a proper husband, insisted on these holidays. She had to admit she looked forward to them. Though she also looked forward to returning home, as she was now, coming over the hill with her nose pressed up against the carriage window to catch her first glimpse of dear Three Gables down in the valley.

She would miss the little girls until she saw them again in four months, but not the way she missed her menfolk. Geoffrey was waiting on the steps when the carriage drew up. At twelve, he usually counted himself too old to hug his mother, but he made an exception for her return.

He had something more important on his mind, however, barely giving her time to kiss Gideon's cheek and ask how he had been in her absence. "Mother, we got a box from Mr. Ashby," he said, pointing to the item in question, which was about the size of a hatbox.

"Do let your mother get out of her dusty things," Gideon told him. "I would not let him open it, Regina, because it was addressed to you. How are your friends and the little girls?"

"All well, and they looked after me wonderfully. I am pleased to be home, though. Geoffrey, I shall go up to wash and change. If you fetch a bar to pry open the lid of the box, we shall open it before dinner."

"Your son is impatient, madam," Gideon teased, as the boy ran from the room as if someone had set fire to his shoes.

"Our son is twelve," she replied. She was the only mother Geoffrey had ever known. Gideon had been his father since shortly after his birth, since his real father had not been able to offer him a loving home. He had been two when Regina met him, and she a bride of seventeen. If she sometimes, especially when she saw Cordelia's little daughters, wished she had given birth to a child or two or three, she loved her son, and she relished the role of godmother.

She wondered what treasures would be in today's parcel. Regina now had several brooches, a pair of earrings, and a hair ornament, all with various forms of shoes. Several letters ago, Elijah had written that, while he had started the practice and still found at least half of the little trinkets, Lord Arthur had taken on the quest with enthusiasm, and never saw a place selling baubles and curios without stopping to ask if they had anything in the shape of a shoe. They also never failed to enclose a gift for Geoffrey, Gideon's ward, and for Gideon himself.

In her turn, Regina had embroidered bed slippers and hand-kerchiefs for them both. It seemed very little in return for a window on the whole world.

That's what she told Gideon, when he said she didn't deserve to be stuck in the country with no better company than an invalid and a schoolboy. She had the world at her fingertips in Elijah's letters, she told him.

Furthermore, she was not chained to Gideon's bedside. She went out to visit the neighbors. She joined in with village society. She traveled to see Cordelia. She had not seen her mother since the day of her wedding, but her brother visited often, even now he had reached his majority.

Compared to what might have been, she had a wonderful life. Almost as excited as Geoffrey, she hurried upstairs to wash and change, so she could find out what was in the box.

The following evening, she began her reply to the delightful letter that had been not the least of the box's treasures.

Dear Elijah and Arthur,

Gideon has asked me to thank you for the hookah. He is looking forward to trying the hashish you sent and agrees it will be useful when he cannot sleep.

Our son Geoffrey is delighted with the camels. He has added a camel brigade to his collection of hussars and foot soldiers, and they are currently wiping the playroom floor of Napoleon's troops.

I thank you for the little brass shoes. They are a delightful addition to my collection and take pride of place on the bookshelf near my favorite reading chair, along with the Holland clog you found in Egypt, the Murano glass shoes from the street peddler in Sardinia, and the little pottery booties you found in Baghdad that came all the way from China.

Every time I see them, I think of my friends, so far away. What a privilege to be able to not only travel to all those distant countries through your stories and illustrations but be reminded of them every time I look up from my book or put on one of the brooches or other adornments you have been so kind as to send.

Yes. she was very fortunate.

Ceylon, August, 1816

Dear Regina,

Your letter with your sad news arrived today. Rex and I did not want to waste a minute before writing to send our sincere condolences on your loss. We feel we have come to know your husband a little through your letters. He was a fine man, and I am sure will be greatly missed. I trust you, your son, and your brother have been able to comfort one another.

We have been here in Ceylon for six weeks, and I've enclosed several of Rex's sketches of the local inhabitants. The peacock lives in the compound where we are staying and keeps us awake at night with the most awful braying screeches. Yesterday, we saw the elephants from the construction site near our temporary home being taken down to the water to wash and relax after working. And the monkeys are everywhere. Even as I write, one is watching me from a nearby branch. He hopes I might share some of my watermelon.

Rex has just come in to say he can get this letter into the governor's mail bag, so I'll close now, and write in more detail later.

My deepest sympathies.

I remain, your sincere friend,
Elijah Ashby

Rex had brought a runner with him. Ash addressed and sealed the letter and handed it over. The runner saluted, flashed them a cheerful grin, and took off out the gate of the compound.

Rex used a foot to hook a chair closer and sat on the other side of the table Ash was using as a desk. He poured himself a glass from the jug on the table, sipped, and held it away from him to examine it. "Nice," he proclaimed.

A rattle. A beaded curtain covered the entry to the house from the veranda where they sat, and it shifted in the occasional breeze. This time, though, the disturbance was human—a slender brown hand; Rex's current mistress was watching her protector from behind the curtain. Rithya had been a gift from an Indian potentate, who had been delighted to find that his English visitor was the youngest son of a British duke.

The official from the East Indian Company who had brokered the introduction had apparently interpreted the word *duke* as *maharajah*. Rex had protested that he was merely an unworthy fourth son. "But it seems that Indian princes are even more impressed by titles than my father," Rex told Ash. "He said I was being modest, and that the usual East Indian officials are all merchants with an unwarrantedly high opinion of themselves."

Rithya had been with them for nine months. Rex had never

kept a mistress for so long. Ash kept waiting for him to announce it was time to give her a large dowry and hire a local matchmaker to find her a husband, but Rex seemed to be fonder of the girl than ever. She was certainly very attached to Rex.

If Rex knew he was being watched, he chose to ignore it. "Should I arrange to travel up into the mountains? It's cooler up there, apparently. Rithya is feeling the heat."

"It'll be Spring in England when that letter arrives," Ash commented.

Rex blinked at the *non sequitur*, then followed the new conversational thread in his usual obliging manner. "I miss it, sometimes. England, I mean."

"We've been gone a long time. More than fourteen years."

Fourteen wonderful years, on the whole.

Which was why Rex's next remark surprised him. "Do you ever think about returning to England?"

"From time to time," Ash answered.

Often. Daily. He'd loved seeing the world, but on hot days like today, he remembered England with an ache—a hollow longing that had mysteriously increased with the news that Regina Paddimore was now a widow.

More fool him. No doubt she had married again before the letter reached Ash. Or perhaps caring for an invalid all these years had put her off marriage for life. If so, would he be able to change her mind?

"Perhaps we should go home," Rex said. "Ash, Rithya is with child." He took another sip.

Ash had no idea what to say. *It is a wonder this hasn't happened before.* At least, not to his knowledge. Rex seldom slept alone, but as far as Ash knew, none of his discarded lovers had been pregnant.

"Lost for words?" Rex's smile was more wry than usual. "I felt the same when she told me." He pushed up from his chair and paced. "I'm going to marry her."

"Marry?" Ash's head filled with all the standard objections, most of which he profoundly rejected. Society would say a duke's son couldn't marry his mistress, or a native girl, for that matter. But what were those rules worth when it came to human feelings? "Do you care for her, Rex?"

"Are you asking do I love her? I'm not sure what that means. But I know I cannot abandon my child, Ash. Nor Rithya, either. In the lands of the East, a concubine is honored almost as much as a wife. She has rights, and her children can inherit side by side with the children we would call legitimate. But English law regards her as nothing, and any child we have as less than nothing." His face took on the pinched look that accompanied any mention of his ducal father. "No child of mine will feel unwanted, nor will I allow them to be brushed aside like trash."

He took his seat again and leaned forward, staring intently at Ash. "If anything happens to me, I want you to take Rithya and the child to England and set them up there with anything they need. Promise me, Ash."

Ash nodded. Probably for the best. Rithya would not be welcomed back to her previous home, and she had no other. And the child would be half-English. "I will, but I'd rather you stuck around to see to the task yourself."

Rex grinned. "That would be my preference." Then the grin faded. "My father won't be pleased, but what can he do? Cut off my allowance? I don't need it. And Ash, you should go home even if I don't, now your childhood sweetheart is free."

"By the time I can get there, even if I took the fastest packet ship, she'll be married again, Rex. I'll stay with you if you don't mind. But yes, I'd like to go home."

Rex's mood lightened. "How do you feel about going up through India and beyond to the Silk Roads? Perhaps head west for a while and then strike north for Russia? I believe we can take a boat most of the way from the Caspian Sea to the Baltic Sea. We haven't been that way, and we can sail for England from St. Petersburg or one of the other Baltic ports."

He switched to Hindi, speaking slowly so that Ash could

understand. "Rithya, I know you're there. Come out and join the conversation. We need to talk about getting married the English way as well as yours. And how do you feel about going to England?"

Chapter Ten

REGINA WAS DELIGHTED to attend the Stancroft house party. Her hostess Arial, the Countess of Stancroft, had become a dear friend the previous Season, as had Arial's friend Margaret, Countess Charmain, who lived nearby. Cordelia, Marchioness of Deerhaven, and her marquess were also guests.

Regina attended in half-mourning, the whites, mauves, purples and greys a relief after the dull black of the past two months, as the nation grieved for poor Princess Charlotte, who had plunged the country into mourning when she died in childbirth two months earlier.

For the most part, the gathering had been as enjoyable as Regina hoped. Then John Forsythe, Deerhaven's brother, was caught with a young lady in his bed. Forsythe proposed, of course, and if Regina and her friends were convinced that the minx had crept into the bedroom uninvited, Forsythe was too honorable to denounce her.

Now most of the guests were gone. John and his bride had said their vows in the Stancroft family chapel and were on their wedding journey. Even the bride's parents had left, taking with them the elderly suitor who had been their preferred applicant for their daughter's hand. It was a sour note on which to end the house party.

However, the party was about to take on a new lease of life, with a much more cheerful and more innocent set of guests. The Deerhaven coaches had rolled up not half an hour ago, bearing the Deerhaven progeny, come to join their parents for another two weeks at the Stancroft estate. The marquess and his wife had seven daughters and twin sons of not quite a year old.

After enthusiastic greetings, the Deerhavens escorted their offspring up to the nursery floor, accompanied by Lord and Lady Stancroft and Pansy Turner, Lord Stancroft's stepsister, who lived with them.

Margaret refused the invitation to join them. "I had better make my way home," she said. "It looks as if it might snow."

"I'll see you to your horse," Regina told her.

By the time Regina had said goodbye to Margaret and ascended to the nursery floor, it had already taken on the state of ordered chaos that surrounded the Deerhavens. The schoolroom group had gathered with the nursery babes to enjoy the attention of the adults—fifteen children in all, for the Deerhaven nine augmented those who lived in the house. The Stancrofts' had a little son of their own as well as guardianship of the earl's two sisters and Arial's three cousins.

The children saw Regina first. "Aunt Ginny," called one of them, and she was immediately swarmed. Even in the years of her seclusion, she had made an exception once a year for a brief trip to the Deerhavens, and in the last two years, since Gideon's death, she had spent weeks at a time with her godchildren and their sisters.

Since Lord Stancroft's two sisters met the Deerhaven schoolroom crowd last year, they had spent so much time together, they had soon taken to calling her Aunt Ginny too, as had Arial's three little cousins.

Regina shushed the competing voices trying to compress a month of news into a few sentences. "Young ladies! You may each take it in turns to tell me all about what has happened recently. Take a moment to decide who will go first." She turned to smile at her friends, with the two-year-old Deercroft child on her hip and the four-year-old clinging to her other hand.

"Our apologies for the hellions," said Deerhaven. He had caught up one of the twins. The little boy was gumming the collar of the dignified and elegantly dressed marquess with every evidence of enjoyment. Blond curls and a pointy chin. Lord Martin, the younger born.

"I am thrilled to see them," Regina confided. "My goodness, Cordelia, how the boys have grown! I cannot believe it."

Miles, the Earl of Spenhurst (dark hair and rounded chin), was in his mother's arms, but squirming to be put down.

"We can walk him, Mama," offered the oldest daughter. Cordelia lowered the infant to the ground, and he set off gamely around the nursery, lurching wildly from one sturdily planted foot to another, pausing to find his balance, then lurching again. A sister on each side held on to a hand, stopping him from crashing to the floor.

"Miles is determined to be the earliest of our children to walk," Cordelia confided. "Whereas Martin is more of the view that the world can be easily enjoyed from a sitting position."

From the cradle in the corner came the sort of mewling noise that presaged an infant about to wake and demand attention. Lord Stancroft swooped on it and lifted his son, the little Viscount Ransome, just five weeks old.

He touched noses with the baby, prompting a giggle, then nuzzled his neck, which set off a whole barrage of them.

Regina swallowed a lump in her throat. She had determined long ago not to deny herself the company of children just because she had not given birth to any.

A chortle from Arial's little son brought Regina back to the present. She had to swallow a lump in her throat. Geoffrey had been an adorable toddler, but smaller babies always set off an ache in the empty place that longed for motherhood. Of course, she was thrilled for her friends. But since Gideon had died and Geoffrey became a young man, her longing for more children was getting worse, not better.

"Arial, he is a treasure," she told her friend.

Arial beamed. "They both are."

Arial was besotted with her husband and he with her. Regina suppressed a sigh.

"Hand me that chubby little giggle bunny, Peter," Arial commanded, holding out her hands for Harry, as the little viscount was called by his parents. "Ladies, will you excuse me while I feed his little lordship?"

"Of course, Arial. Regina, shall we go downstairs and order tea? Arial can join us down there when Harry is fed. Deerhaven, you and Peter are welcome, too."

"Stancroft and I are off to his study to discuss important manly things," Deerhaven told her, his eyes twinkling.

"Like brandy and horses," added Stancroft, whom all the friends apart from the dignified marquis called Peter.

"I am promised to the young ladies," Regina reminded Cordelia.

"Twenty minutes, girls," Cordelia proclaimed. "You may have your Aunt Ginny for twenty minutes, and after that, she is promised to me."

She blew them a kiss, and she and the men left Regina in the playroom, where she was soon ensconced on the sofa with a girl tucked into each side, one on her knee, and the rest sitting cross-legged on the floor at her feet.

Half an hour passed in a flash, though Regina didn't realize it until Arial returned. "Here is Harry for his Aunt Ginny's kiss," she announced, "and then I must carry her away to tea with your Mama."

Regina dutifully kissed the little fellow, and then each of the little girls wanted a kiss as well, which Regina passed out while Arial handed Harry to his nurse.

The two friends went downstairs arm in arm, but Regina's

mind remained upstairs with the children. Perhaps it was not too late. Perhaps she should consider finding a husband. One who found her desirable. One who could make her a mother.

A mother again, she added, with a silent apology to dear Geoffrey.

She would not marry any of the admirers who currently made her the object of their gallantry. Most of them were not serious and would run a mile if they suspected she thought of marriage. Those who had proposed were mostly after her money, or someone to park in the country to look after their children. David Deffew would marry her in a heartbeat, but he was a man she would never consider.

She could set aside his actions when she was little more than a girl. He had apologized profusely, and it was a long time ago. She could not, however, find anything about him to like. He had been pursuing her since she reentered Society after Gideon died, and she would not have even given him the time of day except that she felt a debt towards him for her part in his father's death.

As it was, she had done everything short of barring him from her house to make it clear she was not interested. Nonetheless, he had proposed three times. She had refused each time, most recently telling him that she would never consider his suit, and he should stop asking.

Of course, the thought of Mr. Deffew sent her mind winging to his stepbrother. *Elijah is coming home.* She shook it off. She might feel that she knew him through his letters, but in truth, they had not spent much time together since she was ten. Just the length of a single dance, on her seventeenth birthday, nearly sixteen years ago.

Besides, his last letter had been sent ten months ago, from some port on the Caspian Sea. Who knew whether he was truly coming back to England, and whether he would have any interest in Regina if he did? She refused to believe anything had happened to him and his friend. Elijah Ashby and Arthur Versey were the darlings of the English-reading world. If they had met with disaster, it would be on the front page of every newspaper.

And here she was, thinking about Elijah again, instead of considering her lackluster reaction to the men who had pursued her since she returned to Society. The fault must be with her, for they all left her cold.

Downstairs with her friends, she shook off her slight melancholy and told them her plan.

"A ball for your birthday!" Arial exclaimed. "How exciting."

"A masquerade ball," Regina corrected. It was Arial who had given her the idea. Her friend was badly scarred on one side of her face and wore a half mask to hide the damage. This meant that, wherever she went, even those who had never met Arial knew who she was and remembered last year's nasty lying rumors—that her burns and her own ugliness had driven her mad, that she had purchased a husband, that she was as much a loathly lady in her personal habits as she was in looks.

An event where Arial could avoid the staring and the comments might please Regina's friend: one where everyone was in costume, and many were wearing masks.

Regina had never organized a ball, though she had attended balls in her one Season before she married and last year when she came out of mourning. "I will need to ask my brother for permission to use his ballroom, since my townhouse is not big enough for what I have in mind."

"If he will not agree, you may hold it at our townhouse," Cordelia suggested. "We will be in Town by the beginning of March."

Regina beamed. "Thank you, Cordelia. I'm sure Kingsley will not mind, but I cannot tell you how grateful I am."

"What can I do to help?" Arial asked. "Peter and I will be there about the same time."

"I shall come up for the event," Margaret said. "Count on me from the beginning of April, Regina."

In moments, Cordelia had fetched paper for making lists, and the four ladies were hard at work.

March, 1818

NOWHERE ELSE SMELLED like England. It was raining, but Ash rode anyway, the better to enjoy the sights, scents, and sounds of his homeland. His childhood memories had been created in the tame and gentle lands of England, in very similar countryside to that their little line of carriages and horsemen was currently traversing on their way from Ipswich to London.

Rex had put his riding horse on a lead rope when the rain first began, retiring to the family carriage where Rithya, Caroline, and little Gareth traveled in as much comfort as Ash could procure on their behalf at short notice.

Caroline had been born in February of 1817. Rex had taken a house in a small village in Kazakhstan when Rithya adamantly refused to travel any further. "I am as large as an elephant and far less useful, Rex. Until this child is born, I am staying here."

Besotted with his baby daughter, Rex had quelled his restlessness until Rithya pronounced herself well enough to travel. They set off again, with a wet nurse, a train of pack animals, and a small army of local guards.

After that, Rex traveled as if possessed. No more stopping for weeks or even months at a time, to see the sights and get to know the locals. "I want to leave St Petersburg before the Baltic ices over," he explained.

In Turkmenistan, they heard about an Englishman who ran shipping on the Caspian Sea, paradoxically known as the King of the Mountains. The man they found in a small port on the eastern shores proved to be the son of the rumored king, though from the olive cast to his skin and his heavy eyebrows, his mother was not English. Turkmen, perhaps, which would explain why he was here. He was able to supply space for their party on a ship sailing for the mouth of the Volga River, and also advice on dealing with Russian officials as they traveled up through the waterways of that enormous empire.

The river travel took longer than expected, and they spent

Christmas at the Winter Palace of the Tsar in St. Petersburg.

Tsar Alexander was delighted with his visitors, whom he proclaimed he knew well, for he had read all of their books. Rex in particular was a favorite, his lineage making him, in the tsar's eyes, "his British cousin."

The nearby port was frozen over. Indeed, the ice blocked much of the sea for hundreds of miles. The tsar assured them they could stay as long as they wished, but Rex insisted on taking an overland route, by *troika*, to Klaipeda, which was ice-free. Somehow, he managed to charm the vehicles and their teams, an escort, and a ship out of the tsar.

Perhaps it was because Rithya was heavy with child again, and the childless tsar and tsarina were enchanted with Caroline, and anxious to do all they could to make sure Rex was back in England "for the birth of your heir, my cousin."

They traveled into storms. Rithya was horribly ill, which was perhaps why, when they docked in Rotterdam to avoid the worst of the weather, she went into early labor, giving birth to Gareth. He was tiny, but strong, and a patch of fine days gave them the opportunity to make the crossing to Ipswich.

Traveling by gentle stages, they spent two nights on the road and were now approaching London. Their sixteen-year journey was all but over.

They stopped at an inn on the outskirts of London to meet the solicitor Rex and Ash shared. Ash had sent a message from Rotterdam, asking him to purchase Rex a townhouse and set it up ready for their arrival, and the solicitor was waiting at the inn with the address and the keys.

Rex ordered another riding horse. "I'll go on ahead with Ash," he told Rithya. "We will make sure everything is ready for you and the children. You enjoy your tea, my dear. Take as long as you like." He saluted his wife's cheek and went on to kiss Caroline and Gareth. Rex had taken to fatherhood like a duck to water.

It was a fifteen-minute ride to the townhouse. Ash held the

horses while Rex mounted the steps to the door. It opened before he had a chance to put his key in the lock.

"Lord Arthur Versey?" asked a man with a South-Asian look and the accent and stance of an English butler.

Rex nodded. "Send someone to take the horses back to the Angel in Highgate," he commanded.

"Yes, my lord," the butler replied. "You have visitors waiting in the drawing room." He must have signaled to a footman, for one sidled past Rex and ran out to take the reins from Ash.

Ash followed Rex into the house. Rex was asking the butler who the visitors were. "Your sister and her husband, my lord. Lord and Lady Barker."

Ash thought he was going to say more, but Rex's face lit up and he interrupted. "Do you hear, Ash? Elaine has come to greet us." He turned back to the butler. "And your name is...?"

The butler bowed. "Gampaha, if it pleases you, my lord." A name from the isle of Ceylon, which explained his appearance.

"Ash, this is Gampaha. Gampaha, my friend, Mr. Ashby. Lady Arthur, the children, and the rest of our retinue will be here in the next half hour or so. Come on, Ash, let's go see my sister."

The butler ran ahead to open the door, and they entered into a room crowded with people. Rex stopped two paces inside the door. Ash counted. Seven people. Not that large a crowd, after all.

"Arthur?" said one of the ladies.

Rex's frown suddenly cleared, and he stepped forward with his hand out. "Elaine!" The lady grasped his hand, and another lady and gentleman hurried up, saying their names, while Rex shook hands or kissed cheeks. He was then presented to the lady and three gentlemen who had not come forward to claim him as family. Ash heard my husband, Lord this; my wife, Lady that.

"And this—" Rex proclaimed, putting his hand out towards Ash—"is my friend Ashby." Ash was introduced around and discovered that those who had come to greet the returned travelers were only some of Rex's large family—Lord and Lady

Barker, another sister, and her husband, one brother and his wife, and a cousin who represented the eldest of the brothers.

That was the second surprise they had for Rex. "Did you come here to warn me that the duke still doesn't want me in the country?" he asked.

One of the sisters said, "You haven't heard? His Grace died a year ago, Artie. Percy is Dellborough now and is very proud of his brother the travel writer."

The cousin spoke up, "He sent me to let you know, Arthur, that you and your wife—" he bowed to Ash—"and your friend are very welcome to stay in the family townhouse."

Rex said he was pleased to be welcome once again in Dellborough's London home, but he would keep his own household. He started asking after other relatives and family friends, and Ash watched on, torn between mystification and envy at the way Rex had been drawn immediately back into the network of Dellborough connections.

Ash had no family. Apart from those under this roof, the only people he knew in England were Regina Paddimore and the vicar. And he knew from letters that the vicar had long since retired to the midlands, where he lived with a daughter and her family.

Lady Barker must have taken pity on Ash, for she took him to one side to find out about their recent travels. She interrupted when he mentioned the children. "Arthur!" she called. "Mr. Ashby tells me you have a son and a daughter!"

At that moment, the door opened again, and the butler announced, "Lady Arthur, Miss Caroline, Master Gareth."

Rithya entered the room with the grace and carriage of a queen, leading Caroline by the hand, followed by the wet nurse with Gareth. She surveyed the room, and only someone who knew her well would have detected the nervousness in her eyes.

Rex stepped forward to take her hand, with the proud and fond smile he kept just for her and the children. "There you are, my dove. You are just in time to meet some of my family." He presented everyone to her, as if she was the highest-ranked lady in the room. Cunning devil. His relatives would go away thinking she must at least be a princess!

The ladies cooed over the children. Gareth wanted nothing to do with these new relatives. Rithya explained that his wet nurse had been about to feed him, and after a few minutes, she extracted him from Rex's arms and carried him off. Caroline was in her element with a whole room of adults to charm.

"Arthur is going to have his hands full with that one," commented one of the brothers-in-law to Ash. "I never thought I would see the day when that rascal was married with two children."

"He was twenty years old when he left England," Ash pointed out. "Nearly half a lifetime."

The brother-in-law nodded slowly. "You make a good point. We tend to think of the youth we knew, even though we have all been following his adventures through letters and your books. You will find that most of London thinks they know both of you, Mr. Ashby. Prepare to be lionized."

Chapter Eleven

Lady Barker—Elaine—had been able to discover that Mrs. Paddimore was in residence, and that today was her afternoon for receiving calls. Ash had seen enough of English Society in far-flung corners of the world to know the process. The butler took Ash's card, and beckoned Ash to follow him up the stairs and into a drawing room that managed to be both elegant and comfortable.

Catching her at home and receiving was a mixed blessing. It had insured his immediate entry, but meant he was now afloat in a sea of unknown faces.

Not that he gave any of the others more than a cursory look. He had eyes only for Regina. He had not seen her in sixteen years, and she was now very much an adult rather than a girl on the verge of conquering Society, but she was even lovelier as a mature woman than she had been when he was last in England.

There were perhaps a dozen men and four other ladies in attendance, but he could not have described anything about them. Odd. He had long since developed the habit of cataloguing the people present, the contents of a room, and every possible exit. His travels had taken him to places where his life depended on such awareness.

At this moment, however, everything and everyone else was

just a background for Regina. Her flawless skin, her dark hair in an artful coil on the top of her head. Her blue eyes, sparkling as she conversed with the lady next to her. Her plush lips, curved in a gentle smile. One of the shoe brooches he had sent her was clipped in her hair.

The butler announced him. "Mr. Elijah Ashby." The room silenced as if by magic, and everyone turned towards the door, their mouths hanging open. Regina leapt to her feet and hurried towards him with both hands held out.

"Elijah!" she proclaimed. "How wonderful! I read in the newspaper that you had returned to England but did not expect to see you so quickly! I am so glad you called. Please, come and allow me to introduce you."

She was smaller than he expected. Over the years, he had forgotten how diminutive she was, not just short but also slender, though in a thoroughly womanly fashion. *She is still a sylph.* The force of her personality, coming through in every letter, had somehow led him to expect a larger presence. The scent was the same as he remembered, though. An English garden, with a touch of something that was pure Ginny.

"Ladies, allow me to present my friend, Mr. Ashby. Mr. Ashby, my cousin, Mrs. Austin, and the Ladies Deerhaven, Charmain, and Stancroft, all very dear friends."

Ash made his bow.

Lady Deerhaven was a regal lady with the slight padding of a matron and a kindly smile. "Regina and I have been reading your books since the very first," she claimed. "How lovely to meet you in person."

Lady Charmain was a statuesque blonde with eyes of a vivid blue. "Mr. Ashby, it is a delight to meet you."

Ash did his best to look Lady Stancroft in the one eye that showed. The other was hidden by a pretty half mask that covered one side of her face. A fine tracery of purplish scars hinted at the story the mask had to tell.

He was next introduced to Lord Deerhaven and Lord Stancroft, presumably the husbands of the two ladies. They welcomed him back to England. Lord Charmain, if there was one, was not present. Regina continued to introduce him around the room, and he continued to be polite about remarks that praised the books and to deflect questions about his and Rex's plans for the future.

Then they reached a short balding man who was vaguely familiar and whose face came into full focus when Regina said, "And, of course, you know David Deffew."

Daffy Down Dilly, as Ash lived and breathed, there with an oily smile on his face and his hand out ready to claim his part in the fêted return of the famous author.

"My dear stepbrother," Dilly announced to the room, as he clasped Ash's hand and held it too long. Ash inclined his head slightly and gave a tug on the hand to free it. He would not make a scene in Regina's drawing room.

Ash continued to follow Regina around the room, acknowledging the rest of the introductions while wondering what on earth Deffew was doing here. Was he courting Regina? Elaine had said the bees had gathered last year, some meaning marriage and some a less permanent arrangement. Regina had encouraged none of them.

Surely, Deffew did not think to compete with some of the other men even in this room? His family had been on the fringes of Society and the bare bones of their backsides when Ash knew them. Perhaps that had changed? If not, he had nothing to recommend him. He was as much of a dandy as ever but had aged poorly—his thinning hair slicked over a bald pate, and his brightly-colored waistcoat stretched over a torso that had long given up any pretensions to a waistline.

As for character, the man Ash had known sixteen years ago had been a cypher, adopting his morals, his manners, and his ideas from anyone he looked up to or feared. Mouth, at the time, was both. If Dilly was that way as he approached thirty, sixteen years was unlikely to make a difference.

To be fair, I barely know Regina or what she wants in her next husband. Ash's heart objected. Through her letters, he felt he knew her better than he knew anyone else on earth, except perhaps Rex.

Ash found himself ensconced in the place of honor next to the hostess, fielding questions about his most recent voyage. "We were most recently in Russia," he explained. "We have the manuscript for a book on our travels through India and on into Central Asia and have begun one on the trip up the Volga River to the tsar's court, and then down to the Nordic Sea."

He answered some eager questions and told a couple of anecdotes about the tsar's court. His audience appeared appreciative. Nonetheless, he was pleased when Lady Deerhaven stood and announced to the room at large they had all been there quite long enough and should leave Mrs. Paddimore to enjoy her reunion with her childhood friend.

Everyone stood and began saying their goodbyes. Everyone except Dilly. Lady Deerhaven said, "Come along, Mr. Deffew, you too."

"But I am family, you know," he insisted. "Ash will not mind if I remain to hear the more personal stories."

Ash turned his most practiced social smile on the wretch, baring his teeth in a far- from-sociable grin. "Another time, perhaps," he said. "I do not wish to keep you." And never a truer word was spoken.

Deffew was obviously not any cleverer than he had been sixteen years ago, for he said, "I don't mind waiting. Truly. Perhaps we could go out for a drink after you and the charming widow have completed your reunion."

"That will not be possible," Ash told him, keeping his smile pasted on for the sake of the audience.

"Do stop delaying, Deffew," commanded Deerhaven. "Come along." Deffew had, of course, risen to his feet when the ladies did, and now Stancroft and Deerhaven stood, one each side of him, and marched him out the door. They did not precisely lug him by the elbows, but they certainly managed to give the impression they were keeping that option open. In moments, the room was emptied of everyone except "my cousin, Mrs. Austin." Presumably, she belonged in the house. A companion, perhaps?

"You cannot imagine how delighted I am to see you," Regina said as soon as the last of the guests disappeared. "I have been worried, and then when I saw in the paper that you had arrived... But they said you reached London just yesterday! And yet here you are! So soon. I mean, not soon. Such a long time after your last letter."

Her blush was adorable. Ash wondered how far down her chest the color flowed. "I have sent several, but I thought them unlikely to arrive before me, if at all. They will have been passed from one petty potentate's messenger service to another. And those I sent in Russia are probably in the hands of the tsar's secret police. I did send one from Rotterdam, but..." He shrugged. "I am sorry you were worried."

That was not true. He was delighted she cared enough to worry. *Which does not mean she will see a nobody like you as a desirable suitor. She is a viscount's daughter, wealthy, and a beautiful woman, besides. And you were raised the next best thing to a servant.*

Regina's blush deepened. "Your letters have meant so much to me, Elijah. You cannot imagine."

She looked down at her clasped hands. "I suppose I should call you Mr. Ashby."

"Perhaps in public," ordained Mrs. Austin, "but since you and Mr. Ashby have been friends since childhood, and the friendship was encouraged by dear Gideon, calling one another by your personal names would be entirely acceptable in private."

"If you say so, cousin," Regina replied, "I know it must be true." She looked up through her lashes at Ash, smiling, and his throat was suddenly dry. "It does seem silly to call you Mr. Ashby when we have been Regina and Elijah to one another for decades."

"Not in public, however," Mrs. Austin warned. "Mr. Ashby,

you can expect to be invited everywhere, for you and Lord Arthur are great favorites in Society, and I daresay you have many stories to tell. Are you planning to stay in England for long?"

"I have not made plans," Ash said, honestly, but his eyes were on Regina, and if his mind was still thinking of all the reasons why she would not be interested in a man like him, his heart had already decided he would not leave England again without discovering whether he and Regina might possibly have a future.

Regina sent for refreshments, and Ash spent another hour in that pleasant drawing room talking about everything under the sun. He only left when Mrs. Austin reminded Regina of an evening engagement. Before going, however, he gained Regina's agreement to ride out the next day. Somehow, between now and then, he had to beg, buy, or borrow a carriage.

Chapter Twelve

REGINA WENT UP to change for dinner, her mind full of Elijah, comparing him to the boy she knew when they were both children and the young man with whom she had walked at her ball. This new version of the man took her breath away. He was taller, broader, far more confident. But he still had the charm and kindness of those earlier selves. He still spoke with her rather than to her, as if she had ideas and opinions of her own that he was interested in hearing.

Regina had had her fill of encounters in which her role was listener and her supposed admirer's idea of a conversation comprised a self-interested monologue with easy compliments scattered like raisins in a stodgy dough.

It didn't hurt that Elijah was handsome and a bachelor. *Pull yourself together, Regina. Undoubtedly, now that he is back in England, he will be looking for a young bride—not a long-in -the-tooth widow.* It was not, by all accounts, as if he needed her money, unlike most of the suitors who had made respectable offers since she returned to Society.

She pasted a smile on her face and went downstairs to present herself for inspection to Mary Austin, who looked up from her book for long enough to say all the right things.

Mary was a distant cousin of Gideon's, and his pensioner. The elderly widow had traveled several days by stagecoach to pay her respects at Gideon's funeral and had afterwards come down with an ague. She and Regina had had a fortnight together before she was well enough to return to her home and had kept up their relationship by correspondence.

When Mary commented she had never been to London, Regina had invited her. "I will enjoy the company," she had said. Mary had agreed on condition that she would not be expected to attend everything Regina went to. "I am not as young as I used to be," she said. "My idea of a pleasant evening is a warm fire, a good book, and a cup of tea."

"The Stancrofts this evening, is it not?" she said, after Regina had twirled around to show her all sides of her gown and hair. "You shall have a pleasant time, then."

"You are most welcome to come, Mary," Regina reminded her.

"Thank you, dear, but the opera three nights ago was my late evening for the week. Today, too, has been very exciting, with your young man returning from abroad. I do like him, Regina."

There was a stir in the hall, and then a familiar but unexpected face appeared around the edge the door. "Here you are, Mother. Cousin Mary."

"Geoffrey? Come in, darling. What on earth are you doing here?"

The boy opened the door further so he could enter. He was at the tall and gangly stage, fast transitioning to adulthood. He could not really have grown three inches since she saw him at Christmas, could he?

"Come and sit down. Have you eaten?" He was probably hungry. He seemed to always be hungry.

"I should not sit down in my dirt, Mother. I will just go up and change, shall I?"

Now that she came to look at him, Geoffrey was a bit disheveled, his coat dusty and his cravat limp and crumpled.

"Very well, dearest. Just tell me why you are in London during term time." She narrowed her eyes. "You have not been sent down, have you?"

Geoffrey flushed. *He has been sent down.* "Geoffrey!"

"It is not like that," he protested. "Well, it is. But there were reasons."

Regina nodded. "You shall tell me about them. Go and wash, my dear, and I will order your dinner."

"But you are dressed to go out, Mother, surely? I do not wish to spoil your evening. We could talk in the morning?" He sounded hopeful.

Regina was having none of it. "Good try, Geoffrey. I shall send my apologies, and we shall talk this evening."

"Probably for the best," Geoffrey muttered. He sketched a bow and as he did so, his right hand, which he had been holding behind his back, came into view, covered in bandages.

Regina gasped. "Geoffrey! Your hand."

"Part of the story," Geoffrey said, hiding it behind his back again. "A doctor has set the bones, Mother. You do not need to worry." He was backing towards the door as he spoke, and he sidled out of the room on the last words.

Regina exchanged glances with Mary, her eyebrows raised. Mary grinned. "You heard the boy. You do not need to worry. That will be quite some story, I think."

Regina sighed. "Little boys are easier," she said.

She sent a message to Arial Stancroft, explaining that Geoffrey had arrived unexpectedly, and apologizing for upsetting Arial's table, then another to the stable to cancel the evening's carriage. The cook would need soothing. Regina went down to the kitchen in person.

"Master Geoffrey has arrived home unexpectedly, and so I will not be going out this evening," she told that august personage. "We shall need dinner for three, rather than one."

The cook stared at her, mouth open.

"I do apologize," Regina added. "We will be satisfied with whatever you can manage at such short notice."

"We'll make sure the young master does not starve," the cook assured her. Geoffrey's appetite was legendary, and he was generous with his praise. Fortunately, the cook adored him.

"He appears to have broken his hand," Regina added, "so he may be in need of some help with cutting meat and the like."

"Hmm." said the cook. "I will see what I can do."

Sure enough, half an hour later she served a very credible first course—an oyster soup, a roast of beef, some of it already sliced into bite-sized pieces, a savory pie with shredded meat and potatoes, a bowl of buttered carrots and peas, and apple tarts.

Geoffrey, now neat and tidy, attacked the food as if he had seen none for a fortnight. He managed credibly with his left hand, apologizing before he picked his piece of pie up so he could take mouthfuls directly from the slice. "I left on the noon coach," he explained, once he'd eaten enough to slow down between mouthfuls, "so haven't eaten since breakfast."

"Coaches do stop at inns along the way," Cousin Mary commented.

Geoffrey shrugged. "No money," he explained. He looked at Regina, his mouth in a wry twist. "That is part of the story," he told her.

"Which can wait until after dinner," Regina told him.

Whatever his story, it did not affect Geoffrey's appetite. He made good inroads into the first course and took two slices of the chocolate tart that followed.

When she was sure he had eaten enough, Regina rose.

"We will take tea in the drawing room, Wilson," she said.

"I shall have a tray in my room," said Mary, "and leave you and Geoffrey to your chat."

In the drawing room, Geoffrey prowled while the tea makings were brought in. When the maids had left the room, Regina patted the seat beside the couch.

"Come and sit down, my darling."

Geoffrey straightened. "I would prefer to stand, Mother."

Regina inclined her head. "As you wish."

"The short story is that I was sent down for fighting. I—Ah—broke someone's jaw."

Regina froze, unable to react for a moment. Which was probably just as well because it gave her time to regain control. Her stomach roiled and her emotions surged between anger and horror, but she knew from experience that he would close up and stop talking if she showed any reaction.

"That's why I have no money. I gave it all to pay for the doctor and for the nurse who was going to look after him while he recovers." Geoffrey swallowed and shuffled from one foot to the other.

Regina waited. Let him tell his story in his own words, and then ask questions.

After a moment or two, Geoffrey took a deep breath and continued. "The Chancellor said that was part of my punishment for resorting to brute violence instead of using my brain. He told me to go home until my hand healed, and to talk to you about what Richard Deffew said." He sat down like a puppet with its strings cut, flopping any old how into a chair.

"Richard Deffew?" Regina commented. "That would be the gentleman whose jaw you broke, I take it." Mr. David Deffew had mentioned having a nephew at Cambridge.

Geoffrey nodded. "Although he is no gentleman, Mother. I did not mean to hit him so hard, except he deserved it."

Regina remembered the threats David Deffew made when he tried to coerce her into an elopement all those years ago. She had a good idea of what Richard Deffew might have said to spark Geoffrey's temper. Her boy was generally easygoing and slow to anger, but his wrath burned hot when it did erupt. She took a deep breath.

She and Gideon had only once talked about the identity of Geoffrey's progenitor, but as the little boy grew, William had guessed, and undoubtedly, once Geoffrey came down from Cambridge and began mixing with people who knew the current Lord Kingsley or the former one, his true relationship with

Regina would be obvious to all.

William and Regina had had a single conversation on the topic, too. "People will know he is our half-brother, Regina," William had said. "I won't deny him if that is what you are afraid of. Mama will not like it, though."

Mama and Regina had been ignoring one another for years. Regina could not see that changing. "I believe we should warn Geoffrey," she told William.

William quirked a half smile. "I will leave that to you, sister," he replied.

It seemed she was too late. However, best to know what was said, before she at last told Geoffrey the truth of his origins.

"What exactly did Deffew say?"

Geoffrey blushed. "I won't repeat his foul words, Mother. But in essence, he said you are my mother in truth, and you were married off to Father—Gideon Paddimore—because you were ruined beyond recovery, and he was your father's..." He hesitated, looking for a word. "Your father's intimate friend." His blush burned deeper.

Regina raised her eyebrows. She had expected Gideon's reputation to be called into question, but not her own. "I had just turned fifteen when you were born," she pointed out. "Rather young to be steeped in sin."

"Yes," Geoffrey said, but the relief in his tone indicated that the accusation had bothered him. "I knew he was lying, especially when he said Uncle William must be my father because I look so much like him."

Regina's eyebrows shot up further. "That would have made him a very precocious twelve-year-old," she said. "To set the record straight, Geoffrey, I did not give birth to you, and William is not your father." She paused, wondering how to broach the truth.

Geoffrey gave her an opening. "Do you know, Mother? Who my real mother and father were, I mean? Only, I do look like Uncle William."

Regina took a deep breath. *Gideon, I wish you were here.* "You know that we always told you your father took you into his arms, his heart, and his life when you were but a few hours old." She held out a hand that trembled rather more than she wished.

Geoffrey took it. "Yes, and you did the same when I was two years old, and you married Father."

"I did," Regina agreed, and continued with what she needed to say. "Gideon was there that day because, when the mother who gave birth to you died shortly afterwards, the midwife sent for her lover."

Geoffrey's hand gripped hers and his eyes burned. "My father."

Regina nodded. "Your father. Gideon was with him when he got the message. Your father was married, Geoffrey. He could not take you home, he refused to put you into an asylum, and he was reluctant to leave you to paid care. But Gideon had already, as he told you, taken you into his heart. He claimed you as his ward, and from that moment on, you were his son in everything but blood."

Geoffrey's focus was on the man who had given him up rather than the one who had taken him in. "Did my real father want nothing more to do with me?" he asked, a tremble in his voice.

"He visited you often, my darling, until the day he died when you were only two years old." Regina had given Geoffrey a handful of clues, but he still didn't put them together.

"Father told you all of this." It was a statement, not a question.

Regina nodded again. "Certainly. He insisted on telling me the whole after he asked me to marry him, and before I accepted. He thought I should know that I would be raising my half-brother as my son."

Geoffrey blinked, his face blank. He repeated the words as if they did not make sense. "Half-brother."

She watched the realization dawn on him.

"You and I have the same father? And Uncle William? Does

he know?"

"Yes," Regina told him. "He knows he is your brother, and he loves you. He told me weeks ago that I needed to tell you about your origins before you came up to London, where people might see the family resemblance. I am sorry I did not do it earlier, Geoffrey."

Geoffrey was generous. "You couldn't expect Mr. Deffew to come visiting his son and tell him lies about you."

Regina refused his invitation to shelve responsibility. "I could have armed you with the truth, and perhaps saved you a broken hand. I was afraid you would not... That you would look at me differently when you knew." Unaccountably, now that the confession was done and Geoffrey had not rejected her out of hand, she felt tears welling in her eyes.

Geoffrey was alarmed. He grabbed her other hand. "Do not cry, Mother. You are my mother, for you are the only one I've ever known, and I love you." He blushed again, for he had given up such displays of affection when he'd gone off to school six years ago.

Regina's smile was a little watery. "And I love you." She had one more thing to tell him and then all the secrets were bare. "Geoffrey, Gideon *was* my father's—our father's—intimate friend. That much of what Deffew told you is true. I promised you the truth, and now you have the whole of it. I hope it will not make you think less of Gideon. He was the best man I have ever known. He was kind, generous, and honorable. He saved me when liars tried to destroy my reputation, and he became my dearest friend."

Geoffrey was slow to respond. "He was all that you say," he said at last. "But, Mother, how am I to respond when people make such accusations?"

Regina smiled. "As Gideon would have. As he did, when a man tried to blackmail him into allowing my abduction and releasing my dowry." Should she tell him the identity of the man? No. He would ask, then, why she tolerated the Deffews, and that would lead to why she felt she owed them a debt for her part in their father's death.

Besides, as Gideon had told her all those years ago, "We may despise and detest them, Regina, but we do not need to entertain Society by allowing it to show. I plan to behave with civil dignity when we happen to meet, but that does not mean I will ever trust them again."

She could give her son the benefit of her husband's wisdom on the matter of responding to blackmailers. "Tell them they can think and say what they like, but they should remember that, if they attempt to tarnish the name of one you hold dear, you, your mother, and your uncle will use our wealth to destroy them."

Geoffrey grinned. "Much better than a broken jaw," he said. "And I can just imagine that the slimy toad crawled away on his belly."

Regina remembered David Deffew's face just before he fled her mother's house. "Rather quickly," she confirmed.

"Is that why you married Father? Because he saved you?"

More truth. But no names. It was ancient history, and she did not want Geoffrey to make a crusade of it. "The blackmailer had previously tried to compromise me and had spread lies throughout Society that caused people to question my virtue, Geoffrey. You have asked before why we do not see my mother."

She could see the distasteful thought surfacing on Geoffrey's face. "Because our father was unfaithful, and I am the result. And I suppose she did not like Father for the same reason."

Regina narrowed her eyes as she thought carefully about her next words. "The break is on my side, Geoffrey. She would have visited had I invited her, or so she said in her letters." Which Regina had never answered, until in the end they stopped coming.

"I have not spoken to her since my father's funeral, Geoffrey. She tried to force me into the carriage of the man who assaulted me and tried to blackmail me. She did everything short of locking me in my room to prevent me from marrying Gideon, who was a kind man and a good one. She did not like Gideon, so thought instead to force me to wed a repellent swine who only wanted me for my money."

Mother had hated Gideon and could not see any goodness in him. Now that Regina was older, she could understand, a little. Like many women, Mother looked at her husband's infidelities and blamed the object of them rather than her husband. At least a mistress was kept out of sight. But Gideon was Lord Kingsley's closest friend, and even though he mostly avoided the Kingsley house, he was an ever present third in Regina's parents' marriage.

She gave a short laugh into her son's silence. "I have always taught you to forgive, have I not? Not to bear a grudge? I am a poor example, my darling."

He sat down on the arm of her chair and gave her an awkward hug with his left arm. "It must have been horrid for you, Mother. But you had Father and Uncle William. And me. You will always have me."

He looked away for a moment, his cheeks flushing slightly. His gaze when he turned back to face her was almost shy. "I am glad we share the same blood, Mother. I have always wondered why my family did not want me, and knowing that you did... I am glad. That's all."

She put a hand on his cheek. "I am glad, too, Geoffrey. I love you."

REX SIGHED AS he took a seat in the room that had been designated a study for him and Ash. It still lacked desks and shelves, but a couple of mismatched chairs at least allowed the two friends to escape the chaos in the rest of the house.

"If I had known setting up house in London at the start of the Season was going to be such a challenge, I might have suggested staying in Ipswich," he complained.

Ash smiled. He knew what was really bothering his friend. Rex had taken far greater inconveniences in his stride during their travels. "It's the ladies, is it not?"

"I might as well have taken Deerhaven up on his offer of accommodation," Rex growled. "I would have as much say there as here, with Elaine and Rithya in one another's pockets. Making lists!"

Rex's wife and his sister had taken to one another immediately. When Rithya realized that the townhouse was poorly furnished and only half-staffed, she had enlisted Elaine's help. Rithya still tired easily after her confinement, but Elaine had arranged for what seemed like every merchant and warehouse in London to bring samples, and the employment agencies to send candidates.

The ladies had been having a marvelous time.

A knock on the door heralded Barker, Elaine's husband. He didn't wait to be invited in but opened the door immediately. "I came to see where my wife went off to after breakfast and almost got roped into offloading some of the new furniture they bought yesterday. I told them I had an important errand."

"Shouldn't we help?" Ash asked.

Barker looked horrified. "And move every item around every room a dozen times while they try them out in different places? I sent for half-a-dozen footmen from my place to help yours. That's contribution enough. Do either of you happen to have an errand I can claim as an excuse?"

"Ash needs to buy a carriage and team," Rex offered. "He is taking a lady driving this afternoon."

"Excellent!" Barker gave a sigh of relief. "Ash has to go because he is buying. I know where to go, and Rex, you're coming along to advise on the horses. They cannot object to that. And afterward, I shall take you to my club for lunch."

The ladies, both wearing aprons and a beam of satisfaction, accepted the excuse with such alacrity that Ash suspected their plan all along had been to drive the men out for the morning. He kept the observation to himself, however.

The three of them crowded into Barker's curricle, with no room left for the groom. "Make yourself scarce, Tom," Barker told the man. "If my lady catches you, she'll have you moving furniture." The groom touched his cap and disappeared down a lane towards the mews.

Ash had heard of Tattersalls, but never been there. He looked around in fascination as they entered a courtyard surrounded on three sides by pillared arcades and centered on a facsimile of a Greek or Roman temple, a circle of pillars topped by a dome.

Barker explained that the buildings around the courtyard comprised stables, a carriage house, a counting house, and subscription rooms. "The auctions are on Mondays and Thursdays, so we're in luck. Let's take a look and see if there's anything you'd like to bid on."

They checked the carriages first, and it didn't take Ash long to decide that any of three low phaetons would suit him.

Barker and Rex wandered off to look at a landau. Rex wanted one for taking his family on outings. Ash continued to examine the phaetons, scrutinizing them with the eye he had developed through countless trips into potentially hostile territory, when a breakdown might have had fatal consequences.

"You should get a high-perch phaeton, Ashby," said a voice from his past. Sure enough, Matthew Deffew was leaning against a nearby wall. "Excellent for taking a drive with the ladies." Like his brother, he had aged. Indeed, he must be approaching fifty. He still looked fit, but was burlier than before, and what hair Ash could see under the hat was iron gray peppered with white.

His brother was with him. "Or a curricle. They're very fashionable, too," Dilly insisted. "A renowned author like yourself doesn't want one of those boring low-built things."

Mouth bared his teeth in what was more of a leer than a smile. "A high-perch," he insisted. "Makes the ladies shriek and cling to your arm," he explained.

Ash gave a slight bow. "Gentlemen."

"I know a carriage maker who could whip you up a nice high-perch phaeton in no time," Dilly offered. "Any color you like. Red wheels are very dashing."

Ash acknowledged the remark with an inclination of the head. "I intend to buy one of these but thank you for the advice."

"Suit yourself," Mouth said. "It seems a very tame choice for a person who claims to have had the adventures you have written about."

"A vehicle like these would be all right for messages and the like, I suppose," Dilly allowed. "But not for driving in the Park. One has to be up to the nines, there. You should come and see mine, Ashby. I drive in the Park most afternoons. It is the place to be seen."

"Hyde Park," Mouth explained to Ash, then reminded his brother. "Ashby has not been in England long enough to know the fashionable places."

Ash was listening with only half an ear. Some of the spokes on the second of the three phaetons had a scattering of tiny holes surrounded by wood-colored dust. Furniture beetles. The holes showed that they'd gone, but Ash would want to replace the spokes to be certain there were no more larvae growing vigorously within, waiting for the opportunity to spread in a new home. That one went to the bottom of his list, then.

Dilly was twittering on about meeting Ash at Regina's. Ash was not paying attention until he heard Dilly say: "... so I thought it only fair to tell you that we have an understanding."

Ash straightened and studied Dilly with his brows raised. "Is that right?"

"Yes, that is right," Dilly insisted. "So, if you have hopes in that direction, you may forget them."

Mouth nodded. "Very fond of my brother, is Mrs. Paddimore."

Ash contemplated telling the pair that he was buying a vehicle so he could take Regina driving. *No. It would be more fun to say nothing and hope our path crosses theirs this afternoon while I am out with Regina.*

Dilly had drifted off on another tangent. "I suppose you need a safe vehicle to drive Dellborough's brother. I had thought, after sixteen years of nursing the Versey imbecile, you would have been happy to hand him over to the care of his family and look for a real job."

Ash raised his brows still higher. Rex and Barker had come up behind Dilly as he spoke, and Barker was turning red with rage while Rex was gesturing for him to be quiet while trying not to laugh.

Mouth's eyes had widened in alarm, and he said, "David, that's enough."

But Dilly talked over the top of him. "Is it true that the half-wit has married a black woman? I don't suppose Dellborough will keep you on after that," Dilly continued. "You should talk to Matthew. He might be able to find you a job as a clerk or something."

Rex leaned forward so his head was just by Dilly's shoulder. "He will not be needing another job," he murmured.

Dilly started, and spun around, his eyes widening. "I do not know you, sir, and you are interrupting a private conversation. Oh. Lord Barker. I did not see you there."

Barker looked Dilly up and down, then stepped past him, his attention on Ash. The cut direct and performed with precision.

"Are you ready to look at some horses, Ashby? Lord Arthur and I are done here."

Rex gave Dilly a consoling pat on the shoulder as he passed. "The landau is not quite what I had in mind," he said to Ash. "Do you remember the carriage the Duchesse de Monterosa used in Alexandria to take her children to see the crocodiles? I'd like something a bit closer to that for my lady wife. Something that will fit the whole nursery party, including footmen."

He sighed. "And Lady Arthur wants some sort of provision on the back to carry our baby carriage and all the other paraphernalia that is apparently essential for a thirty-minute drive in the

Park." He didn't look at Dilly as he added, "A princess is a great catch, but being raised in the lap of luxury does make her very particular in her tastes."

"I was telling Lord Arthur he should commission one," said Barker to Ash, ignoring the Deffews as if they did not exist, "and he can use our barouche while it is being built."

Mouth pulled Dilly a few feet away and whispered to him. Ash heard the word "apologize."

When Barker said, "Let's find a team for your phaeton," and started to walk away, Mouth stepped in front of him, saying to Ash, "Will you not introduce us to your friends, Ashby?"

Ash asked, "Do you wish to meet the gentlemen, Rex? Barker?"

Barker snarled deep in his throat. Rex grinned. "By all means." He waved a lordly hand.

Ash said, in proper form, "My lords, allow me to present Mr. Matthew Deffew and Mr. David Deffew. Gentlemen, Lord Arthur Versey, Lord Barker."

Mouth bowed, and nudge Dilly. "I beg your pardon for what I said, my lord," Dilly hastened to say, "I did not realize you were listening."

Rex's eyebrows shot up as his eyes widened. "And you think your comments would have been appropriate if I had not overheard? How kind of you to confirm my initial impression, Deffew."

"The man's an idiot," Barker grumbled in an undertone. Dilly pretended not to hear him.

"Just so you know," Rex confided to the Deffew brothers, "my half-wittery has been much exaggerated. As an example, chosen at random, I never insult people behind their backs, but if I were to do so, I would check my surroundings first. In some of the places Ash and I have been over the past sixteen years, insulting a member of a wealthy and influential family would lead to dismemberment and death, rather than the mere financial and social ruin a family like mine has at its command. And insulting that man's wife? The same, but with blunt knives."

Dilly was frowning, clearly trying to understand whether he had been threatened. Mouth, though, had no doubt. He bowed. "My brother has learned his lesson, my lord, I assure you." His eyes told a different story, burning with banked wrath.

"Has he?" Rex asked. "We must hope so. Good afternoon, gentlemen. Come on, Ash. We have a carriage and team to purchase, and then lunch at Westruthers."

Chapter Thirteen

REGINA WAS ABOUT to go above stairs to prepare for her outing with Elijah, when her brother William arrived. As Geoffrey's titular guardian, he'd received a stern letter from the university, and had come to read the boy a lecture.

Cousin Mary took one look at his scowl and excused herself to go and talk to the housekeeper.

Geoffrey had been reasonably cheerful until then, despite a sleepless night, the pain in his hand keeping him awake for most of the night. William's lecture on propriety sent him into a sullen temper.

"Had the pair of you seen fit to share the truth with me, brother, I might have taken a different approach when Richard Deffew called my sister an incestuous slut." He suddenly remembered Regina was in the room. "I apologize for my language, Mother. Regina, I mean."

William opened his mouth and then shut it again, finally saying, "Oh." He then, the cad, turned to Regina and said, "I thought you were going to tell him?"

Regina glared. "We had that discussion three weeks ago, William. Did you expect me to tell him by letter? If Matthew Deffew had not seen fit to share his scurrilous version of the story with his son, we would have been having this discussion when I next visited Cambridge, and Geoffrey would not have an injured hand."

"Hmm," William said. "Broke your hand, did you?" He raised an eyebrow and attempted to remain stern, but a smile twitched the corners of his lips. "Broke young Deffew's jaw with it, I gather. Must have been a good blow!"

"William!" Regina would never understand men. "I thought you agreed with me that this was not the way to quell gossip."

William had the grace to look sheepish. "Yes, I suppose. But you have to admit our boy was provoked." Then he compounded his crime by adding, "Pity we can't do the same for the little rat's lying father."

Regina threw her hands up in the air. "Men! Thinking that a fight solves anything. I am going up to get changed for an afternoon drive with a friend."

"Anyone we know?" William asked.

Regina wanted to keep her escort's identity from her menfolk. Which was silly. It was not as if Elijah was courting her. And even if he was, William and Geoffrey had no reason to object. And even if they did... *What a ridiculous train of thought.* "Elijah Ashby."

"The travel writer that you and Father used to correspond with?" Geoffrey asked. He turned to William. "I have read all of his books, Unc... um..." He blushed over his own hesitation and then rushed on. "His and Lord Arthur Versey's, that is."

In a moment, the two men were exchanging views on the adventures recorded in Elijah's books. Perfect amity was restored. Regina rolled her eyes and went up to change. She would have to hurry to be ready on time.

In the event, she was a little late and Elijah was early. She came downstairs to find him in the drawing room with Cousin Mary, Geoffrey, and William, the four of them in eager conversation about the political and strategic importance of Central Asia.

He was the first to become aware of her, and stood, followed a heartbeat or so later by her menfolk.

"Mrs. Paddimore, you look stunning," Elijah told her.

She had dressed with particular care in a new carriage gown of pale blue, with military style braiding and decorations on the bodice and sleeves, and a line of rouching just above the hem. The matching hat was a close-fitting white bonnet with a small hem and a jaunty cockade of ribbons in the same blue as the gown.

The admiration in Elijah's eyes more than repaid the effort.

"I apologize for keeping you waiting, Mr. Ashby," she said.

"The results were well worth it, Mrs. Paddimore. Besides, I have enjoyed rekindling my acquaintance with Lord Kingsley and meeting young Mr. Paddimore after our many years of knowing one another only through letters."

"Mr. Ashby says he will introduce me to Lord Arthur, Mother," Geoffrey said, his face clear of the shadows from their earlier conversation.

Regina was about to suggest that Geoffrey not make a nuisance of himself. Perhaps Elijah guessed, for he hastened to tell her, "Rex will be keen to meet Geoffrey. Lord Kingsley, too. We both felt that we knew them. A day that one of your letters arrived, bringing the air and taste of home, was always a good day for us."

"Likewise for our family, Mr. Ashby. You gave us a window on the wide world, did he not, Geoffrey?"

Geoffrey nodded, eagerly. "That is what I have been telling him, Mother."

Cousin Mary said, "You and Regina should go for your drive, Mr. Ashby, before your horses take a chill."

Elijah shrugged. "The groom is walking them, but if you are ready, Mrs. Paddimore, I would be delighted to show you the phaeton and pair I purchased this morning."

That was a cue for Geoffrey and William to follow them out into the street, where the points of the carriage and the horses had to be noted and discussed.

"Very tidy," William approved, but Geoffrey appeared disappointed in the carriage, though he admired the team.

Pressed, he allowed that he thought high-perch phaetons more the thing, or even a curricle. "I think low phaetons are more for ladies or dull old sticks."

"Perhaps I *am* a dull old stick," Elijah suggested, clearly amused.

Geoffrey flushed. "Not you, sir. I misspoke."

Poor boy. His first actual meeting with his hero, and he'd put his foot in his mouth.

Instead of becoming annoyed, or teasing Geoffrey some more, Elijah took pity on him and explained. "I was looking for stability and comfort, Mr. Paddimore. The four wheels and the low body give me both, but the carriage is still light enough to be maneuverable in tight city streets and in traffic. The curricle, with only two wheels, is more maneuverable but less stable. And the high-perch phaeton can be top-heavy. Perhaps I am being overcautious but, if I have learned anything in my travels, it is that anything that can go wrong, will eventually go wrong. I would not risk your mother's safety just for the sake of cutting a dash in front of people whose opinion doesn't matter to me."

Which rather implied that he had purchased the phaeton and team just for this afternoon's ride. William clearly thought so, too, from the expression on his face as he looked away from admiring the horses to glance between her and Elijah. Geoffrey, who really did have to learn to think before he spoke, blurted, "You bought them for my mother?"

Elijah's grey eyes seemed to heat as he looked into her own, confirming Geoffrey's assumption even as Elijah's words put his purchase into a more acceptable framework. "I needed a vehicle so I could get around town without relying on a hackney. I bought one this morning because I have invited your mother for a drive this afternoon."

She spoke quickly, before any of the gentlemen could embarrass her further. "We should not keep the team standing any longer," she said.

"Allow me to help you up," Elijah said, offering his hand. When she was settled, he spoke to the groom. "Meet me back here in..." He raised an eyebrow and asked Regina, "one hour and a half?"

She nodded, and the groom touched his cap and stepped away from the horses' heads.

ASH HAD TAKEN the team out after he had bought them, just to get the feel for them and the carriage. He'd driven the route they now took from Regina's townhouse to Hyde Park, so he was able to take the necessary turns without hesitation and could divide his attention between the traffic and the lovely woman beside him.

"It is a pleasant afternoon for a drive," he said.

Her eyes twinkled. "Are we to discuss the weather, like polite English people?"

He laughed. "Whatever you prefer, Regina."

"So, I am back to Regina? I thought when you addressed me as Mrs. Paddimore, that perhaps I had lost your favor, Elijah."

A sideways glance from those blue eyes hinted that she was teasing him, emboldening him to reply, "I was trying to keep your favor, Regina, and that of your cousin. She did insist that I address you formally except in private. Are Lord Kingsley and young Geoffrey to be admitted to our conspiracy of friendship?"

She pursed her lips in thought, sending a bolt of desire that had him shifting slightly to ease the fit of his trousers.

"I shall consider it," she said. "Had you truly already planned to buy a carriage when you invited me to drive with you?"

Ash had to pay attention to the team for a moment, when they took exception to a dog that darted out of an alley, barking.

Once he had them well away from the noise, he said, "I had not thought of it. I went home and threw myself on the mercy of

Rex's brother-in-law, who took me to Tattersalls this morning. He offered to let me borrow something, but the rest of what I told your son was quite true. It made more sense to have my own rig. Rex is also looking for a carriage—something his wife and children can use to get around. Your son would be pleased to know he is considering a high-perch phaeton for his own use."

The horses had settled enough that he was able to look away from them to aim a question at her. "Would you have preferred to drive out in a more fashionable style?"

Regina shuddered. "No, thank you. I am far too small to get up into one of those things without a ladder."

Ash had a brief vision of lifting the lady from the ground up into one of those ridiculous vehicles. He would have to apply his hands to places he should not be thinking about. Not, at least, while driving through the streets of London in tight pantaloons with never a bed in sight. And not without an indication from the lady that she favored him as more than a childhood friend and a storyteller.

He turned in through the gates of Hyde Park. He had better find a new topic of conversation, preferably one that didn't heat his blood.

"The brothers Deffew are of Geoffrey's opinion about my choice of carriage," he told her. "They were at Tattersalls and surprisingly friendly." He chuckled. "At least until Dilly—David, I mean—made some insulting remarks about Rex and his wife without realizing that my friend was standing right behind him."

"Dilly, Elijah?" Regina said with a chortle in her voice. "True. He is not the brightest candle in the hall."

So much for Dilly's suggestion he had some claim on the lady. Ash had not believed him, but he was pleased to have it confirmed. She would not speak of a man she planned to marry with scorn, even such gentle scorn.

He turned out of the slow line of carriages into a quieter lane, where they could move at a steady walk and have less risk of being overheard. "I used to call him Daffy-Down-Dilly when I lived with them. In my mind, I mean. It was a minor and unspoken rebellion."

She tucked her hand into his arm and smiled up at him. "Ah. The country name for the daffodil, or narcissus as it is more properly called. A man in love with his own reflection, and foolish enough to waste away while admiring it. And his older brother? What name did you have for him?"

"Mouth Almighty," he admitted, helpless to do other than return the smile. "He spoke as if his every pronouncement was handed down from on high, on tablets of stone."

The chortle became a full laugh, but she sobered. "They were not nice to you, were they? The Deffews? When you lived with them?"

Ash shrugged. "It is ancient history, Regina." He volunteered another nickname. "I used to call the major Major Defect."

"Gideon, who generally had a kind word to say for everyone, found Major Deffew below contempt." She lowered her lashes to look down at her hands. "You may have heard that the major is believed to have died at the hands of the same highwayman who shot and crippled Gideon."

She still wasn't meeting Ash's eyes. Something about that brief account bothered her. Grief for her husband, Ash supposed.

She cast her gaze up into the trees they were passing. "As for his sons, I believe the younger one is merely a fool, while the older is a villain. When we were in town, before Gideon's accident, he used to insist on being polite to them, showing no open enmity, for he said that snakes bite when they feel threatened. I do likewise now I have returned to Society."

She sighed. "Though I wish Dilly would take the hint from my repeated refusals of his pr– invitations, and turn his attentions elsewhere."

What began with "pr"? The word that came to mind was proposals. Plural, as in more than one. Repeated, which implied at least three.

The carriageway had looped around to rejoin the more fashionable and therefore busier route that they'd escaped.

"Look," Regina said. "Speak of the devil and smell brimstone."

Sure enough, Mouth and Dilly Deffew rode towards them side by side—Mouth on a solid-looking bay and Dilly on a flighty chestnut that Ash could tell, even from a distance, was all show and no substance.

Dilly saw them first, his reaction communicating itself to the horse, so it danced sideways, fighting the bit. While Dilly was distracted getting the beast under control, Mouth saw Ash and Regina. His eyes narrowed, but he nodded in welcome. "Mrs. Paddimore. Ashby."

Ash returned the nod, as did Regina. As they came abreast of the brothers, Mouth turned his horse to fall in beside them, as did Dilly a moment later.

"So, this is why you wanted a phaeton," Mouth accused.

Dilly had a complaint. "I say, Mrs. Paddimore. I have asked you to drive with me I don't know how many times."

Regina ignored him, instead addressing Mouth. "How is your son, Mr. Deffew? May I hope his condition is improving?"

The look Mouth shot her was heavy with loathing, but his response was polite enough. "Very uncomfortable, Mrs. Paddimore. I trust that his assailant has been properly punished for his unprovoked attack."

Regina stiffened beside Ash, and the hand that was still tucked into his arm gripped hard enough to pinch, but her voice remained steady as she said, "Unprovoked, Mr. Deffew? An overreaction on Paddimore's part, certainly, and so I have told him. But no gentleman could ignore an insult to the lady who raised him as a mother."

Dilly turned on Mouth. "What has that limb of Satan done now? Mrs. Paddimore, I apologize for my nephew's disgraceful behavior."

Mouth's frown deepened. "Richard has a broken jaw, thanks to young Paddimore."

Regina was quick to reply, "And Geoffrey has a broken hand. They will both heal, and one hopes they will learn from the experience."

"Not done to insult a man's mother," Dilly insisted.

Mouth glared at him, then spurred his horse into a fast trot. Dilly stared after him for a moment, then lifted his hat to Regina. "Your servant, Mrs. Paddimore." He nodded to Ash. "Ashby."

Ash watched him chase after his brother then gave Regina a wry smile. "Your son broke his hand on Richard Deffew's jaw?"

"He did, and do not say he did the right thing. He has already heard that from William, which is not at all helpful."

"Would it be intrusive to ask about the insult?"

"Young Deffew told Geoffrey I was his birth mother and William his father. He used rather crude terms, I gather, which my son would not repeat." Or not to her, at least.

Ash whistled. "That would do it. No wonder your son punched the other lad."

"It is, I hardly need say, completely ridiculous, as well as disgusting."

"Yes." Ash allowed the horses to drop to a slow walk and pulled them to the side of the road so another party could pass. Once they were well ahead, he added. "That kind of filthy accusation comes from a depraved mind. Mouth's, probably. Quite apart from the fact that you are brother and sister, Geoffrey is what, eighteen or nineteen? You and William were both still children when he was conceived."

Regina frowned. "It is because he has my coloring and William's build," she admitted.

It is because Mouth is a nasty man. But what Regina said was true, as far as it went. "He looks quite a lot like William, apart from the coloring, and his eyes. He has his mother's eyes. Mouth should know that. He and Lord Kingsley came to blows when she refused Mouth's advances and he attempted to force the issue."

That startled Regina. "Deffew assaulted Geoffrey's mother? When? Wait! You know who she was?"

"You don't?"

"Gideon would never say. He said she was dead, so there was no point in telling me."

Ash didn't think much of that reasoning. As far as he could see, there was no point in not telling her. A mistress had a son. Nothing scandalous about that. The shocking thing was who fathered the boy. But perhaps she did not know that, though surely, she must have guessed by now.

"She was a widow in the village, one of your father's tenants," he told her. "Officially." He pulled the horses to a stop so that he could give her all her attention. "Most of us knew he was her protector. You did know that Lord Kingsley was Geoffrey's father?"

Regina nodded, completely unabashed. "Gideon told me before we married, and even if he hadn't, I would have guessed once Geoffrey grew old enough for the resemblance to be startling. For I know William was not old enough. When did my father and Deffew fight over the widow, Elijah? Before Geoffrey was born?"

"Yes. I was still living in the village, and the Deffews were boarding with my mother, so that would make it... seventeen ninety-five, Regina."

Regina shook her head, but in wonder rather than disbelief. "Some five years before Geoffrey was born, that would have been. My Papa had a mistress in the village all that time! And I never knew. He must have been fond of her too, for they sent for him when she lay dying, and he visited Geoffrey, Gideon said, until he died."

"He was not a profligate, as I understand it," Ash assured her. "He had one long-term mistress and—" he paused again, to choose his words, in case he was breaking open another secret— "... a close relationship with another person."

Regina nodded. "Gideon. I have often wondered how he felt sharing my Papa with my mother and with Geoffrey's mother. He also, Gideon told me, occasionally had short-term affairs with ladies of the ton. He craved variety, Gideon said. Poor Gideon. Poor Mama!"

She said nothing further for at least a minute. Ash busied himself setting the horses to walking again and turning on to a road that would take them back into the carriageway that led to the gate nearest to Regina's townhouse.

"What does your mother think of it all?" he asked.

Regina expelled breath in an impatient noise. "I have no idea, Elijah. I have not spoken to my mother since she conspired with David Deffew to have me abducted to Scotland and married perforce, after he had compromised me."

Ash's hands clenched on the reins, and he had to calm his surge of anger in order to get the horses back under control. By the time he had succeeded, she was telling him the whole story. The fake message. The forced kiss. The avid gossipers. Her father's heart attack and death. Dilly's arrival with a coach and four and her mother's insistence that they must marry.

She spoke of Gideon's offer of a cordial marriage—a partnership that offered her his name and protection.

She did not say what she contributed to the deal. Her dowry? As far as Ash knew, Gideon Paddimore had been a rich man before he married. Certainly, Regina was now a wealthy widow, or Dilly would not be so eager to lay claim to her. The hope of an heir, perhaps? Gideon had Geoffrey, but perhaps he wanted a son of his own blood?

They turned back into the main ride.

"Enough of that," Regina said. "Ash, I wanted to personally invite you to my ball on our birthday. I have sent invitations to you and to Lord and Lady Arthur."

"I cannot speak for Rex and Rithya," he told her. "But I would be glad to come. May I presume on an old promise and claim a dance?"

"I would be disappointed if you did not."

Chapter Fourteen

REGINA WAS ONE of a score of ladies invited to Lady Barker's At Home to meet Lady Arthur Versey over tea and cake. The travelers had been back in England for two and a half weeks, but Lady Arthur had been recovering from the birth of her son and months of travel. This would be her first public appearance.

Since Regina was not well-acquainted with her hostess, she assumed she had been included because Elijah had suggested her. After all, in the eyes of many, she had lost her status as the daughter of a peer when she married a commoner, and one in trade, at that. One, furthermore, who could buy and sell most of his so-called betters.

Most of the ladies present had far more illustrious connections. However, her three particular friends were there, so perhaps she owed her invitation to Cordelia, Arial, and Margaret.

Lady Barker presented her to the guest of honor. "Dear sister, may I make known to you Mrs. Paddimore?"

Society had been buzzing with speculation about Lady Arthur. She was as fashionably dressed and coiffed as any other lady in the room. Regina had already guessed her identity, as the warm brown tones of her skin set her apart in the sea of pale faces.

She was a princess of a principality in India, that much

seemed to be accepted beyond a doubt. The circumstances of her marriage to Lord Arthur changed according to the storyteller. Regina's favorite was the tale that Lord Arthur had seen her on the back of an elephant in a procession, peeking out from behind the curtains of her *howdah*. He had fallen in love and wooed her with poetry smuggled into the harem by a eunuch guard.

"Mrs. Paddimore, I am very pleased to make the acquaintance of the dear friend of our Mr. Ashby," said the lady of the hour, putting paid to the rumor that she spoke no English. She spoke it well, though with a slight intonation that hinted of distant lands.

"And I, my lady, to meet you." Elijah had written about Lady Arthur a number of times.

"I must thank you for your invitation to your ball," Lady Arthur said. "My husband and I are looking forward to it."

Today's news made her fret that the ball might not go ahead, but that was nonsense. Of course, she could solve the problem. She smiled at Lady Arthur. "I am so delighted you can come. May I ask after the children, Lady Arthur?"

Lady Arthur's dark eyes lit with pleasure. "Ash has spoken to you of Caroline and Gareth? They are well, Mrs. Paddimore. Gareth is gaining weight at long last."

"He was born early," Regina commented. "Mr. Ashby mentioned that. It must have been a worry for you."

Lady Arthur nodded, decisively, and said to Lady Barker, "See, Elaine? I knew that, if Ash liked her, we would be friends. Mrs. Paddimore, I must allow my sister to make me known to other guests, but I would like to speak further with you. Would you care to call tomorrow afternoon? I shall ask Ash to bring you if you are available."

"It would be my pleasure, Lady Arthur," Regina agreed. Elijah had already arranged to take her driving, so they would merely be changing the destination.

She would enjoy knowing the lady better for Lady Arthur's own sake. She would not consider that a closer acquaintance with

Lady Arthur might be beneficial to her future.

It was too early to decide her future belonged with Lord Arthur's best friend. She had seen Elijah every day since he made his first afternoon call, most days more than once. They had been driving twice, the second time stopping at Gunter's for an ice. They had taken Geoffrey to Astley's and to a balloon ascension.

They had been to the British Museum, conducted on a personal tour by one of the curators. The man would have shown them every exhibit donated by the famous travelers, but they manage only seven, for every item Elijah and Rex had collected prompted half a dozen anecdotes about the land of origin, the friends' adventures in that country, and all the lovely things they had left behind.

The curator began surreptitiously checking his pocket watch after two hours, and Elijah promised to bring Regina back another time.

Elijah had also called, with flowers, during her visiting hours. Dilly Deffew, arriving yesterday at the same time, spend the next thirty minutes glowering at his stepbrother. Regina was going to have to do more to depress Mr. Deffew's aspirations.

Even if Elijah was merely amusing himself, Deffew would never do, and it was unfair of her to allow him to continue to believe she favored him, and that her refusals had just been female coyness. Although she had told him she would never marry him, so how much more forceful could she be?

Was Elijah serious? He had not spoken of his intentions nor made any attempt to as much as steal a kiss. Not steal. Steal was the wrong word, since she would give a kiss freely if she thought it would be valued.

It would be easy to find the opportunity. Mary had come down with a cold, and had gone to Three Gables to convalesce, and Geoffrey was out more than he was at home. All she needed to do was manufacture a reason to be alone in a room with Elijah, and let things happen.

Even thinking of the possible consequences of that plan made her feel warm and trembly.

She reached her three friends, who had saved her a chair in their group of four. "Solemn thoughts, Regina?" asked Cordelia, which reminded Regina of another hiccup in her current plans. She had put off dealing with David Deffew out of sheer inertia, but the latest problem to rear its head was not as easy to manage.

"My mother is in town, ladies. She is staying with my brother William, so I am going to have to move my ball. Cordelia, is the offer of your ballroom still open?"

Cordelia was quick to reassure her. "It is, of course. We can send out a note to those who have been sent invitations."

"Surely your mother…" Arial's voice trailed off. "I beg your pardon, Regina. You know your own business best."

Regina needed her friends to understand. "I do not want to put my mother at outs with my brother. He has walked a careful path over the years, remaining close to both of us. I would never ask him to choose between us."

When William came to her this morning to say that Lady Kingsley had arrived unannounced, he had not asked for her to move the ball, but the relief on his face when she offered to speak to Cordelia spoke for itself.

She shrugged. "Besides, I want Geoffrey to come to my ball, and I do not know what my mother might say if she was forced to confront him."

Her friends nodded thoughtfully, and Margaret asked what Regina had already wondered. "You don't suppose, do you, that she has heard the rumors about his parentage?"

"I do not see how she could have avoided it," Regina agreed. Richard Deffew's scurrilous assumptions were doing the rounds. Regina and William, after discussing the matter with Geoffrey, had immediately told several of their friends the truth. Mother might, indeed, have heard the competing stories. Perhaps she had known the truth all along. What she planned to do about it, if anything, was another matter.

Cordelia changed the subject. "Come to my house tomorrow

morning, Regina, and we shall inspect the ballroom together. With only a week to go until the ball, we have no time to lose." She shot Regina a sideways look and a sly smile. "Unless you are engaged with Mr. Ashby, of course."

Regina's lips wanted to twist into a fatuous smile, but she would not allow them to do so. Nor would she respond to her friend's teasing. "Tomorrow morning will be excellent. Arial? Margaret? Will you join us?"

ASH AND REX had been summoned to the Foreign Office to make a report on the political situation in Russia. The tsar's lack of a son to succeed him could mean a contentious succession, but both of Alexander's brothers had declared their disinterest in becoming tsar. "They are serious," Rex assured the man they knew only as *Tolliver*. "I don't blame them. I wouldn't want to rule Russia, either."

They talked for some time about that vast and fascinating land, and about what the travelers had observed on their long river journey and in the tsar's court. Eventually, Tolliver's questions ran out.

"Your country thanks you, gentlemen," he said. "May I suggest a destination for your next journey?"

"No next journey," Rex informed him. "I am a married man, and Ash has aspirations."

Tolliver steepled his hands before his nose, his elbows resting on his desk, as he examined Ash. "Your first engagement after your arrival was a visit to Mrs. Gideon Paddimore, and you have since been seen escorting her to both day and evening events. Am I to wish you happy?"

Ash felt his cheeks heat. "I have not determined the lady's sentiments on the matter, sir. But my own are fixed."

Tolliver nodded. "Very well. That will be all, gentlemen.

Thank you for calling."

With that dismissal, they made their way through the winding corridors of the anonymous old building. The quickest way from there to Rex's townhouse led through a courtyard where some maintenance was in progress. A scaffold reared against the wall behind them and the one to their left.

Two levels of planking up, a man was chipping away at stone, shaping a replacement for a window frame currently under repair. He'd made considerable progress since they'd passed him earlier, on their way to the meeting.

They stopped for a moment, drawn by the endless fascination of watching craftsmen at work. Perhaps he felt the weight of their eyes, for he looked over his shoulder. His eyes widened, and he shouted a wordless alarm.

Ash threw himself one way and Rex the other. Just in time. A large block of stone crashed right where they had been standing.

In no time at all, workers had converged, loudly protesting that they had been nowhere in the vicinity of the stone when it fell. Ash and Rex assured all and sundry that they were unharmed. Somewhat dusty, but not injured.

After they'd disentangled themselves from the conversation, they went on their way, Ash wondering, "Was that deliberate? And if so, was it for you or for me?"

Rex shrugged. "Or a case of mistaken identity. I can't think of anyone who is that annoyed at me."

"No one in India? A couple of those workers had the look."

Rex shook his head. "I cannot think why."

Ash thought about his own possible enemies. "The only person in England who might want me dead is Dilly Deffew."

Rex examined him, head tipped to one side. "Because he realizes that Mrs. Paddimore favors you?" he asked.

It was a cheering thought. If Dilly was desperate enough to attempt murder, perhaps Ash really did have a chance with Regina.

THE MEETING ABOUT the ball went well. Most of the arrangements Regina had made would transfer easily from the Kingsley residence to the Deerhaven mansion, and she and her friends had plans for all of the difficulties they could foresee.

Arial had brought her husband's stepsister with her. Pansy Turner had been involved in a poisonous whispering campaign against Arial last year, but in the end, she had warned Arial's husband Peter of a plot against his wife.

Arial said she owed Pansy her sanity, and possibly her life, so she had accepted the woman's sincere contrition, and hoped her friends would do likewise. Regina would be polite while reserving judgement until she saw the supposed positive change for herself.

She entered her own house just as Geoffrey descended the staircase. They had seen little of one another in the two weeks since he arrived. Once the pain in his hand began to dull, he had been eager to see something of London, and William had offered to show him around. Since then, it seemed, that if she was home, he was out, and the reverse.

He looked tired. Perhaps she should have a word with William about not allowing him to burn the candle at both ends. "Good morning, Geoffrey. How are you enjoying your stay in London?"

He started, as if his mind had been far away. "Is it you, Mother?" His smile did not reach his eyes. "I am having a very educational time, thank you. What about you? You are very busy are you not? Out again with Mr. Ashby this morning?"

"Not this morning. I was visiting the Countess of Deerhaven to see her ballroom." She started up the stairs. "I plan to ring for a tea tray. Will you join me?"

He turned and fell into step beside her. "That is right. You mentioned that you needed to change from William's ballroom."

Which raised a question. William had eagerly accepted her

offer to move the ball to avoid offending her mother. Surely Geoffrey's visits to William would offend her even more? "Have you met Lady Kingsley? Was she nice to you?"

He did not answer for a moment as he moved past her to open the door into the drawing room and to stand to one side so she could enter. He followed her and tugged the bell pull before taking the chair on the other side of a small table from hers. "I have not been meeting William at his house," he said. "We have been to his club, and to Tattersalls, and to a couple of other places."

He was not meeting her eyes. What had he and William been up to? Perhaps it was better if she did not ask. The parlor maid arrived in answer to the bell, and Regina ordered tea for two and something to eat. She did not have to ask for a substantial meal. Once Cook knew that Geoffrey was with her, she would send up enough food for an army.

Once they were alone again, she asked, "You do not mind that I am spending time with Mr. Ashby, do you?"

Geoffrey shrugged. "I like Mr. Ashby. William says you deserve to think about yourself for once, and I agree." His color rose and he stammered a little—a habit she thought he had long since overcome. "If you and Mr. Ashby want to marry, I don't mind."

Regina was touched. "Mr. Ashby and I have not discussed marriage. But thank you, Geoffrey. If I should take a husband, your blessing would be very important to me."

He cleared his throat, and his voice deepened as he said, "You have my blessing. If you need it."

She asked about his plans for the rest of the day, and Geoffrey countered by asking about hers. "You will remind Mr. Ashby that I would like the opportunity to be presented to Lord Arthur?" he said, when he heard about her plans for the afternoon.

"Yes, of course. And he and his wife will be at my ball, of course. You can meet them then, if not before."

He asked a few questions about the ball, in between demolishing two large pieces of savory tart, a sliced bun laden with meat and pickle, two apples, three small sultana cakes, and a boiled egg. He washed all the food down with three cups of tea, declared he felt much more the thing, and excused himself. "I hope you enjoy your afternoon, Mother."

He had avoided most of her questions, giving only the most general of answers. He was up to something. She had better have a word with William.

Chapter Fifteen

A SH AND REX debated their possible enemies all the way home but came to no conclusion.

Ash shrugged. "It was probably just a poorly secured stone, and someone at the other end rocked the plank. I am taking Mrs. Paddimore out in half an hour. I'll have to go straight there."

Rex pointed at Ash. "Not in those clothes, you won't."

Fair point. All one side was smeared with mud and other substances from the courtyard. Rex was likewise grimy.

By the time Ash had washed, changed, made some arrangements to ensure her safety, and driven to Regina's house, he was ten minutes late. He tossed the reins to the groom and hurried up to knock on the door.

Regina was just coming down the stairs as the butler admitted him, in a delightful ensemble of a shade to complement her eyes. She took his breath away every time he saw her. Would familiarity dull the impact? It had not done so yet.

"Mr. Ashby! I was concerned that I had kept you waiting."

"Sadly no, Mrs. Paddimore. I arrived but a moment ago, full of apologies because I was delayed. I inadvertently got mud on my trousers and had to go home to make good, so I was fit to be your escort."

She let her eyes rove over his apparel and said, "Well worth the wait."

Two could play at that game. He scanned her slowly from the toe of her pretty boots to the delightful bonnet that framed her face, and replied, "My sentiments exactly." He could only hope that the exchange heated her as much as it did him.

"GO AWAY, ASH," Rithya told him when he had delivered Regina safely to her drawing room. "Mrs. Paddimore and I have much to talk about, and do not wish to have an audience. Rex is in your study."

There Rex was, attempting to read the draft of the chapter that Ash had finished when he woke up this morning—the one that they had scoped out one evening earlier in the week. That was the way they worked. They would decide together what the chapter would cover, then tell each other stories while Ash made notes. Then Ash would go away and write a first draft. After that, he'd read the chapter aloud to Rex and they would both suggest refinements.

Rex was frowning at the draft. "I cannot make head or tail of this," he grumbled.

"No need," Ash reminded him. "That's what you have me for."

"Dellborough has arranged for us to speak to his club." From his voice, the engagement was for the guillotine. "Said he was proud of me. Said he didn't know I had it in me." He looked up from the sheets of paper in his hands, his eyes bleak. "He thinks I am an author."

"You are as much of the author of our books as I am," Ash protested. "Mine might be the hand on the quill, but they write your words as often as mine. You see things that I don't. Your descriptions are much more detailed than mine. And I could not do your sketches to save myself."

"I cannot even read what you've written." Rex sounded un-convinced.

"If you were blind, and dictating your ideas to me, would you still think you weren't the author?" Ash asked. Rex hadn't had one of these bouts of self-doubt for years. The expectations of family could be hard.

Rex looked up for the first time, a slight smile twitching one corner of his lips. "You have a point. I am feeling sorry for myself, Ash. You get to listen to it because you are my friend."

"I *am* your friend," Ash agreed, twitching the first draft out of Rex's hand. "But I am also your partner, so let's get to work."

Within minutes, they were in a vigorous argument about the weather on the morning they left Saratov for the next leg of their Volga journey. Ash knew Rex's correction was right, but he held out for his own faulty memory because his friend needed the satisfaction of a robust debate followed by a victory.

THE SENIOR FOOTMAN was waiting for her when she let herself into her townhouse. "Mr. Deffew has called, madam, and insisted on waiting for your return." Wilson the butler, who was on his half day, would have politely closed the door in Mr. Deffew's face, but poor Charles did not yet have the confidence.

Regina's surge of irritation was out of all proportion. She was already disappointed that Elijah had merely dropped her off, and not asked to come in. This would have been the ideal opportunity to get him alone.

However, she had decided it was time to send Deffew pack-ing, and what better time than the present? "In the drawing room, Charles?" she asked.

"Yes, Mrs. Paddimore. Do you want me to send a maid up to sit with you?"

She paused on the stairs. What she had to say was best kept

between the two of them, particularly if he would not take a polite hint and she had to be blunt. Dilly Deffew would not take kindly to being scolded in front of a servant. "Not just yet, Charles. Give me ten minutes, and then come yourself. If Mr. Deffew has not left by then, I may need your help to remove him from the house." She stopped again a couple of steps higher. "Oh, and Charles? He is never again to be allowed into this house if I am not present."

When she got to the drawing room, she stopped at the door but against the wall where she couldn't be seen by Dilly, who was roaming the room, picking things up to examine them, then putting them down to move on to the next, appearing for all the world like a customer in a warehouse. Regina watched in silence from the doorway for a moment, her ire rising.

Perhaps she made a sound, for he spun around, dropped the ornament he was holding—one of a set of two glass slippers—and fumbled to catch it before it fell to the carpet.

He grimaced and then replaced the expression with an ingratiating smile. "Mrs. Paddimore! Lovely as always!"

"Mr. Deffew." She crossed the room and held out her hand for the glass slipper.

He put his hand behind his back. "I will see about having it fixed for you, my dear. Better still, I shall buy you something better to replace it. Royal Worcester has a lovely range of china figurines. Very fashionable. Much better than a knickknack like this."

Regina glared. "The object is irreplaceable, Mr. Deffew. It is a memento from someone I care about. Give it to me now, please."

He expelled a noisy breath. "Very well. If you insist."

He put it in her hand—mostly intact, but one of the delicate ties that arched from one side to the other had lost most of its curve. She would need to be careful until the piece could be found. Or pieces. It might be able to be repaired. Someone might cut their foot.

For the moment, she took the poor damaged item to a little

cabinet just inside the door and popped it into a drawer. As she slid the drawer shut, Deffew grabbed her from behind, wrapping his arms around her, trapping her arms at her side, and pressing her against the table.

He crooned in her ear. "Regina, my love. How can you treat me so coldly? Have I not loved you faithfully all these years?"

Regina stamped backward with her feet. "Let me go, you oaf!"

He shoved his hand over her mouth and pressed his body into hers, pushing her thighs hard up against the cabinet, so it rocked and the vase of flowers on top of it threatened to topple.

"I have been patient, Regina. I was prepared to give you time. But you are making a fool out of me, running around town with that sniveling servant Ashby. It is time for you to learn you are mine." He bent her forward, so her face was pressed up against the wall. The vase gave up the struggle and fell over, spilling water and flowers to the floor.

Regina could feel his other hand scrabbling at her calves and then her thighs. She bit down on his fingers, and—when he yanked them away—screamed at the top of her voice.

She heard the bang when the door burst open and another crash. Some part of her that was not panicking catalogued a further breakage to Deffew's account.

Then he was gone.

Regina rested a moment more against the sideboard, taking a deep breath to calm herself before turning towards the sounds of blows against flesh.

Elijah had Deffew by the cravat, holding him up while his other fist pounded the man's face again and again.

Charles watched, his face white.

Deffew's struggles were growing weaker. "Elijah," Regina said, and then again, louder. "Elijah! Don't kill him. Not in my drawing room." Not anywhere, she should have said. She could not bear it if Elijah had to flee England. Unless he took her with him.

The thought had her fighting back tears. "Please, Elijah."

Perhaps it was the quaver in her voice, but his fist ceased its stern punishment and the grim rage ebbed from his expression. "I beg your pardon, Mrs. Paddimore." He let go of Deffew's cravat and the worm collapsed spinelessly onto the carpet, sobbing. "Shall I take him out into the mews and kill him there?"

Regina's gasp and Deffew's whimper sounded together, but the dance of humor was back in Elijah's eyes. "Or shall I call the constable? Assault is a serious offense." He stirred the wailing idiot with his toe.

"Charles, see Mr. Deffew to the door," Regina said. "I have new instructions for you. He is not to enter this house again. Ever."

"You have to marry me," Deffew said, the words garbled and muffled as he spoke around whatever injuries Elijah had inflicted. "You owe me." She could see another thought dawn on him. "When I tell people how Ashby found us, you will be ruined if you don't marry me."

He flinched at the scorn in her glare, or perhaps at the fist Elijah raised.

"You tried that sixteen years ago, you benighted fool," Regina scolded. "Do you think your consequence is greater than mine? If you say a single word about what happened here today, I shall tell the truth about the highwayman who shot my husband, and we shall see who is ruined."

Deffew, already pale, whitened still further. He made an inarticulate sound of protest.

"Nothing happened here today," Elijah said. "I was in the room the whole time, was I not, Charles?"

The footman nodded, a grin spreading slowly over his face. "Yes, sir. And I was, too. Chaperoning my lady, like. Since she had two gentlemen callers."

Elijah offered Deffew his hand. The man took it cautiously and allowed Elijah to help him to his feet. Elijah leaned close to Deffew's ear. His voice was a low and lethal whisper, but Regina heard every word. "If you say one word that casts discredit on Mrs. Paddimore in any way, I shall hunt you down, Deffew. I have learned much in my travels. I shall take you apart, and no one will ever find the pieces."

Deffew backed away, white showing all round his irises.

"Charles, take out the trash," Elijah commanded. The footman took Deffew by the arm and marched him out the door.

Regina collapsed onto the sofa and burst into tears.

Chapter Sixteen

I N A MOMENT, she was a warm fragrant bundle on Ash's lap, her curves draped across his torso, her arms wrapped around him, her face tucked into his shoulder as she cried.

He patted her shoulder, murmuring comfort. "There now. You're safe now, Ginny. He's gone. He won't bother you again. I have you, my darling. I have you."

He had not seen Regina so discomposed since she was a child, grieving the loss of a kitten. He wished he'd hit Deffew harder. He'd thought he and Charles were in time, but if the swine's violation had gone beyond what he'd seen, the dog would die for it, Regina's opinion notwithstanding.

Charles poked his head around the door, his eyes widening in alarm when he saw the state of his mistress. Ash pointed to the brandy decanter he could see on a sideboard. "Two," he mouthed, ceasing his patting to hold up two fingers then resuming again, barely breaking rhythm.

Charles nodded and tiptoed to the decanter to pour two glasses of brandy, then tiptoed back across the room to place them on a side table next to Ash's elbow, setting them down so carefully they did not clink.

Ash briefly wondered whether the young man wanted to save Regina the embarrassment of knowing her emotional collapse had been witnessed, or whether he feared she might expect him to do something about it if she knew he was there. Whichever it was, he faded back across the room and out of the door, pulling it shut behind him.

The footman was not important. Not when the lady he loved was in his arms, her soft curves molded to his body, the aroma of roses, honeysuckle, and something indefinably Regina filling his nostrils. He yearned to hold her closer still, to show her how much he desired her, though the way her lovely rear pressed into his groin, she would notice soon enough.

She was still crying, but the angry storm was gone, fading into heart-wrenching sobs that twisted Ash's gut even more than the initial outburst. "There now, Ginny," Ash soothed. "Let it out, dearest. You're safe now, my love."

She turned her face up at that, drawing back so that her tear-drenched eyes could meet his. "Am I, Elijah?"

"Yes, of course. He has gone, and I won't let him near you again."

She thumped his chest softly, an action so reminiscent of the child Ginny that he had to repress a smile. "Not that," she scolded. "The other."

He retraced his words in his mind. "My love?" At her tiny nod, he repeated, "My love."

She raised her eyebrows in question, the imperious gesture only slightly marred by the shuddering breath of a leftover sob.

"I love you, Ginny. Did you not know?"

She thumped him again, another gentle reprimand. "You never said," she grumbled. "You never even tried to kiss me." The last two words were disrupted by a hiccup, but he understood them well enough.

"I am abjectly sorry, Ginny," Ash told her, managing to keep his voice suitably solemn while his heart was attempting to break out of his chest and into hers. *She has been waiting for my kisses! Missing them, even.* "I have never courted anyone before. I am clearly not very good at it."

She hiccupped again as she put up a hand to cradle Ash's cheek. "I am sorry to be so cross, Elijah. I hate hiccups. I hate crying, and it always give me the hiccups." She proved it with another shuddering hiccup.

"Have a sip of brandy, beloved," he suggested, and he picked up one of the glasses and held it to her lips. "It might help. And if it doesn't, perhaps a kiss will cure them."

Ash was very aware that she had not returned his declaration of love. However, she wanted his kisses. He would start there and hope for the best.

Ginny took the glass from his hand and had another sip, followed by another hiccup.

"It will have to be the kiss, then," he suggested. He lowered his head to hers, slowly, giving her plenty of time to turn him away. Instead, she lifted her face to bridge the gap, her mouth reaching inexpertly for his.

He pressed kisses to each corner of her mouth, then settled his mouth over hers, stroking her lips with his. She clutched him, some of the brandy spilling from the glass so she drew back, apologizing with another hiccup.

Ash put the glass out of harm's way and drew Ginny to him again. This time, he ran his tongue across the seam of his lips, seeking entrance. She hummed but didn't open. If he hadn't known she'd been a wife for more than three years before her husband's accident, he would have thought she'd never participated in a kiss.

"Open for me, sweetheart," he suggested, his lips still touching hers as he spoke.

"Open what?" she asked, and he took the moment to slip his tongue inside, into the soft warm cave of her mouth, gently teasing the sensitive skin inside her lips and at the roof of her mouth. She tasted as wonderful as she felt: a deeper richer version of the Ginny element of her perfume.

She tensed at first, but as she relaxed into him, she opened wider, the hum becoming a moan of pleasure that sent a bolt of lust to his most irresponsible organ. She pressed her body to him, her breasts plastered against his chest, her hips rubbing against his groin as she moved in concert with his tongue as it slid in and out between her lips in a rhythm old as humankind.

When her tongue followed his as it moved away, darting out to touch his lips, he could feel the shy caress strike like lightning down through his body to his groin. Then she followed that up a moment or two later with a more daring foray, until their tongues danced, surging forward, and retreating, in a partnership that nearly consumed the world.

Nearly. Some part of him remained sensible enough to remind him not to rush her. She was, as unlikely as it seemed, an innocent. He kept his hands gentle, his touch forming soothing circles on her back. Over her clothes. *Soon*, he promised his baser self. Soon, he would have her naked on her back, and worship her as she deserved. *I hope.*

He drew back enough to place a reverent kiss on the corner of her mouth then follow with a row of kisses down her neck. She cast her head back and arched her neck for his ministrations. Perhaps a little farther? He was about to tug the bodice of her gown out of the way so he could kiss the tops of her breasts, and perhaps even lower, when he heard the head footman loudly and somewhat frantically say, "Wait a moment, Lord Kingsley! Let me announce you!"

"Thank you but I'm fine, my man." The door opened with a rattle, and there was a masculine gasp. Ash looked up to see Ginny's brother in the doorway, his mouth open, consternation in every line of his body.

He pulled himself together before Ash could speak. "I need to speak to you, Regina," Lord Kingsley said. "I'll just wait in the hall, shall I?"

ELIJAH WAS LOOKING worried, but he had not removed his arms from around Regina. She reached up and kissed the corner of his mouth. "I need to go and wash my face. I must look a mess."

Either the kiss or her statement made him smile. "You look beautiful, as always," he assured her. "Perhaps a little rumpled and tear stained. Should I expect your brother to challenge me to a duel or demand a quick wedding?" A grin then, a touch wistful. "A quick wedding would be nice, but I would rather court you properly and then propose in due form."

She had to kiss him again, for resolving all her doubts about his interest in her. He took the kiss over and deepened it, then pulled back reluctantly. "I love you, Ginny. But you had better go and tidy up. Your brother looks as if he has something on his mind. Shall I go home and leave you to your discussion?"

As he spoke, he helped her off his lap, and stood as she did.

"No, do not go," Regina begged. "Stay, Elijah, if you do not mind. If you are able."

His smile was tender. "Able and willing."

"Tell William we are courting," Regina suggested. "He has no authority over me, but he does worry."

She lifted her chin and puckered her lips, and he bent so that she could reach his mouth. A small peck, and she left the room to find William pacing the hall. "Regina…" he began, then stopped. "You have been crying. You never cry."

"I need to wash and put myself to rights, William. Keep Elijah company, will you? I will be five minutes and no more. Oh, and gentlemen? Use the little sitting room. A glass ornament was broken on the rug before the fire in the drawing room. I shall send a maid to sweep it for pieces."

She instructed one of the parlor maids, and went up to her room, where she splashed water on her face and brushed her hair back into a tidy plait, which she bound around her head and pinned in place.

Looking presentable again, she descended the stairs some five minutes after she'd left the room. Within the sitting room to which she'd directed them, Elijah and William were sitting relaxed back in their chairs, each sipping from a glass of brandy as they talked.

Elijah saw her first and stood, William following a second behind him.

She took her own seat on the sofa, and said, "Please be seated, gentlemen."

William leaned forward in his chair. "I have to talk to you about Geoffrey."

Elijah began to rise. "Shall I wait in the next room?"

Regina put out a hand. "Stay, please. William, you can speak freely in front of Elijah. Is Geoffrey making a nuisance of himself? I am sorry—I didn't think. He seemed so pleased to be spending so much time with you. I should have asked you if it was convenient to have him with you so often."

William shook his head. "It's worse than I thought then. That is to say, he hasn't made a nuisance of himself at all. Regina, I've barely seen Geoffrey in over a week."

For a moment, she could not take it in. "But he said... He told me..." Her hand reached for Elijah's with no conscious thought and his firm grasp anchored her enough to get her thoughts in order. She turned her head to look at Elijah. "Ever since he arrived in London, Geoffrey has been, at least as I thought, visiting with William every day, and often staying with him overnight."

William shook his head. "That is not true. He did so a couple of times at the beginning, yes. But when he heard Mother had arrived, he said he would not impose. I don't know where he has been, but it has not been with me."

"He has been lying." She took a deep breath, letting the reality settle. "To do what, William? Do you know?"

"I know where he was last night. That's why I came. When he saw me, he begged me to tell you I'd been with him. I told him to go home and tell you the truth, and I'd visit today to make sure he had done so. But I asked Charles, and he said Geoffrey hasn't been home since he rose yesterday morning."

Regina fixed on one part of that, her alarm rising. "Where was he? Somewhere he shouldn't be?" Her mind teamed with possibilities, each worse than the last.

"A gambling den?" Elijah guessed. "A cock fight?"

"A bare-knuckle match," William admitted.

They were all illegal activities, but a bare-knuckle match was not so bad, was it? At least it was not a brothel! She let out a breath she didn't realize she'd been holding.

William grimaced. "He was with a group of boys around his own age and a bit older. I didn't know any of them." He added, "They were all half-cut." He shot an apologetic glance at Regina and clarified. "Drunk, Regina."

Regina gripped Elijah's hand tighter, using it as an anchor for her spinning thoughts. "Drunk?" Her voice shook, but she swallowed, and it was firmer as she said, "But at least together. At an event like that? Safer."

William looked doubtful. "Perhaps. But men in a drunken group can be very stupid."

"I see." She had heard stories, though she had no personal experience. She had been insulated from wild young men as a debutante, and as Gideon's wife. And even in his youth, William had been sober and responsible.

Now that she was a widow, she was both too old and too respectable to move in the same circles as such youth.

Elijah opened his mouth and then closed it again.

"Say what you're thinking," Regina coaxed. "I *did* ask you to stay."

"Is this behavior you would have expected from him?" Elijah asked. "Deceit? Lying? Asking his guardian to lie for him?"

"Not normally," William declared. "Not at all."

Regina shook her head. "This is my fault. I should have realized he would not come to your house with Mother there. I should have checked on where he was spending his time." She had been so absorbed in her ball and her friends—no, she would be honest, if only to herself—so absorbed in *Elijah* that she had neglected Geoffrey.

"*I* should have asked after him," William responded. "*I* am to blame." He looked at miserable as Regina felt.

"What exactly is the problem here?" Elijah asked with a reasonable tone that cut through their self-recriminations. "Geoffrey has been enjoying the pursuits of a wealthy youth in London. Yes, he deceived Regina in order to do so, but it sounds to me as if he knew what her response would be. I don't see that anyone is to blame for his choices except Geoffrey himself."

Regina's mouth dropped open. "But he lied," she stammered.

"Which was wrong, of course. But he is very young, Regina."

William was staring at Elijah as if he had said something wondrous. "You're right. He has always been so good, so biddable, we didn't expect... He must be punished for lying, of course, but he should not be afraid to tell us that he wants to go out with his friends. A boxing-match. Nothing wrong with a boxing-match," He looked slightly abashed, and the look he cast his sister was wary. "I was there myself."

Were they right? Her heart recoiled at the idea of the dear boy roaming unprotected around London. "But he might be hurt, Elijah. And who are these friends of his? How do we know they are not leading him astray?" Elijah did not have children. How could he possibly understand?

Elijah grimaced, and again, Regina asked him to speak his mind.

"Yes," William agreed. "You are nearly family, from what I saw when I walked in."

Regina felt the heat rise in her cheeks at his sly rebuke. William continued to address Elijah. "If you have any ideas about how to handle this, I'd be grateful." He raised his eyebrows, looking at Regina, and she nodded.

"*We* would be grateful," she said.

"It is just that he is eighteen, and has lived away from home at university for, what, five months? I assume he started in

October? Or is this his second year?"

"No, you are right. He has been..." She trailed off, suddenly realizing what Elijah was saying. "He has been accustomed to making his own decisions about how to spend his time, to being trusted as an adult."

"Answering only to the proctors if he is out in the streets at night without his gown," William acknowledged. He sat back in his chair again and sipped his brandy. "I remember how heady it was to be in rooms in Cambridge, away from home. I'll speak to him about how wrong it was for him to use me as an alibi. He'll take it better from me." He leaned forward and put his brandy down before saying, "Now, what is this that Ashby tells me about Deffew? Do I need to call him out, Regina?"

Men! "No, William. Putting your life and my reputation at risk by dueling is not required."

William made a rude noise. "If that is the way you talk to Geoffrey, Regina, it is no wonder he sneaks out behind your back."

"I will have you know—," Regina began, then noticed Elijah grinning at the pair of them. *He thinks this is a laughing matter, does he?* She raised her brows, indignant, but he disarmed her by leaning forward to kiss her cheek. He said, "I have always wanted a to feel like part of a family."

Chapter Seventeen

T HE NEXT MORNING, Ash and Rex sat in one of the lounges at Westruthers with the president of the club, who had invited them to visit and given them a guided tour along with an enthusiastic explanation of the benefits of membership. "I speak for us all, Lord Arthur, Mr. Ashby, when I assure you that we would be delighted to welcome you as members."

He gestured towards the stack of their books, which he'd produced for signing as soon as they entered this room. With the flyleaf now sporting a personal massage from Ash and an autograph from each of them, they had now, the president assured them, become a club treasure.

"Several gentlemen have vouched for you," the president continued. "Viscount Barker, the Earl of Stancroft. There will be no problem with your election."

He did not need to work so hard to win their agreement. The lunch the friends had shared with Barker had been advertisement enough, and they had since met a number of the members, all of whom spoke highly of Westruthers.

"We are delighted to accept," Rex said, though it was probably Ash, a single man sharing a home with a young family, who was likely to make the most use of the facilities. At least for the time being. He would need a house of his own before he married, and he smiled at the thought.

They said their goodbyes and made their way out of the club.

Ash was still thinking about his courtship of Regina. He was not sure he had grounds for optimism. Regina had accepted several of his invitations, yes. But she had other suitors. More handsome, wealthier, better connected. Why should she choose an orphan of no particular family who had to work for his living?

She found him attractive; he couldn't doubt the purely feminine interest with which she regarded him. But she didn't flirt. She did not employ any of the many ways a woman indicated that a man's attentions would be welcomed.

She had not returned his declaration of love. She enjoyed his kisses, though. Returned them, too. She had agreed that he might court her. She'd insisted on him staying for a family meeting. Yes. On the whole, he thought his hope was not misplaced.

He wondered about Deffew's claim that she owed him because of Paddimore's accident. What was that about? Perhaps she would have told him if Kingsley had not interrupted their embrace. Or perhaps, the embrace would have led to things other than talking.

He descended the steps to the street with his mind joyfully employed on imagining those things, oblivious to his surroundings until Rex's body crashed against his and they tumbled to the footpath. Even as he fell, his mind replayed the sharp bark of a rifle, heard through the din of the busy street. As Rex rolled off him and he took cover behind a cart parked in the road, he was already scanning the rooftops on the other side of the road.

A dark-clad figure holding a rifle clambered up a roof on the other side of the street and disappeared over the ridge. A moment later, the person topped the ridge behind and presumably kept going

Rex had hurried back up the steps and was exploring the dent the bullet had gouged in one of the stone pillars that held up the portico. "Definitely a bullet." he reported.

"Definitely a rifleman," Ash said. "I saw him running away."

Rex was scanning the ground. "It dropped here." He stooped and came up again with a lump of misshapen lead.

"Good reactions," Ash told him.

Rex shrugged. "I saw a glint off the barrel. On the way down, I thought—it couldn't be a rifle. Not in London!"

Ash was still scanning the rooftops. "I cannot see any movement." He grinned at his friend. "I'm glad you didn't stop for second thoughts. Was that for you or for me?"

Rex shrugged. "Or a case of mistaken identity. I have to say it rather confirms that the falling stone incident outside Tolliver's was no accident."

"Lord Barker mentioned a firm of enquiry agents, Rex. I think we should call them in."

A few pedestrians had stopped to stare, but most of the traffic—foot, hooved, and wheeled—continued, oblivious to the attack. Two of the men were lascars by their dress and complexion, like those present when the stone block narrowly missed them after the meeting with Tolliver. These were unlikely to be the same two. London attracted people from all over the world, and many British ships sailing to and from India and nearby lands employed locals from those parts as sailors.

In any case, there was nothing to connect two men in the street to the man on the rooftop. Ash shook off his momentary distraction and followed Rex across the road.

By the time Ash and Rex made their way around the row of buildings opposite the club, the gunman was long gone. As they looked up at the back of the most likely house, Ash noticed a groom watching them from inside a stable that let onto the alley.

"Hey," Ash called. "Did you see a man come down of the roof here?"

The man shuffled a few steps forward and reported seeing a man drop from the roof onto an outbuilding and from there into the alley, where he had mounted a waiting horse and ridden off.

The groom couldn't describe the man except in the most general terms. Medium height. Heavy build. Dark clothes. A hat.

No, he didn't see the man's face or any other features that might distinguish him. No, he didn't try to stop him. Wasn't his business, was it?

And that was it. Nothing to give them a lead.

"We'll see what the enquiry agent turns up," Ash said.

"We'll have a chance to catch the villain when he tries again," Rex said, ghoulishly.

WHEN SHE WOKE the next day, Regina's first thought was of Ash's kisses, and her second of Geoffrey. When she asked her maid whether the young master had come home, the answer was in the negative.

Unsettled by her physical yearnings, worried about Geoffrey, she decided to tidy her desk drawer—a humdrum task that might at least keep her occupied in one place instead of pacing to and fro like a wild beast.

In the back of the drawer, tied with string, was a bundle of letters. Her mother's letters, mostly from the early year of Regina's marriage. Her words to Geoffrey about holding a grudge, and William's expression whenever he spoke of their mother, which hinted at the pain their estrangement caused him, came back to her.

She sat down and read them all again, starting with the first one she received, in which her mother wrote of her fear that Regina would have a marriage like her own, in which her husband found love elsewhere, and she was all alone. At the time, Regina had been angry at the insult to Regina's father, but as she read the letter again, her heart ached for her mother.

By the time she had finished them all, she was crying. Her poor Mama. Her loneliness showed through the stiff and courteous questions about Geoffrey and Gideon, wry observations about life in the village, intelligent comments on current affairs.

Why had Regina never seen it before? Gideon had, she realized. He had told Regina that Mama was grieving—not just Papa's death, but the sorrows of her marriage, which was so much less than she had hoped. That had fueled her anger, her grasping after Mr. Deffew as a suitor, her insistence that her world would come to an end if Regina did not elope with the horrid man.

Regina had first scoffed and then become so upset that he'd let the matter drop.

Her mother had written for the last time after Gideon was shot, when everyone, including the doctors, expected him to die. Regina had returned the letter unopened with her first reply to any of her mother's letters wrapped around it. She could remember the precise words. "Leave me alone. I do not wish to hear from you."

Regina blinked back tears. She had been so unfair! If only she could go back and respond differently. She swallowed against a suddenly thick throat. Poor Mama. Regina took a deep pained breath and shut her eyes. Would she be willing to forgive Regina after all these years? Regina had to try.

Geoffrey appeared late in the morning, slinking into the house with an expression Regina could only describe as surly.

He stopped in his tracks when he saw Regina descending the stairs. *Calm and welcoming*, she reminded herself. "Good morning, Geoffrey."

"William says I owe you an apology for deceiving you," he grumbled.

"Yes," she agreed. "And I owe you one for being so protective that you thought you needed to sneak behind my back instead of coming out like a man and telling me your true plans."

Geoffrey blinked, and then his face cleared. "Ouch," he said, with the rueful grin she loved. "That apology had a sting in it."

"That wasn't the apology, clod pate." She composed herself, her hands folded at her waist, her head meekly bowed. "Dear

Geoffrey, I'm sorry that I acted in a way that made you believe I would not support your going out with your friends."

Geoffrey took her cue, thank goodness, bowing from the waist while sweeping his arm back as if it held a plumed hat. "Dear Mother, I am sorry I lied to you about my whereabouts and my activities." He straightened again and grimaced. "Uncle William said I can hardly expect you to treat me like a man when I sneak off like a boy."

"We shall both try to do better then," Regina said. "Have you breakfasted, Geoffrey?" Her boy looked pale and tired, but she would not comment on that. Not now they had established peace between them.

"Nothing for me, Mother. I have a bit of a headache. I might just have a wash and go to bed."

The after-effects of much drinking, perhaps? She had heard other women complain of such headaches in their husbands, sons, or brothers. "I will send Charles up with some tea, Geoffrey. I understand drinking several cups can help."

He looked at her suspiciously, and then nodded. "Thank you. I may have dipped a little deep last night. But they are excellent fellows, Mother. Now that I am not keeping them a secret anymore, I shall be able to introduce you, and you shall see for yourself."

"I shall look forward to it," Regina told him.

"You are dressed to go out," he commented, then flushed. "Not that *you* need to tell *me* where you are going, Mother."

"To order some items I need for my ball, dear. Mr. Ashby is taking me in his phaeton."

"Oh yes. The ball. It is in a few days, is it not?" He was making a visible effort to appear interested, while suppressing a yawn that showed his true interest was his pillow.

"On Tuesday night next week. May I hope you will be present? And would you like to invite your friends?"

He blinked a couple of times, surprised. "I can ask them," he replied, cautiously. "I do not think it is the kind of thing they enjoy. I will be there, Mother, of course."

At that moment, the knocker sounded, and Wilson appeared from the butler's little room to answer the door.

>>>><<<<

WHEN ASH ENTERED the house, Regina stood at the foot of the stairs, her bonnet dangling by its strings from a hand that also held her gloves. She was dressed in blue again—this time in several shades. Her outer garment was a redingote slightly darker than her eyes; it skimmed lovingly over her delectable curves. Under it, she wore a gown in a light shade trimmed with some sort of braid in a deep blue that matched her gloves and the sensible boots on her tiny feet. Flowers in all three blues festooned one side of the straw bonnet.

"Mrs. Paddimore, what a charming outfit."

He drank in the sight of her for a moment before taking note of her foster son. Geoffrey Paddimore looked pallid and rumpled, as if he had just arrived home after a night out. At least he was home.

"Good morning, Mr. Paddimore. I hope I find you well?"

The boy had excellent manners in spite of his greenish tinge. "I am, Mr. Ashby. And you, sir?"

"All the better for seeing your lovely mother," Ash told him, and winked at Regina.

She stretched up and young Paddimore lowered his cheek for her peck of kiss. "Go and get some sleep, my dear," she advised. "Will I see you for dinner?"

"I would like that, Mother. Could it be an early dinner? I am meant to be meeting some of the fellows this evening at about eight."

"Wilson," Regina told the butler, "Would you let Cook know that we will need dinner for six o'clock? Will that be early enough, Geoffrey? Oh, and can you have someone take up a pot of tea to Mr. Paddimore's room?"

"Thank you, Mother," the young man said. "That will be excellent." He finished on a yawn, which he attempted to hide behind his hand.

"It will suit us, will it not, Elijah? Mr. Ashby is escorting me to the theater this evening. To Drury Lane, to see *The Bride of Abydon.*"

Paddimore smiled at Ash over Regina's head. "We are going to the theater too, but not such a grand one. The East End, for the pantomime and burletta. Have a good shopping trip, Mother."

He stepped lightly up the stairs, and Regina crossed to where Ash waited by the door. "Let us be off, Elijah. It is a lovely day for a drive, even one with shopping!"

As they left the house, Ash scanned the surroundings, but saw no suspicious movement. Fullaby was on horseback, farther down the street, his nod confirming he'd seen nothing suspicious. Two of Rex's grooms were also in the vicinity, mounted and alert. The periphery was also guarded by some of the town-house's footmen, out of livery but hardly anonymous. Their stature and way they walked screamed "footman," and the attention they paid to Ash and Regina signaled to any observer that they were not casual passers-by.

Still, it was the best Ash could do at short notice, and he and Rex had agreed that a second attempt so soon after the last was unlikely. Later today, he'd look into finding some men who would better serve to thwart another attempt on his life. If, in fact, he had been the target. Rex was seeing the enquiry agent this afternoon. Perhaps the man could find out who was attacking them and why.

He helped Regina up into his phaeton. Her own carriage was drawing up behind them and would follow to carry her parcels.

"Do you know those men?" Regina asked, peering at the nearest footman.

Ash hesitated only a moment. His urge to protect her was

natural. But keeping her in the dark was not the way to do it. She was an intelligent, adult woman. Knowing about possible danger was the first step to countering it.

"They're working for me, Regina. I don't believe you are in any danger, but we think someone took a shot in my direction earlier today, and I wanted to take every possible step to ensure your safety."

She gasped. "Someone *shot* at you?"

"They missed," he assured her. "If I was, indeed, the target. They may have been shooting at Rex, or it may even have been a case of mistaken identity."

"Did you report it to the magistrates?" She gave a sharp nod. "Yes, of course you did. You are not fools."

Ash shrugged. As to that, he and Rex had argued about it. Rex said they and their runners had next to nothing to go on. Ash said they had nothing to lose. "Yes, we went to the nearest police office and reported to the magistrate. He said he'd send some constables to look at the scene and ask some questions. He didn't sound hopeful."

Regina frowned and pursed her lips. "You don't think he will find anything."

"We have called in an enquiry agent," Ash reassured her. "We'll see what he finds out. We've also agreed neither of us will go anywhere without a set of watchers who will be able to see any danger as it approaches." He grinned at the thought of the reception he and Rex planned.

"You look as if you hope they will try again," she observed. "I have never seen a wolf smiling, but I imagine the expression might be similar. You hope to catch them in the act, do you not?"

She was a smart lady. "I hope the enquiry agent will find out who they are before that is necessary. But we will catch them in the act if it comes to it."

Regina was silent for a few minutes. Ash focused on his team, easing them past other traffic, conscious always of Fullaby ten yards ahead and the two grooms following behind. The footmen were jogging to keep up, weaving in and out of pedestrians. If anything happened, their priorities were Regina's safety first and then pursuit and capture of the assailant.

Regina had clearly been thinking with some purpose. "Do you have any idea who might want you dead? You have only been back in England a matter of days. Could it be someone you've somehow offended during your travels?"

"Not that I know of. Not sufficiently to have them pursue me across the world. And the same applies to Rex. Perhaps it was a case of mistaken identity after all." He decided not to mention the people who might or might not be from India, and who might or might not have been present for both attempts.

"I suppose it could be someone in England who wants something they think you have," she mused.

"Or something they want that they think they'll get more easily if I am out of the way. Or Rex." *Like Dilly, for example.*

But his suspicion about Dilly was ridiculous. *Wasn't it?*

They had turned on to the busy thoroughfare that contained the first of the shops on Regina's list.

"You will be careful?" Regina asked him, touching his arm. "I would hate it if you were hurt." Her tone of deep concern had him glancing at her before turning back to the horses. Worry for him filled her eyes. Worry and... love?

And that was promising, wasn't it?

THE FIRST SHOP was followed by a second, a third, and then more. "Are you sure this isn't boring for you, Elijah?" Regina said again, the fourth time she had asked in the past hour and a half. "I can continue on my own if you would prefer."

"I am content," Ash told her, as he had said before. It was true. He was enjoying watching Regina with the merchants, asking questions about quality and construction, decisively selecting what would suit and rejecting what didn't, bargaining to establish a price.

She knew precisely what she wanted, and what she was prepared to pay for it. The truth was, he realized, he just enjoyed
watching Regina. She filled his thoughts, day, and night, and
when he was with her, she absorbed so much of his attention that
he had to remind himself to keep up his guard against any further
attempts at harm.

"Unless I am in the way," he added, suddenly thinking that
her concern about his entertainment might be subtle hint that she
would prefer his absence.

Her smile soothed that doubt, and she accepted his assistance
to mount into the curricle. "Not at all. I am enjoying your
company. Two more stops, then. The china merchant, and then
Fourniers to finalize the catering."

Ash rounded the carriage and leapt up beside her. "Monsieur
Fournier is your chef for the evening?" He gave the horses the
signal to move away from the curb. They were ahead of Regina's
carriage for the moment, as it was still being loaded, but his own
guards were still in place around them.

"Not precisely." Regina tucked her hand into his arm, and he
could feel his body heating on that side. She seemed oblivious,
continuing, "My own cook, as well as William's and Cordelia's
are all contributing to the supper, but Monsieur Fournier will be
supplying several of his signature dishes, including a dessert that
he has promised will be truly spectacular, but has refused
otherwise to discuss!"

Ash was astounded. "He won't tell you what he is making for
your own ball?"

Regina's eyes twinkled as he looked down into them. "He is
an artist, you see. 'Madame shall be pleased with my creation,' is
all he will say. And, indeed, he has the finest of reputations,
Elijah. The Duchess of Winshire herself employed him until he
married her secretary, and both the Duchess and her son have
invested in his restaurant!"

The china warehouse took up a whole building, with one side

on the riverbank and the other fronting a street of shops and display rooms. Ash drew the curricle up outside of the display room for the china merchant.

He hurried around to assist Regina down from the carriage, one of the grooms trotting forward to take the heads of his team. She nodded her thanks to the groom, and he blushed as he nodded back.

"What is the mission here, Ginny?" Ash asked.

"Vases. I have a mind to decorate the ballroom with spring flowers, which William, Geoffrey, and Deerhaven can supply in great quantity from their estates. But even all three households can barely supply enough vases, and they will be a mishmash of sizes, shapes, and colors. I hope to find some inexpensive, round, white vases that will not take attention away from the flowers."

She repeated the requirement to the salesman who hurried to serve her as soon as they entered, and soon she was happily examining a range of samples.

Ash followed her around the room for a while, but his eye was caught by a display of china ornaments. They illustrated popular tales. There was the Green Knight in battle with the Black. Thomas the Rhymer being tempted away by the Fairy Queen. The Laidly Worm about to be kissed by Childe Wynde. And Cendrillon sitting on the kitchen floor leaning against a large pumpkin, with a tiny dancing slipper on one fair hand.

Ash managed to catch the salesman to one side while Regina was giving her footman instructions for the careful transport of the vases she had chosen. "I will have the Cendrillon," he told him. "Wrap it after the lady and I are gone, and I'll be back later today to pay for it and collect it."

Cendrillon would make a perfect birthday gift for his Ginny.

Chapter Eighteen

OVER DINNER, GEOFFREY entertained Regina with stories of his various adventures since he had arrived in London. Or, at least, that was his intention.

Regina's vague disquiet about his unknown friends turned to alarm as he spoke of stupid stunts and risky wagers—of stealing a couple of milk cows from the St. James Park herd and harnessing them to a friend's curricle in place of his pair, of riding a horse backwards down Bond Street, of nailing a dozing night watchman into his sentry box.

Since these were the pranks he felt comfortable sharing with her, she was sure there were others, much worse. Still, remembering the discussion with Elijah and William, she kept her opinion to herself. *Perhaps it is perfectly normal behavior for a wealthy young man. But those poor cows. The poor watchman.*

"I will look forward to meeting these friends of yours," she told him

Geoffrey nodded, eagerly. "Oh, they are great sports, Mother. I'm sure you will like them."

They were all known by nicknames, apparently. Chalky, Muggers, Thatch, and Dex. Since Geoffrey now proudly bore the soubriquet *Padders*, Regina assumed all of the boys' surnames had been shortened.

When she met the young men, they would be introduced by

their proper names, and she could then find out something about their families. This would either soothe her worries or introduce new ones, yet still, she would have to do nothing. It was very hard to let go, and to allow Geoffrey to make his own mistakes.

She managed to smile and nod and keep any critical outcry to herself. She could not help, though, saying to him as he left for his evening out, "Do be careful, Geoffrey. I could not bear for you to be hurt, or worse."

He kissed her cheek, a rare gesture of affection. "You do not need to worry about me, Mother. I know what I am doing. Have a good time out with Mr. Ashby." He accepted the coat and hat that Charles offered him and paused in the doorway. "Don't worry if I am not home in the morning. We'll probably be out most of the night, so I'll sleep in a chair in Thatch's rooms."

Don't worry, he said. As if Regina could switch her concern about him off like a tap.

She went upstairs to allow her maid to put the final touches to her appearance for the theater. They were attending with a party—Rex and Rithya, of course, and some other members of Rex's family.

Geoffrey's accounting of his activities continued to niggle in the back of her mind. It wasn't until she was coming downstairs again to wait for Elijah that it occurred to her she'd never heard him mention any of the young men before. Not in his sporadic letters from Cambridge. Not during his week-long break at home over Christmas. Were they all new acquaintances? And if so, how did she meet them?

She set the question to one side so she could focus her attention on her escort and his party, and it wasn't hard to do so when Charles let Elijah in the door just as she descended the last flight of stairs. He stopped to watch her, a glow in his eyes that spoke of desire and affection.

"Mrs. Paddimore," he told her, "I shall be the most envied man in the theater."

"Just the theater, Mr. Ashby?" she teased. "Not the whole of London?"

He was ready with a response. "The whole of London, delight of my eyes, has no idea what it is missing."

This was Regina's first visit to the theater this Season. It had been a favorite activity when she and Gideon lived in London, and before her marriage, during her first Season, she and her mother had often prevailed upon one of her mother's admirers to escort them.

Never before, though, had she been a guest in such a capacious and well-appointed box. The Dellborough box was to the right of the stage and consisted of a spacious room with an apron front at the same level of the stage, and a retiring room behind, where servants waited with refreshments for the guests.

Rex presented her to the Duke and Duchess, a stately couple some twenty or more years older than Rex—indeed, their son had been born just three years after Rex; he was present with his Countess, the mother of the next generation of Dellborough heirs.

The box's inhabitants were of nearly as much interest to the audience as *The Bride of Abydos*, which was the main feature of the evening. An adaptation of the Byron poem, with the tragic ending switched for the happier closure of Byron's *Corsair*, it soon had Regina forgetting the sea of watchful eyes.

The play leant itself to the modern innovation of gas lighting, with both dawn and dusk scenes profiting from changes in the lighting. The scenery was beautiful, the costuming gorgeous, and the music pleasing. Edmund Kean played the hero, Selim, and he was always worth seeing, especially when playing opposite the beautiful Charlotte Mardyn.

ASH PAID LITTLE attention to the performance. His attention was totally caught by Regina. She stared enchanted at the stage, her expressive face showing every emotion the actors and the music induced. He could not look away.

In the tiered galleries along both sides of the theater, denizens of the fashionable world preened and postured for one another. Far above, those who could not afford admission to the galleries looked down from their high perches, enjoying the spectacle of the audience as much as what happened on the stage. And from the floor of the theater, working-class men and women rubbed shoulders with young gentlemen out on the town.

Here and there, others focused on the actors and their enactment of Byron's romantic tale but few with the concentration of his Ginny.

He loved her. He wanted a lifetime with her. He wanted that focus directed towards him as he made slow deliberate love to every portion of her delectable anatomy. Small as she was, he might have to worship some places more than once to draw out the time.

When the curtain closed for the intermission, Regina roused only slowly from the spell the show had cast. Servants passed around glasses of wine, and Ash took one for her and placed it in her hand. "Thank you, Elijah," she murmured, her eyes still far away.

People crowded into their box to pay their compliments to the Duke and Duchess of Dellborough, and to meet the two adventurers. Regina responded with perfect courtesy to greetings from those she knew and introductions from those she didn't, but Ash sensed she was simply waiting for them all to go away and for the play to return.

She roused when one of the visitors condescended to Rithya, speaking loudly and slowly as if she thought Arthur's wife to be deaf or stupid. "You must be very glad to be in England, Lady Arthur. Lord Arthur was kind to bring you here."

"To the theater?" Rithya asked, with perfect English enunciation, her eyes glittering. "Yes, my husband is very good to me."

The interlocuter drew back, and then commented to Regina, "Her English is quite good, is it not?"

"Certainly, far better than my Hindi," said Regina. She smiled at Rithya. "As you explained to me, my lady, in your country, ladies of your class are expected to master several languages—written as well as spoken—as well as musical instruments, dance, and artistic endeavors."

Rithya returned the smile. "And science, mathematics, politics, geography, and the like. It is to make us better companions to our husbands and mothers to our children."

Regina nodded, decisively. "We English could learn from that example. Many of our girls have little education and must bore their husbands to tears."

Rithya's smile turned wicked. "We also study the arts of the bedchamber," she said. "Boredom in that area of marriage is fatal to one's happiness, or so I have been told."

Rex must have also been listening to the conversation, for he turned away from his own, picked up his wife's hand, kissed it, commented, "I am not bored," and returned to what he had been saying.

At that moment, the orchestra began playing again, and the red-faced lady stammered to her own husband that it must be time to return to their seats. He obliged, offering her his elbow, but mouthed to Rex as he left, "Lucky man!"

The box swiftly emptied of its visitors, several of them casting approving glances at Rithya or envious ones at Rex. As they took their seats again, Regina bent closer to Ash and whispered, "Rithya's comments and Rex's will be repeated all over the theater, and most of the *Ton* will have heard by noon tomorrow that Lady Arthur is an accomplished and educated lady."

"Better still, they'll all be talking about how Lord Arthur is a very happy man." Ash smiled and reached out to press her arm, delighted that the lady he loved shared his appreciation of Rithya's deft management of her detractors.

As the lights went up on the stage, she sat back in her chair and composed herself to sink into the story again. Regina was an accomplished and educated lady herself, and if that did not yet include an education in the arts of the bedchamber, Ash knew he too would be a very happy man, if she allowed him to amend the lack.

Chapter Nineteen

L ADY CONLEY'S VENETIAN Breakfast was a crush, which was no doubt gratifying for Lady Conley, but set Regina's teeth on edge. Her size meant all she could see before and behind her were the torsos of other people and, if she looked up, the underneath of their chins. She had been trying for half an hour to find Arial, who was supposed to be here this afternoon, but the inability to see through the crowds was impairing her search.

The event spilled over all seven rooms on the first floor of Lady Conley's townhouse, and Regina had been into every one, though Arial might have been on the other side of any of the rooms she passed through, and Regina would have missed her.

In the final room, a doorway connected to the gallery that formed a bridge over the front hall and a landing for stairs down and up. The gallery offered a quicker path back to the first room than the tortuous route from room to room across the front of the house.

Regina slipped out of the crowd and took a deep breath in the privacy of the gallery. She stopped partway across the bridge to look down into the front hall, currently occupied only by a footman who stood by the door.

On either side of her, the hum of voices and clatter of crockery continued, cresting and sinking in waves, with the lulls allowing her to hear a bar or two of music. In one of the front rooms a trio of musicians on pianoforte, violin and cello did their poor best to entertain a crowd more interested in conversation and gossip.

Here, though, she was in an oasis of—if not silence—at least calm.

Glancing up, Regina saw a little group of chairs on the landing a third of the way up to the next floor. It would be rude, surely, to enter the private part of the house? But the space appeared so inviting, and she was not looking forward to returning the maelstrom.

It was the work of the moment to dart up the first flight of stairs and sink into one of the chairs, which was as comfortable as it looked. She sat back and closed her eyes.

As always, as soon as she was still, her three main preoccupations demanded her mental attention: Geoffrey, who had continued to keep her informed about his coming and goings but had still not brought his friends to meet her. Her ball, which was the day after tomorrow, and everything seemed to be happening as it should, which perversely made her convinced that she was forgetting something. And—of course and always—Elijah.

She wished Elijah was here. He had had another engagement, but he was joining her for dinner. She wished she was with him now. She wished they were together and in private so they could share another of those drugging kisses.

He loved her. He had made it clear. And she loved him, even if she had not said the words. When he asked her to marry him, the answer would be "yes."

"Why the smile? Thinking of me, Regina?" The loathsome tones of David Deffew broke into her thoughts and her eyes sprang open. He was lowering himself into the chair beside hers and reaching for her hands.

She pulled them out of his reach and stood. "Mr. Deffew. I will leave you to your solitude. It is time I returned to the party."

She had no expectation that it would be that easy, and sure

enough, he leapt to his feet and put his body between her and the stairs. "Now, Regina, don't rush off. Surely you will allow me to make an apology for my over-enthusiasm last time we met?"

"Over enthusiasm? Is that what we are calling it? You assaulted me, Mr. Deffew, and would not stop when I asked you to do so. And I have not given you leave to address me informally."

Deffew's nostrils flared. "You encouraged me until Ashby came back. We had an understanding." His voice whined. *He really is a worm.*

"I treated you with the same civility I treated anyone else, Mr. Deffew, and I did not encourage you. Indeed, I refused each of your proposals. Now, please get out of my way. I wish to leave."

Below, the door on this side of the gallery opened, letting out a burst of noise. Deffew grabbed her in his arms, trapping her own at her sides so that, struggle as she might, she could not stop him from raining kisses on any part of her twisting head that he could reach.

"My love," he near-shouted, projecting his voice to reach the witness who had just entered the gallery, "you have made me the happiest of m—Arghhh!" His arms loosened and Regina darted out of reach as he twisted to look behind him.

Pansy Turner stood on the stairs; a long hat pin held before her like a weapon. From the way Deffew clutched his thigh, she had used it to stab him, and God bless her for it.

"You bitch," Deffew roared. "You *stuck* me!"

Miss Turner lifted one eyebrow. "Oh dear. I slipped."

He glanced at Regina, and smirked. "Miss Turner, you can be the first to congratulate us—"

"He is lying, Miss Turner. He assaulted me, when I have already made it clear that I would not marry him if he was the last man on earth."

"You *have* to marry me," he sneered. "You will be ruined if you don't. Miss Turner is my witness that you were in my arms."

Miss Turner shook her head. "On the contrary, Mr. Deffew. I was sitting with my friend Mrs. Paddimore the whole time. I am her witness that *you* are lying."

"Again," said another voice—one Regina had not heard in years. "Lying again, Mr. Deffew? Have you still not been able to find a woman who will marry you without you blackmailing her into it? Hello, Regina."

She had changed so much. Her hair had turned grey, her face was lined, and she appeared to have shrunk. Somehow, Regina had never thought of her mother growing old without her. Regina swallowed a lump in her throat. "Hello, Mama."

Her mother smiled but kept her gaze on Deffew. "I was here the whole time, too, of course. Go away, Mr. Deffew. Far away. I still have friends enough to see you drummed out of London and will do so if you do not leave of your own accord."

Pansy had eased herself past Deffew and was standing beside Regina, her hat pin at the ready. Deffew stared at her and then back at Lady Kingsley. "But...you are not telling the truth."

Lady Kingsley snorted. "Pot, meet Kettle. Goodbye, Mr. Deffew."

"Making a nuisance of yourself, are you, Deffew?" The newcomer was Peter Stancroft, and Arial was beside him. "Would you like me to remove him bodily, ladies? I would be happy to oblige."

At that, Deffew broke, scuttling past Lady Kingsley and down the stairs on the other side of the gallery. They could hear him calling for his hat and coat.

"Thank you." Regina smiled at each of her rescuers in turn, then let her eyes rest on her mother. "Thank you so much. That could have been very unpleasant."

Miss Turner wrapped her shawl around Regina's shoulder, murmuring something about buttons. "May I see to your hair, Mrs. Paddimore?"

One side was falling down about her shoulders and the other was undoubtedly rumpled after her struggles. Arial and Miss Turner took a side each, and soon had it smoothed and repinned.

"I'm glad we came out," Arial said. "Although Lady Kingsley

and Miss Turner seemed to have everything well in hand."

Regina's smile broadened. "And Pansy's trusty hair pin. Mr. Deffew found it most discouraging."

Peter gave a bark of laughter. "Well done, Pansy!"

Miss Turner's smile at Regina was shy. "I am pleased I could help. Keep the shawl, Mrs. Paddimore. Arial, darling, are you ready to go home?"

"More than ready," Arial said fervently.

The Stancrofts and Miss Turner took their leave. Her mother put a hand out to touch Regina's arm. "May we talk, Regina?"

Regina nodded. It was time and past time that she and her mother bridged the gap between them. "I do not wish to go back into that crowd, Mother. Would you consider coming home with me? We could have tea and a chat."

Her mother looked relieved. "I would love that."

ASH HAD RATHER hoped that Geoffrey Paddimore would not be at home for dinner. At the very least, he could count on the boy going out as soon as he had eaten, leaving Ash alone with Regina. The smile he had been wearing unbidden every time he thought about their kisses spread across his face as Wilson opened the door to let him in.

"Good evening, Wilson. Would you hold these for a moment?" Ash handed the first footman the large bunch of roses he carried, fresh from the hot houses of the Duke of Dellborough. Red for love and romance, pink for grace and admiration, yellow for friendship.

He put the box he was carrying onto a large cabinet and shrugged out of his coat. "Would you put this somewhere safe and bring it in when I ask for it? It is for Mrs. Paddimore." It was her birthday present, all ready for their actual birthday the following morning.

He hoped she would be delighted with it. If Paddimore was not at home, or went out after dinner, her gratitude might take a tangible and delightful form.

"Of course, sir." Charles handed over the flowers and took Ash's outdoor wear. "Sir? We have unexpected guests for dinner. Mrs. Paddimore's brother and her mother."

There went Ash's *tête-à-tête*. He nodded, hoping that his disappointment did not show on his face. "And Mr. Paddimore?"

"Sent a message saying he would not be home, sir," Charles disclosed. "Go right on up, Mr. Ashby. Mrs. Paddimore said to tell you not to stand on ceremony."

Another hopeful sign. A departure from social custom afforded only the closest of friends. *Or lovers.* Ash bounded up the stairs to the drawing room. The door was open, and when he looked inside, Regina rose to greet him. "Elijah! Come in. Mother, I have someone I would like you to meet."

He had last seen Lady Kingsley at Regina's ball, the day Regina turned seventeen and Ash twenty-one. In his memory, she was a mirror image of her daughter. He supposed most people would say Regina was the reflection of her mother, but to him, Regina would always be the first, the original, the only.

The resemblance had been muted by time. The black hair was now iron grey, and the fair skin had crêped and wrinkled with lines of grief and discontent, though this evening she wore the same glow of happiness as her daughter.

"Mother, allow me to present Mr. Elijah Ashby," Regina said.

Lady Kingsley held out her hand. "Mr. Ashby and I have met," she said, dryly, "though he has matured somewhat since then."

Elijah bent over her hand. "Lady Kingsley."

"Well? Go on, Mr. Ashby," she told him. "Give my girl her roses."

It was not the evening he had imagined, but he enjoyed himself. Lady Kingsley proved to have a caustic wit and a keen eye for the idiocies of fashionable life. William was clearly delighted to have his mother and sister together at the same table and let down some of his reserve to share stories of their childhood. And Regina was transcendent with joy to be reunited with her mother.

Even if Ash hadn't found the company pleasant, he would have been pleased because Regina was happy, and her happiness was essential to his.

The evening passed all too quickly, and it wasn't until he and the Kingsleys were leaving that Ash noticed the box, still on the cabinet where he had left it.

"Your birthday present!" he said to Regina. "I almost forgot." He picked it up and brought it to her.

"Come along, William," Lady Kingsley commanded. "Give Regina a few minutes with her swain. She is perfectly capable of opening a birthday present without our assistance."

Wilson's lips twitched as he opened the front door for the lady. "Something amusing, young man?" she demanded. But her eyes twinkled, and the glance she cast her daughter could only be described as doting. "Happy birthday for tomorrow, Regina. I will see you at your ball."

Then they were gone, and Regina drew him back into the drawing room where she opened her present, and his daydreams about kissing her again came true in his arms.

Chapter Twenty

REGINA LOOKED AT herself in the mirror, wondering whether the change she felt was visible on the outside. Her hair had lost its pins in her drawing room, and now tumbled about her shoulders. Her lips were slightly swollen from Elijah's kisses.

Apart from that, the physical differences remained hidden beneath the robe she had donned when she stripped off her gown. Her breasts, which Elijah had caressed with his hands and then his mouth, felt swollen, the nipples drawn into tight sensitive nubs. The cotton of her chemise abraded them as she moved, and it was delicious.

Her miniscule experience had not led her to expect such delights, though Gideon had assured her they awaited if she ever chose to take a lover. Since she had not, Deffew's assault just before her father's death had remained her only measure of romantic intimacy until Elijah's first kiss a few days ago.

As wonderful as that had been, it had not prepared her for tonight's pleasures.

Lower down, her womanly place—untouched by any man— was also swollen, soft, and warm. It ached, and the ache was both a void and a pleasure. She knew what filled it. Gideon had explained how mating worked between men and women. She had not liked the sound of it, and since she knew Gideon had only theoretical knowledge—she did not want to think about his actual experience—she had ignored his assurances and assumed it would be something to endure rather than to crave.

Curse Elijah's gentlemanly forbearance! Or, perhaps, curse her own innocence. Elijah had kissed and caressed her until every particle of her flesh was putty in his hands, yearning for more, and then muttered something about respect and taking their time, and put her from him.

"I would love to continue this, Ginny," he had said, and the fervency in his eyes confirmed his words. "I will, if you will permit, when it is the right time. But for now, I had better walk home and hope for a cold shower of rain to restore me to some sort of decency. For I am utterly wrecked."

"Me, too," had been the only words she could manage. When would be the right time? She was ready now, bother it.

She was so absorbed in her thoughts, she did not at first register that a dull and distant thud, repeated half a dozen times in quick succession, was the knocker on her front door. A caller? At this time of night?

Perhaps it was just that Geoffrey had forgotten his key, though his note had said he would not be home tonight. Regina pulled the robe more tightly around herself and walked out onto the landing to listen.

Another swift cascades of raps, and then the voice of her first footman. "Yes?"

The voices drifted up through the stair well.

"I must see Mrs. Paddimore," the caller said, through heaving pants, as if he had run a great distance.

"Mrs. Paddimore has retired for the night," Charles replied. "Would you care to leave a message?"

"No, you don't understand," pleaded the caller. "It's her son. There's been an accident. I'm here to take her to him."

Regina was hurrying down the stairs as soon as she heard the word *son*.

"Wait on the step. I will send a maid to rouse her," Charles told the caller, as she came down around the last landing.

She was speaking before the caller came fully into sight. "Geoffrey has been in an accident? What has happened? Is he much hurt? Have you sent for a doctor?"

He was a young man, perhaps a year or two older than Geoffrey. He was undeniably handsome, with pale skin and blue eyes. The dark curls under the hat he removed when he saw her had a white streak just above the temples. His greatcoat swung open over a gentleman's casual wear—pantaloons, Hessian boots, and a coat high cut at the front over a colorful waistcoat. The waistcoat and the immaculately tied cravat hinted at pretensions to dandyism.

His eyes lit up when he saw Regina. "Mrs. Paddimore? I have come to fetch you to your son, ma'am. We think he may have broken his leg. We have sent for a doctor. He is conscious, ma'am, or he was when I left him. He is asking for you."

"What happened? No. You can tell me on the way. I must dress. Charles, send my maid to me immediately." Regina turned away, then remembered her manners.

"Do you need a drink? A place to sit down? Charles will see to you." She blinked and shook her head. "I'm sorry. I do not know your name."

The young man flashed a charming smile as he performed an incongruously formal bow. "I expect Padders—Geoffrey, that is—has mentioned me? Please, call me Chalky." He gestured to his white streak and waggled his eyebrows. "Hence…"

Surely, he would not be so relaxed if Geoffrey was badly hurt? "I will return immediately."

THE HACKNEY WAS cramped and none too clean. Regina decided it was best not to speculate about the origin of the stale odors, some of which emanated from the youth next to her, who lurched against her with each tip and turn of the carriage.

To take her mind off the close quarters as much as to satisfy her burning need to know more, she peppered Chalky with questions. His answers were charming, fulsome, and almost devoid of any actual information.

Alarm on her own account slowly rose through her concern for Geoffrey. What proof did she have that her son was injured, or even that this boy knew him? Yet she had climbed into this hackney without any thought, leaving Charles behind, not even asking for the address to which they headed so that Charles would know where to send help.

Though if Chalky had lied about the rest, he could have given a false address.

"Chalky, where are you taking me," she demanded, determined to wring an answer from him this time.

He flashed his grin as the hackney slowed. "We are here, Mrs. Paddimore."

He opened the door and exited, turning to offer her his hand.

Here proved to be a row of anonymously ordinary houses. In the dark and the rain, Regina had no time to take in more, as Chalky ushered her up the steps, opening the door into a small hall, poorly lit by a single candle shielded in a glass holder.

A flight of stairs, uncarpeted and unpolished, ascended in front of her, and doors stood to either side. Each had an impressively solid keyhole and a knocker. Apartments, then.

Chalky confirmed her assumption, as he finished lighting another candle from the standing one and put a glass cover over the candle holder to shield it from draft. "The apartment we want is on the third floor, ma'am. Shall we?" He waved to usher her ahead of him.

She climbed into the gloom, feeling for each step with her foot, since the candle behind her deepened the shadow before. One flight and a turn. Another flight and a landing. Up and up until she paused at the top of the sixth flight and Chalky passed her with the candle, opened a door out of the landing, and stood aside to let her enter a long passage, lined with more doors.

"It is the third on the left," he said.

She hurried forward, hoping for more light, for Geoffrey, for her own comfortable home with her servants around her.

Chalky lifted the knocker and let it fall. Once. Twice. "Geoffrey will be pleased to see you," he suggested.

Even with that assurance, she hesitated when the door opened, and nobody was there. "What is—?" She got no further. A buffet between the shoulder blades sent her stumbling forward, the door crashed shut behind her, and she heard the click of the tumblers in the lock even as she caught hold of a hall table to stop herself from falling.

She did not need to look to know who had locked the door, or who it was that had tricked her into coming here alone. If she had needed confirmation, it was there in his voice, shrill with glee but still recognizable.

"Now, Mrs. Paddimore, we will finish what we started, and this time, you will have no choice but to marry me."

Chapter Twenty-One

ASH WALKED THROUGH the streets of London in something of a daze. Fullaby followed along in the curricle, shaking his head at his employer's unaccountable decision to walk through the drizzling rain, but making no comment.

All of his intimate encounters had been, at root, transactional, though he had been fond of each of his mistresses and, he hoped, they with him. They said so, in any case. Being with Regina was so different he was utterly at sea.

Their first kiss had rocked his world. It had been a carnal meeting of lips, teeth, and tongues, but he had kissed before. And with women who were far more experienced in receiving and giving pleasure. This was Ginny and that made all the difference.

He had, somehow, managed to keep that encounter to a meeting of mouths. Her innocence helped. She followed his lead, but she initiated nothing. It was, as he'd thought at the time, as if she had never been kissed as a lover kissed.

Unlikely as it seemed, he was even more certain now that his first impression was right. She was a quick learner, though. As soon as their lips met tonight, his self-control almost escaped its leash. He managed to retain enough consciousness to keep his caresses within bounds; to slowly introduce her to the feel of his hand on her breasts, to kisses that crept ever closer before he had one of her lovely nipples in his mouth.

Her fragrance, her soft skin, her moans of pleasure, the arch of her back as she lifted towards him, all tempted him to take it further, but he managed to resist. When she gave herself to him, and he was almost sure she would, it would be a free choice, not one coerced through seduction.

A choice of forever, for he could bear no less. To bed her without promises was to risk destruction. Already, it was too late for him to walk away without a broken heart.

Fullaby drew up beside him. "Sir, you are walking the wrong way."

Ash realized that the drizzle had turned to a serious downpour. Fullaby must have decided he had had enough, and he was right about Ash's direction, too. They were farther away from Rex's townhouse than they had been when they left Regina's.

"Let me drive," he said, and leapt up into the driver's seat of the curricle, taking the reins from the servant.

The wise thing would have been to take the fastest route home, but he could not resist driving back past Ginny's townhouse.

Fullaby cast him a worried look when he made the turn. Ash couldn't possibly subject the poor man to a prolonged loiter outside the building while he dreamed beneath his love's lit window. But he wanted to.

He turned another corner to the street than ran past her townhouse. Wasn't that hackney leaving her house? Yes, because Charles was standing at the foot of her steps, watching with a worried expression as the vehicle turned a corner and went out of sight.

Ash drew up in front of the house. "Problems, Charles?" he called.

The first footman's face cleared. "Mr. Ashby! A man came with a message for Mrs. Paddimore. Apparently young Mr. Paddimore has been injured. Mrs. Paddimore has gone off with the man, and she would not let me go with them. Not enough room, she said."

Ash asked a couple of quick questions, and his concern soon matched the footman's. The young man had never been to the house before, had not given his name, had offered no evidence he was from Geoffrey, and had been the one to declare there was no room for a footman.

"I'll follow them, Charles, to see what help we can offer. Do not worry. I will make sure she is kept safe."

"I'm coming, sir," the footman insisted. "I can hang on behind." Even as he clambered up into the tiger's perch, he turned his head and called back to the house, "Henry, wake Mr. Wilson, and tell him I have gone with Mr. Ashby to make sure our lady is safe!"

Ash touched the horses into a fast trot, and followed where the hackney had gone, and, thankfully, saw it in the distance again as soon as he turned the same corner.

"Let's get as close as we can without being seen," he said to Fullaby.

The foul weather would help. Coming from behind in an unlit curricle, they would have the advantage of invisibility over the hackney. As long as they could get close enough to keep them in sight, he amended, as the hackney rounded another bend and disappeared from view.

Chapter Twenty-Two

R EGINA TOOK TWO quick strides across the room and spun
around to face David Deffew. She had not been a complete
fool. She had taken a moment when she was up in her room to
load powder and a ball into both barrels of the muff pistol Gideon
had taught her to use, and to put it, wooden case and all, into her
largest reticule.

She hadn't wanted the trigger to be accidentally knocked, but
now she wished she could just put her hand into the reticule and
pull it out. Instead, she would need to wait for a moment of
inattention. *Keep the man talking.*

"Why are you doing this, Mr. Deffew? Surely there are other
wealthy widows who would be delighted by your attentions?"

Deffew actually snarled. *"You* were delighted until that
jumped-up servant came back from overseas. Everyone knew
that you were going to marry me at last, as you were meant to.
As you would have, if that blackguard Paddimore had not
interfered."

"You will not endear yourself to me by insulting my husband,
Mr. Deffew," Regina said, coldly. "And you delude yourself if you
think I have ever shown you anything but common civility."

Deffew's face turned puce as he spat out, "You lie! I told
everyone we were going to marry, and now they are laughing at

me. They'll laugh no more when we are married. I'll pay every one of them back. You'll see."

He established a façade of calm with eerie speed, wiping the shrillness from his voice and saying, in an even tone that was all the more alarming for the contrast, "I will have you for my wife, Mrs. Paddimore. Regina. Your husband cost me a father, and so you owe me a bride."

"Your father died attempting—I do not know what he was attempting. He stopped our coach. He told us to get out. When my husband turned to assist me, he shot my husband in the back."

Deffew nodded, the same calm prevailing. "He went to get you for me. I own you. I have owned you since I kissed you before your father died. You will submit to me, or I will give the word and Paddimore's brat dies tonight."

The words on the tip of her tongue were "Over my dead body," but his last comment made them impossible. She was not going to die tonight. Neither, if she had anything to say about it, was Geoffrey. Therefore, Deffew could not, as he said, give the word.

A thought occurred, and she shifted from foot to foot, jiggling and twisting. "Is there somewhere I could...? I do not wish to... That is, the young man came, and I didn't think... and it has been raining the whole time, which makes it worse."

Deffew look bewildered for a minute. She broadened the mime and he chortled. "Say it," he demanded. "Say it, say it. 'Please, David, I want to piss.'" He guffawed at his own words and put on a falsetto. "Please, David, I want to piss." He chanted, "Say it. Say it. Say it and I might let you."

Good heavens. Has the man never grown past twelve? Regina kept the contempt from her face and her voice, though her indignation caused her voice to quaver. "Please, David, I want to..."

She hesitated on the vulgarity, and her tormenter repeated again. "Say. It. Say. It."

"Please, David, I want to piss."

Another lightning change of mood. He straightened and sobered. "I suppose," he drawled, "that you'll be unpleasant to roger if you stink of piss. Go on, then. There's a piss pot behind the screen. While you're there, take your clothes off." The glee reentered his voice. "I'll be waiting on the bed. Remember, if you do as you're told, I'll let your father's little bastard live. For how long, depends on you." Which confirmed that the Deffew men had known who Geoffrey's father was all along, and Matthew Deffew's lie to his son was deliberate malice.

Regina retreated behind the screen, where a washing cabinet stood next to a coat stand. The room's candles were on Deffew's side of the screen. She hoped that meant he could not see even her shadow. She took the chamber pot from the cupboard then pulled the gun box from her reticule.

"I don't hear anything," Deffew shouted.

Regina picking up the waiting jug and poured a thin stream of water into the chamber pot from a height. She then unbuttoned her redingote and threw it to drape over the top of the screen. She opened the box and took out the gun—which was dry, thank goodness. Then she peered through the spaces between the panels of the screen.

Deffew must have decided he had her sufficiently cowed, for he had removed his boots and all of his upper garments and was just unbuttoning his fall. In a moment he would be naked, and at a serious disadvantage.

"Hurry, hurry, I have something for you," he crooned, taking a step towards the screen with his hand inside his trousers.

"I am just undressing," Regina called back.

He stopped, grinning. Regina gave a silent thanks that she'd chosen a gown that buttoned in front. She undid the buttons one handed, not even needing to put down the gun, and let the dress drop so she could step out of it.

That garment, too, went over the screen. "Nearly ready." She made that sound as sultry as she could.

Deffew grinned and unfastened the last of the buttons that

held his trousers together. They dropped, and he was unclothed but for his stockings. He stood next to the bed, stroking his male equipment. Disgusting man.

"Are you on the bed, David?" Regina asked, managing to make her voice a purr, though the words tried to stick in her gullet.

He near threw himself backward, reclining on the pillows. "I am ready for you, my love," he proclaimed.

"And I am ready for you," Regina said, stepping out from behind the screen with her pistol aimed directly at Deffew's groin.

He scooted up the bed, his appendage rapidly wilting. "You wouldn't shoot me," he quavered.

"Try me," she invited. Gideon had insisted that she practice loading and firing the gun until she could do it in the dark and with either hand. She continued to practice twice a week, seldom missing her target, but ever since the night she shot Deffew's father to stop him from putting a second bullet into Gideon, she had suffered nightmares. She never again wanted to shoot a bullet into living flesh and bone.

He deserves it, she told herself, *just as his father did.* "Where is my son?"

"I'm not telling," he grumbled, then brightened. "You are bluffing. Ladies can't use guns."

She had no idea how he might react if she told him she was the one to shoot his father. Probably better to keep that fact to herself. "This was a gift from Gideon, and I have practiced with it twice a week for many years. In case you haven't noticed, it fires two bullets. After I have ensured you will never again assault another woman, I will still have one for your black heart."

He shifted uneasily, put his hands across his groin, and then crossed a bare thigh over the top for further protection. "If you shoot, my men will come to find out what's happening," he said, though the threat would have been more effective if it hadn't been delivered as a tremulous question.

Still, she held her fire, and he held his silence. Each stared at the other. Neither moved.

Until a sudden battering on the door made her start. Deffew moved for the bedside cabinet, and she waved the gun. "Keep your place," she barked.

He sank back on the pillows, but his eyes lit with glee. "They are coming for you," he crowed.

A voice Regina did not know shouted, "I think this is the one, sir. I heard a woman's voice."

»»»«««

TWICE MORE, THEY lost the hackney, as it took turn after turn. The first time, they made a lucky guess and came upon its path from a different angle. The second, they retraced their steps down several streets that proved to be dead ends before they finally found what they hoped was the right direction, when a street worker shivering under a tree on a corner pointed after a hurrying carriage. She accepted the coin Ash tossed her, bit it, and waved them on their way with a grin. "Good luck, guv. Hope you find what you're looking for."

"Stop," Fullaby said, as they passed the third turning along the new street. "Turn back, Mr. Ashby. I think I saw it."

Sure enough, once Ash managed to maneuver the curricle around in the narrow street, he could see a hackney parked outside a house partway along a row of them. As he approached, a man came out of the front door and hurried through the rain to the carriage.

"That's him," Charles shouted. "That's the man that came for my mistress." How he could tell when the man was bundled in coat and hat, Ash did not know, but if it was a mistake, he'd apologize later.

The hackney was pulling away from the house. Ash flicked his team into a sudden burst of speed, passed the coach's tired horse, and cut in front of it. He leapt down, leaving Fullaby and

Charles to deal with the driver, and wrenched the door open.

The young man inside sniffed. "My good man, this hackney is taken."

That was all he had the chance to say. Ash dragged him out by his neckcloth and held him up by it. "Where did you take her? Is she in there? Is Geoffrey Paddimore?"

"Wh–who? I don't know what you're talking about." His eyes told a different story, the gaze past Ash's shoulder redolent of a lie.

Ash smashed the man up against the carriage. "Wrong answer. Try again."

"You can't do this," the man protested. "My father is a viscount! He'll have you in Newgate!"

"Doubtful," Ash told him. "First, you have to live to tell him. Second, you abducted the woman I love, and no one in England will stop me from doing whatever I need to find her. Or blame me for what happens to her kidnapper in the process."

"Here," said the hackney driver. "Wasn't no kidnapping. Lady came along right eager. I wouldn't be doing with no kidnapping."

"He lied," Ash said, without taking his eyes off his victim. "He told her that her son was injured."

"He might be injured by now," the man said, spite distorting his expression. "If the stupid female didn't co-operate."

Ash twisted his hand in the man's cravat until he was choking for breath and banged his stubborn head against the carriage again. "Speak. Who lives here? Where is Mrs. Paddimore."

"It's apartments," the driver offered. "For bachelors. A couple of rooms and access to the kitchen. You need to know the floor and the room number."

Ash screwed the cravat tighter, until the man was scrabbling at his hands and drumming his heels. Then he loosened his grip a little. "Floor?" he demanded. "Room?"

"You barbarian," the boy croaked. "Go to hell."

"After you," Ash replied. "Fullaby, start breaking his fingers."

Ash's man took a step forward and the villain shrank away as well as he could, the color draining from his face. "Third!" he screamed. "She's on the third floor!"

He was suddenly a dead weight in Ash's hands. The coward had fainted.

"Charles, there is some rope in the box under the curricle," Ash told the footman. "Tie this miscreant up." He looked at the hackney driver. "Stay here. We may need your services. I will pay for your time."

The driver nodded, but Ash didn't wait for him to say anything. He was already pounding up the steps, through the front door and on up the stairs, Fullaby at his heels.

Chapter Twenty-Three

"I 'LL START AT the other end, you at this," Ash told his servant. "Knock on every door. If need be, we'll break them all down."

"Those locks won't hold against an assault," Fullaby assured him, and began banging the first knocker.

Ash ran to the other end of the passage and did the same. There was no reply from the first apartment he tried, and no noise from within when he put his ear to the door. At the second, a yawning man with a sheet wrapped around his waist denied all knowledge of Geoffrey or Regina Paddimore or anyone called Chalky and cursed him for mistaking the room.

Before he could try the third, Fullaby called from a few doors away down the passage. "I think this is the one, sir. I heard a woman's voice."

He reached Fullaby's side and shouted, "Regina?"

"In here! I'll try to find the key!"

"Stay back from the door," Ash warned her, and gave the lock a kick, thrusting his foot out from his hip, throwing all his weight behind it.

It crashed open, and he stumbled into the room with Fullaby behind him.

He took the scene in at a glance—Deffew, naked on the bed,

Regina in her petticoat with a pistol held steadily on the wretched low-life.

"It looks like you've rescued yourself, Mrs. Paddimore," Ash said. What a magnificent creature she was!

Regina smiled, but she did not glance away from her prisoner. "I am pleased to see you, Mr. Ashby. This creature and I were at stalemate, and you are just in time to help."

"Fullaby, tie Deffew to the bed posts, if you please," Ash instructed. "Mrs. Paddimore, I can keep the gun on him while you get dressed, if that would suit you."

Regina relinquished the gun to him with a sigh of relief and retreated behind a dressing screen in the corner. The gown that draped over the top of the screen disappeared as she resumed talking. "He threatened to have Geoffrey killed if I would not agree to submit to him tonight and marry him after."

"You always were a rat-faced sniveling coward, Deffew," Ash told the man on the bed, who was now spreadeagled between the four posts as Fullaby finished tying the last knot. He'd used the man's own clothes—the cravat for one wrist, a shirt sleeve for the other, and a stocking for each ankle. Deffew was going nowhere without help.

"He refused to tell me where Geoffrey was being held," Regina continued. "I refused to put down the gun."

Ash bent down to fetch the knife in his boot. "I can help with that," he said.

He approached the bed with the knife held in front of him, smiling at the villain's attempt to shrivel into the sheets.

"Where is young Mr. Paddimore?" he asked, keeping his voice mild.

"You can't make me tell," Deffew squeaked.

Ash's smile didn't reach his eyes. "I am glad I am wearing gloves," he commented to the room at large, before reaching between Deffew's legs and pulling his testicles away from his body.

Behind him, Regina gasped, the soft sound almost drowned

by Deffew's squeal of pain.

"Keep still, Deffew. Keep very, very still." Ash laid his knife against the man's most precious piece of flesh and Deffew whimpered.

"Let's try that again, shall we?" Ash asked. "Tell me where Mr. Paddimore is, in what condition, how he is being held, and how many people are guarding him. Make your information full and accurate. Any hesitation, any inaccuracies, and I will take a slice off your ballocks. I am interested in seeing how many slices I can remove before blood loss causes you to pass out, Deffew."

"Eight is your record, Mr. Ashby," said Fullaby, inventing wildly in the spirit of the moment. Deffew whimpered again.

"The trick, Mrs. Paddimore, is to slice thinly. Rex once managed nine slices." He shook his head in feigned admiration.

Fullaby, in a piece of inspired theater, objected, "It was unfortunate that the man was a mute. If we'd only known he couldn't tell us what we wanted to know... Poor man will never breed again."

Ash, hearing his cue, moved the knife a fraction closer, just nicking the skin. Deffew jerked and screamed, and only Ash's swift reflexes in moving the knife away kept the threat from becoming a reality.

"I'll tell! I'll tell! Please don't cut me." He babbled blasphemy, curses, and prayers, all mixed up until Ash held the knife in the slimeball's view, after surreptitiously cutting his own thumb to add sufficient blood to cow the man further.

Once Deffew started talking, he spilled everything. Geoffrey Paddimore was passed out two doors down the hall, having taken drugs with his drink. One of his so-called friends was with him to keep an eye on him. The rest had set up an ambush for Ash on the lane that led into the mews behind Rex's townhouse.

Ash raised an eyebrow. If he had gone straight home from Regina's, he and Fullaby would have had a fight on their hands.

"You should be dead," Deffew blubbered. "You bastard. You're meant to be dead."

>>>≪≪≪

THEY LEFT MR. Deffew tied to his bed, propped the door back in place, and went to rescue poor Geoffrey. Regina was pleased there was no nonsense about keeping her out of danger, though Elijah insisted she stay behind him and his burly servant and hold her pistol at the ready.

No one had come into the hall to see what all the screaming and yelling was about. Either everyone was absent, which seemed unlikely, or the determined deafness of the residents said a lot about the kind of ruckus the tenants were used to.

Regina expected the men to break down the door to which Deffew's directions led them, as they had to reach her. Instead, Elijah called out, in a fair approximation of Deffew's voice, "Muggers? Let me in."

There was muttering from within and then the scrape and chink of the key in the lock. The door inched open, then Elijah and Fullaby put their shoulders to it, and they were in.

The slender youth who had been knocked back by their entry started to complain; he fell silent when he saw Regina and the gun she held. He backed across the room to the far wall, repeating to himself, "I knew this was a bad idea. I knew I shouldn't go along with it."

Regina handed the pistol and the candlestick to Elijah and rushed to the bed. Geoffrey, in his shirt and nothing else, lay on his back on top of the blankets, snoring.

"His clothes?" Elijah asked Muggers. The boy pointed.

"Help me get him dressed," Elijah said, passing the pistol to Fullaby. "Fullaby, if this person moves, shoot him in the knee."

"I won't move!" the youth insisted.

Geoffrey shifted and muttered as they wrestled him into his clothes but did not rouse.

"What did you give him?" Elijah demanded.

Muggers shook his head. "Not me. I didn't give him anything."

Fullaby jerked the pistol and Muggers added. "Gin in his beer, with a bit of opium in the second tankard, just to keep him from interfering. They promised no one would get hurt. But his mother promised to marry Deffer's uncle, and now she's broken it off, and this was the only way…" He trailed off at a glare from Regina, or more probably at Elijah's snarl.

"I am Geoffrey's mother, and I made Deffew no promises, nor did I encourage him in any way to believe I favored him," she told Muggers.

Muggers hunched in on himself. "I only know what Chalky said," he grumbled.

"And did you think to ask Geoffrey?" Regina asked.

Muggers lifted his head at that. "But Defter is my friend, and Padders is just a nobody. His father was in trade, and Padders is base born, too, Chalky says."

Regina shook her head. It was like talking to a brick wall.

"It's time for us to go, Ginny," Elijah said. He propped Geoffrey up on his feet, supporting him by slinging one of her son's arms around his shoulders. Fullaby returned the gun and candlestick to Regina and took up position on Geoffrey's other side.

"Keep the pistol on him until we are out of the room," Elijah told her. They stopped briefly at the open door then sidled, Fullaby first, through the narrow doorway and out into the passage.

Regina backed her way out, keeping the pistol steady.

"Now shut the door and lock it," Elijah said, and he handed her the key he must have taken from the lock on the way through. "We'll send a constable to collect the pair of them once I have you safe."

"You are limping, Elijah," Regina commented, as she followed the men.

"I lost my heel when I kicked the door in," he replied. He glanced back and smiled. "I'm fine, Ginny."

Thank goodness for that. It looked as if they would escape without injury, for even Geoffrey was rousing enough to lurch from one foot to another and support some of his own weight as they navigated the stairs.

They were descending the last flight when they heard a ruckus outside—shouts, clashing wood, the sudden clatter of hooves and alarmed horse squeals.

"Let me and Fullaby check it out," Elijah said to Regina. "You stay here with Geoffrey." It was a command rather than a question, but Regina accepted it. She would not be much use in a physical fight, short of shooting someone.

Elijah helped Geoffrey to sit on the bottom step, where he collapsed against the wall and sank back into sleep. Elijah and Fullaby slipped out through the front door. In the dark and the rain, Regina could see nothing of what was happening.

She stood over Geoffrey, gripping the pistol in one hand and the candle in the other, straining to make sense out of the sounds from the street.

More shouts. Horses approaching at a gallop. A screamed command, "Run!" Carriage wheels and horses departing at speed.

All the chaos devolved into a low hum of conversation, before the door opened again and Lord Arthur entered, followed by a couple of footmen in Versey livery. "Mrs. Paddimore? Time to go. Lift Mr. Paddimore carefully, chaps. One of you will need to take him up before you."

Regina stepped aside to let the footmen carry out their task. "What has happened, Lord Arthur? Why are you here?"

Lord Arthur's explanation was succinct. "We came upon an ambush near my house. We chased them off and followed them here to find a battle royal going on between them and Ash, but they ran when they saw us."

He opened the door for the footmen to carry Geoffrey out into the street, and then winged his elbow at Regina. "Shall we, Mrs. Paddimore?"

The hackney was gone, and so was Chalky. Once Regina had

been handed up into the curricle next to Mr. Fullaby, he explained that Charles had been trying to fight off the returning ambushers when he and Elijah had burst out the door.

The hackney driver had taken off, and the three defenders had been outnumbered. Things had been going badly for them until Lord Arthur arrived with reinforcements.

The horsemen closed around the curricle, Lord Arthur at their head. Three of the riders had an extra person up in front of them. Geoffrey was unconscious again. Elijah and Charles were both conscious, but Charles was nursing one arm and had a cravat tied around his head as a bandage.

Regina couldn't see an obvious injury on Elijah, but she knew him well enough to realize his stoic expression masked pain.

"What happened to Mr. Ashby?" she asked Fullaby.

"Just the old injury playing up, ma'am. He jarred it when he kicked the door down, then he took a cudgel to the bad thigh. It's not broken, Lord Arthur says. Bit of a rest, and he'll be good as new."

Chapter Twenty-Four

W HEN REGINA INSISTED that Ash be left at her house to see the doctor and to be nursed, Ash had two good reasons to agree.

The first was his disinclination to subject his stupid leg and hip to another half hour on horseback or in the phaeton, when the horse's every step or the carriage's every bounce jolted the bruising. He yearned for a bed, pillows to prop the leg up, and—if at all possible—a cloth full of ice.

The second was the unspoken hope for more kisses.

His first desire came true. A few uncomfortable minutes saw him upstairs in one of the lady's spare bedrooms, stripped of his outer clothing, and resting on a bed, pillows in place, while a servant raced down to the bottom of the garden to the icehouse, fully stocked for the coming ball.

The doctor Regina called inspected all three patients and confirmed that Ash's injury was one of bruising and strain. "Keep your leg up for at least seven days," he commanded. "Longer if the pain does not settle."

Geoffrey was put to bed with a footman to watch him. "Let him sleep it off, Mrs. Paddimore. I do not expect any issues. When he wakes, makes sure he drinks large quantities of water."

Charles needed stitches to the cut on his head. His wrist was sprained, the doctor said, a bad sprain, and he would need to rest it.

Regina came to Ash once the others had been seen to, to let him know how they were. "Lord Arthur says he will be back around noon," she reported. "He was on his way to see the magistrate at Bow Street, and then he is going home to sleep. You should sleep, too, Elijah, if you can. The doctor left some laudanum."

He shook his head. "No laudanum. I'll be fine, Ginny. You need some sleep, too. Go to bed."

She had retreated, and he had not seen her since.

Perhaps he dozed a little in what remained of the night. Since daylight filtered into the room and a maid arrived to stoke up the fire, he'd been awake. He asked for coffee and toast—the pain made him queasy, but he knew from experience that something bland would help to settle it.

The footman who brought it helped him sit up against the pillows and deal with some embarrassing personal business. He'd had worse pain, he decided, as he relaxed back after the ordeal was over, his good hip taking his weight and the cushions readjusted to support the other hip and the knee.

"Anything else, sir? The newspaper? A book?"

"I'd like news of the other patients, and of my good hostess," he told the footman.

Apparently, they were all still asleep. Ash asked for the newspaper. An hour or so later, Regina had still not woken and neither had Geoffrey or Charles. Ash asked for washing water, and his clothes.

"Mrs. Paddimore said you are to remain in bed, sir."

The footman would not budge on trousers and boots, but Ash managed to negotiate a wash and a shave, a shirt—the man found him a clean one from somewhere—a neck scarf and a banyan. It would have to do.

The footman left and returned again with a small stack of books.

Two more hours passed. None of the books engaged his attention. The arrival of a pot of tea and a sugar bun gave him something else to do, and the maid who delivered them said Mrs. Paddimore was awake and downstairs.

Surely, she would come up and see him shortly? He waited. And waited.

When the maid returned to fetch his tray, she said that Mrs. Paddimore had gone out to an appointment. No visit from her, then. No personal message. Certainly, no kiss; not even best wishes for his birthday. He wanted to slither down in the bed, turn his face to the wall, and sulk.

He asked for paper and something to write with. Noon was approaching, even if at snail's pace. Ash should get his ideas in order before Rex arrived with news of their miscreants.

Another ninety minutes crept by. Each time he reached for his pocket watch and saw how little time had passed, he swore he wouldn't do it again. Only to break his word an excruciatingly long minute or two later. Perhaps he should throw the timepiece out the window.

At last, Rex arrived. He sauntered in with a grin on his face as if he wasn't more than an hour past his time. "I met Mrs. Paddimore downstairs. She is just going to remove her outdoor clothes and join us. That way, I can give my report to both of you at the same time. What little I have to report. How are you, Ash? Feeling like the devil, by the look of you."

"It's just bruising," Ash grouched. "I'd be fine if I had something to do."

Rex looked worried. "Do you want me to send for my traveling carriage to fetch you home?"

"No!" That was Regina, rushing into the room with a frown. "Lord Arthur, what are you thinking! The doctor said Elijah was not to be moved at all, for several days, and that he must keep his leg up for a full seven."

Rex, the traitor, took a step backwards and put both hands up in surrender. "I am sure you know best, Mrs. Paddimore."

She frowned at him, then turned her attention to Elijah. "How are you feeling today? Have my servants given you everything you need? How can I make you more comfortable, Elijah?"

The concern in her eyes went some way to soothing his bad temper. "Your servants have been a credit to your hospitality, Ginny." If she could throw away protocol in front of Rex and call him by his personal name, then so could he. "I have been grumbling to Rex because I am bored, but it is uncivil of me, and I apologize."

"Hates being stuck in a bed," Rex confided. "Like a bear with a sore head—snap your head off soon as look at you."

"Not helping," Ash told him.

"I am sorry I wasn't here to keep you company," Regina said, moving closer to the bed. "I woke late and had to rush to a meeting at Cordelia's. We now have the kitchen organized so Monsieur Fournier and Cordelia's chef and my cook all have their own spaces to work. And I did two more errands on the way home, so I do not have to go out again today."

He caught her hand and held it up to his lips. "You do not have to entertain me," he told her, to expiate his guilt at being so ungrateful.

She graced him with a smile. "It is not a question of obligation," she assured him, and her blush settled the last of his irritation.

"Right," said Rex. "Now we've cleared that up, would you like to hear about my frustrating morning?"

LORD ARTHUR HAD had a more difficult morning than Regina, though she would not have thought it possible. She had been solving one last-minute problem after another, all the while wishing her ball to perdition. Elijah would not be there. Ever since he arrived home—in some part of her mind, for the sixteen years since her first ball—she had dreamed of dancing, of waltzing in his arms, and now he would not even be there.

She had to go ahead, of course. She was not concerned with the servants hired on for the evening, the performers, the chefs, and other suppliers. As long as they were paid in full, they would probably quite enjoy the night off.

However, it would be appalling manners to send cancellations to everyone who had accepted an invitation. Only a family bereavement would be an acceptable excuse, and they had all (praise be) survived.

She was also aware she was being ridiculous. It was, after all, only one night. There would be other balls. Elijah was courting her. He had kissed her. His eyes, when he looked at her, spoke of love. That was what truly mattered.

But she still wished she could ignore her own ball and stay home with Elijah.

She was here now, however, and should be paying attention to Lord Arthur.

"So, they didn't investigate at all, last night?" Elijah was asking.

"They hedged around the fact—all sorts of protestations about other priority demands on their time. I asked them what they considered to be more important than apprehending the kidnapper of a gentlewoman." Lord Arthur sighed. "Since they didn't investigate until this morning when I insisted, there was nothing to find. Both of our captives were gone. No one admitted to hearing anything or seeing anything."

With no evidence of a crime beyond Lord Arthur's word, the magistrate refused to order further action. "Do you know what he said to me?" Lord Arthur told them indignantly. "He said I was lucky not to be arrested myself, since all I had witnessed was a street fight in which I myself was involved, and anything I might have been told by the two of you was hearsay, and inadmissible."

Regina could hardly believe it. "They are going to do *nothing*?

They are not even going to call on David Deffew? Or Geoffrey's so-called friends?"

Lord Arthur shrugged. "I couldn't tell them the names of Geoffrey's friends, of course. But no. They will do nothing more without further evidence that a crime has been committed."

"Then we'll have to get further evidence," Elijah said. He shifted uneasily and scowled. "I wish we had been able to take Deffew with us. It wouldn't take much to beat a confession out of him."

Lord Arthur spread his hands in defeat. "The Deffews are gone. House closed up. No one at home." He brightened. "But I've told Wakefield and Wakefield all about it. They are the enquiry people we've hired, Mrs. Paddimore. My brother-in-law recommended them. I hope you don't mind, but I've asked them to send someone over here. I thought it would be easier, since they'll want to question you, your son, and Ash."

Regina assured him she didn't mind. There went her peaceful afternoon with Elijah. The man from Wakefield and Wakefield was coming in a little over an hour, so there was no point in Lord Arthur going home. "I will leave you to keep Elijah company, Lord Arthur, and order some luncheon."

Wilson reported that Charles was comfortable, if frustrated, and that Master Geoffrey was awake and had managed to eat a few slices of toast.

"Please arrange for luncheon for three to be served in Mr. Ashby's bedchamber and let Mr. Paddimore know that a gentleman by the name of Mr. Wakefield is expected at half past two and will wish to ask him some questions."

Chapter Twenty-Five

THE MAN THEY expected sent a woman in his stead. "Mr. Wakefield is reviewing the scenes of the various incidents Lord Arthur mentioned," Mrs. Wakefield told them. "Starting with Orchid Court, where you were taken last night, Mrs. Paddimore. He thinks the servants might be more forthcoming with someone less elevated, Lord Arthur."

Rex looked as if he had bitten into something sour. "I didn't think to talk to the servants," he admitted.

"Why would you, indeed?" Mrs. Wakefield asked.

Rex grimaced. "Because they watch their employers, and the more erratic their employers, the more carefully they observe them."

Mrs. Wakefield raised her eyebrows and smiled. "Quite true, Lord Arthur." She sounded approving.

She did not approve of Regina's efforts to gather all of the witnesses into one room.

"I would prefer to interview each of you separately, Mrs. Paddimore. Your different perspectives will give me a more complete view of the events."

Regina arranged for her to be taken to Regina's own private sitting room, and one at a time, those who were mobile went to be questioned. Charles took the first turn, then went back to bed.

Fullaby was called up from the kitchen to go next.

Geoffrey, Regina, and Rex sat with Ash, and spoke of other things. Or, at least, Regina, Ash, and Rex did. Geoffrey sat with his head in his hands, staring at nothing. Poor lad. He'd had a harsh lesson on false friends.

"You take the next turn with Mrs. Wakefield, Geoffrey," said Regina. "Then go back to bed, darling, and get some more sleep."

Geoffrey looked up, anguish in his eyes. "You should be angry with me, Mother. This is all my fault. You were abducted because of me. Assaulted, because of me."

"No, Geoffrey. I was abducted and assaulted because of Mr. Deffew. He has tried assault before, once in this very house. In fact, it is not his first attempt at an abduction, either."

Geoffrey was called in to see Mrs. Wakefield, and then Rex took his turn.

"This is not quite how I planned to spend this day," Regina admitted.

"I expect you have a great deal to do for your ball," Ash said. "You mustn't feel you have to sit with me, Ginny. I will be fine." Or polite, at least, which would have to do, since his heart sank at the idea of her leaving when he had her to himself for the first time today.

She made an impatient gesture. "That's not what I meant. I cleared my afternoon so I could sit with you, but I thought we would be alone."

Ash suddenly felt much better. He reached for one of the hands she had rested lightly on the bed in front of her and lifted it to his mouth for a kiss. "You planned for us to be alone?" The question came out in a gravelly purr.

She nodded, veiling her eyes with her lashes.

He kissed her hand again. "You have me at your mercy, then, Mrs. Paddimore. At least until Rex finishes talking to Mrs. Wakefield. Whatever will you do with me?"

She looked up, a glint of mischief in her eyes. "Not just until then, Mr. Ashby. Later, as well. I have no engagements this evening, and Geoffrey needs an early night." Her voice, just above a whisper, vibrated through his torso.

Apparently, the pain in his leg and hip was not great enough to completely douse his physical reaction. Not to this one woman. He fancied he could be dead and in his coffin and he would still find her arousing.

"Kiss me, Ginny," he begged.

She stood and leaned over him, then hesitated. "I don't want to hurt you."

"I'm injured at the other end, my darling. This end cannot wait for your mouth." He tugged on her hand, so she fell across the bed. She had to wriggle a bit to line up her mouth with his, and then the world went away, the pain receded. Nothing mattered but their kiss.

Reclined on pillows and trapped by his leg, he could not move her to his shaping, but he didn't need to, for she shifted as his hands loosened her ties, as his lips explored down her neck and across her décolletage. He didn't try to free her breasts, lest they were interrupted, but he slid his fingers inside and she moaned and arched her approval.

"Tonight, I would like to see these," he murmured against her lips. "I could do much more to please you if I could reach them with my mouth, as well as my fingers."

Could he take a more fervent moan as approval of his intentions? He hoped so. He reached up to stroke his tongue into her mouth. She opened wider and sank lower.

It took him a moment to realize that the banging sound was not his heart, but someone knocking. He withdrew his tongue. "Ginny, the door."

For a moment, to his delight, his words did not sink in, and she kept trying to renew their kiss. Then she sprang away, wriggling off the bed and grabbing her shawl from her chair to settle around her shoulders.

"Come in," she called, her voice a squeak. She repeated the words in a more normal voice, and Rex entered the room. "Mrs.

Wakefield is ready for you, Mrs. Paddimore."

"Thank you." She was blushing, and her hair was half out of her pins.

She reddened still more when Ash held out a handful of them that he had collected from the blankets. "I will just go and tidy up," she said.

"I'll say good afternoon, then," Rex told her. "Mrs. Wakefield says she will compare notes with Mr. Wakefield, and one of them will report to us in the morning, so I am going home. I'm escorting Rithya to a musicale this evening."

Which left Ash on his own again, this time with pleasant thoughts to keep him company until Mrs. Wakefield came with her questions.

After she had talked him through the falling stone block, the shooting, the assault on Regina that he'd interrupted in this very house, and last night's chase and rescue, she asked if he had noticed anything else that might be useful.

"The two men from the Indies, or perhaps there were four. I am sure I've seen them elsewhere. But it is hard to be sure. London has so many people of all types. I could be mistaken."

"Give me particular instances, Mr. Ashby. What were they doing? What were you doing?"

He did his best, and she was satisfied at last. She rang the bell. Regina came to show the lady out, as cool and as tidy as she had been before he had kissed her. As always, she looked lovely. He preferred her rumpled from his arms, and with luck, that was how she would be this evening.

Chapter Twenty-Six

G EOFFREY WAS STILL suffering the aftermath of the opium he had been given. He begged off dinner and went straight to bed. Given his usual appetite, Regina would have been worried had not Cook told her he had gone to the kitchen after being interviewed by Mrs. Wakefield, and had spent a couple of hours there, eating meat pies, sampling Cook's baking, and dicing with one of the footmen.

Regina ordered her dinner to be served with Elijah's, in his bed chamber.

She had been wondering all day whether to give him his birthday present. She knew it was scandalous to exchange presents with a man who was not a relative, but she and Elijah were far past that, surely? And even that high stickler, her mother, had not blinked at Elijah giving her the lovely little china Cellidron.

There were further considerations. On the one hand, it might remind him of his injury. On the other, she hoped he would take it as it was meant—as a promise for the future. He had not asked her to marry him. He had mentioned proposing as a future thing, but surely the time had come? She hoped his kisses spoke for him, but what did she know about a man's kisses?

He had clearly done this before. Many times, and, given how

he traveled around, with many different women. His kisses to them had not meant permanence.

Did he want to wed her or simply to bed her? Did men court their mistresses? He knew her to be a widow, and it was true that widows took lovers.

That was another thing. At some point, she was going to have to tell him about her own lack of experience. She trusted him, but not another soul alive today knew the truth of her marriage. Not even Cordelia.

On the other hand, he called her his darling. He kissed as if he was starving and she the only food that could save his life. He called her his *love*.

He wanted to see her breasts! Even Annie, her maid, had only ever caught glimpses. The thought of displaying herself to him in such a way should outrage her, scandalize her. Not make her hot and tingling all over, curious to see his reaction.

She changed into a morning gown—shockingly informal for dinner with a guest. "I shall probably go to bed early after dinner," she told her maid. "Do my hair in a plait, please, and pin it around my head. Leave my washing water by the fire. Then take the rest of the evening off."

Annie's eyes were alight with curiosity, and she had probably drawn her own conclusions about what might happen inside Elijah's bed chamber. Regina reminded herself that she owed no one an explanation, that she was a widow with the freedom to make her own choices as long as she was discreet, that Elijah was too injured for them to go very far with their explorations of one another.

Even so, a lifetime of following the rules for a lady left her feeling nervous and vulnerable as she entered his room, his birthday present under her arm.

GINNY HAD LEFT to change for dinner. Ash asked a footman to help him wash and freshen up. A clean shirt. A slightly more formal cravat. Rex had brought over a bag of his clothes, so the banyan and the waistcoat under it were now his own—the banyan an ornate silk coat from China that he'd bought from a merchant in India.

He took particular care with brushing his teeth and started to shave, but had to let the footman complete the task, because the position his injury forced him into wasn't conducive to a steady hand.

There. A smooth chin and a fresh mouth for the kisses that he hoped would follow dinner. If what he needed to say first didn't send Ginny off to her own room and leave him bereft.

He was going to ask Ginny to marry him. He didn't want to kiss her again without a promise between them. No. That was not true. He wanted to kiss her more than he wanted to breathe. But he wanted far more.

Ash wasn't going to risk kissing her again without first finding out if she was only amusing herself. His heart was on the line. If she refused his name and his ring, but wanted his body, would he agree? He didn't have the answer. He hoped it wouldn't come to that, because he didn't think he was strong enough to walk away, and he knew he wasn't strong enough to survive loving her if she did not love him back.

"Faint heart never won fair lady," he told himself, but the ancient saying gave him no comfort. Bold hearts often failed to win fair ladies, too.

Regina arrived at the same time as the servants with their dinner. She put the box she carried to one side and made light conversation until the servants exited the room. She had changed for dinner, into a gown with long sleeves that buttoned right up to the neck—a charming gown in a pale shade of blue that complemented her eyes. Very demure. Very chaste. Was she sending him a message? Had she already made up her mind to stop what was between them?

Even as Ash reminded himself not to jump to conclusions, Regina gave him a counterargument, leaping up to lock the door so they would not be disturbed.

His face must have shown the question he was thinking, for she blushed and said, "Let us eat first."

First before what? He hoped they were both on the same path!

They ate and talked. In silent cooperation, neither introduced the topic of their relationship or the attacks or the investigation. Instead, Ginny asked about Ash's banyan, which took them to a conversation about China, its exports, and its policy of keeping foreigners away from its lands, except in authorized port towns.

That, in turn, took them into a discussion of Britain's trading empire, which led to Ash expressing his opinion about the Company.

"I do not like bullies," he concluded, "whether they are individuals or organizations. Around the world, our land is regarded as a bully, and the policies of the East India Company are a large part of the reason why."

"England is full of bullies," Ginny argued. "Of course, we export them overseas. Look at the way that owners of businesses treat their workers, householders treat their servants, men treat the women dependent on them, and the aristocracy treat everyone else."

She put up a hand when he opened his mouth to object. "Not all of them, I agree. But we do not, as a nation, treat those we consider lesser than ourselves with any degree of consideration and respect."

He conceded her point but didn't think it was exclusively an English trait. "Name me a nation that does," Ash replied.

"I can name a few individuals who have power but use it for the benefit of others," Ginny said. "Have you eaten enough, Elijah? I will put the trays out onto the table in the hall, if so."

He nodded, and she began stacking the empty dishes and plates onto one of the trays. "Won't those be heavy?" he asked, frustrated that he was unable to carry them for her.

She shook her head. "Not at all. I shall make several trips." She blushed and mumbled, "This way, we shall not be disturbed."

"Why, Ginny," he joked, hoping to ease the tension. "Do you mean to be naughty? I hope so."

She cast him an alarmed glance and her flush deepened. "Excuse me." She unlocked the door and made several trips to clear the remains of their dinner. After locking the door again, she remained just inside it, her eyes wary.

"I embarrassed you," Ash acknowledged. "That was not well done of me. If you wish, I am content just to be with you. We don't have to..." He trailed off, not wanting to offend her again.

"I am not accustomed to..." She tossed her hands up in frustration. "I know nothing about such affairs. I do not think I am cut out for them."

It was a stab to the heart. *Faint heart never won fair lady.* "Not an affair, Ginny. Not on my part. Did I not say I wished to court you? I hope for marriage."

She was staring at him, her mouth open. Not the reaction he was hoping for. He made his last cast of the dice. "I love you," he admitted. "I want to spend the rest of my life with you by my side."

The tension went out of her, and her smile broadened. "You do?" she asked.

"Didn't you know?" He was a little hurt. He thought he'd been wearing his heart on his sleeve. Certainly, Rex thought so.

She shook her head. "I hoped, but I didn't know. You said you love me, but I know men say such things to women they would never marry." She crossed the room to take the hand he held out to her. "I have no experience, Elijah. None at all. I lived isolated for more than a decade, and before and since made many mistakes about what motivated men." She looked at their joint hands rather than into his eyes. "I love you, too."

She glanced up through her lashes and her smile turned teasing. "When you actually propose to me, I might even consider accepting."

Ash could take a hint. "Regina Paddimore, Ginny, delight of my heart, would you do me the very great honor of bestowing this lovely hand in marriage on me, your unworthy but devoted knight?" He kissed said hand.

"Yes," she said, instantly, and pulled their hands away from his lips to cover his mouth with her own.

REGINA WANTED—SOMETHING. THIS, then, was lust. This urgent hunger to touch Elijah everywhere, to be touched, everywhere. Especially on her breasts, which ached for his fingers, and lower, where—according to her purely academic understanding of the matter—he would insert his male organ.

The idea had never sounded in the least appealing, though Gideon had said she would change her mind if she tried it. Gideon had been right about most things, and it seemed her body knew more than she, for that part of her also felt hollow and warm and needy.

It would have to go unsatisfied tonight. Elijah was hurt. Re-membering, she gentled the kiss and lifted her head, thrilled when his mouth followed her up until he could lift his head no further.

"We have to be careful," she reminded him. "You are in-jured."

"I am well enough to kiss my betrothed." He grinned, that wicked look back in his eye. "In interesting places, too, if you co-operate. May I undo your buttons, Ginny?"

She hesitated. She should tell him. She couldn't find the words.

"You do not need to be shy, Ginny. Not with me."

She was, but she would try to be braver. That was, after all, why she had worn a morning gown that buttoned down the front, with nothing beneath it but her chemise and front-lacing stays. She nodded and moved closer so he could reach the buttons with one hand, while his other traced feather-light patterns on the flesh of her neck. She could not keep herself from trembling.

"You are tense, my love. How long has it been for you?"

That was the pertinent question, though Elijah tossed it off without a thought.

When she didn't answer, he looked up into her eyes, his fingers pausing on her buttons. "Since Gideon died? Surely not ever since his accident?"

"N-n-never." She stammered the truth in a whisper.

His eyes widened. His hand fell away from the half-open bodice of her dress. The other cupped the side of her face, keeping her from ducking her head away. "Never, Ginny? Not at all?"

"I..." Her voice came out in a squeak. That would not do. She took a breath and tried again, and this time managed to speak out loud. "I am a virgin. There. I've said it."

His mouth twitched before he could impose a solemn expression on it.

"It is not funny," she scolded, attempting to pull away.

His hand on her nape coaxed her to stay. "Not at all funny. How angry you sounded struck me as just a little amusing. I am sorry I offended you."

"I am not angry," she protested. "I am embarrassed."

She started to do up her buttons, but he covered her hands with his. "Please? You do not need to be afraid, Ginny. Or embarrassed. I will do nothing you do not want and will stop whenever you say."

"I have a birthday present for you," she blurted, darting her eyes to the box she had abandoned when she first came in.

He allowed the distraction. "You have already given me the privilege of being your chosen betrothed, my love. That makes this the second most memorable birthday of my life."

"The second?" she prompted.

He took her hand to his lips again. "The first was the day of my twenty-first birthday, when you and I waited out a dance."

He knew what to say to melt her. She found herself leaning towards him, then straightened. The present! It was no longer scandalous to give it to him. "I have something for you. I will just get it."

He let her go, and she brought him the box, waiting anxiously for his reaction.

"What could it be?" he asked, as he undid the string and then opened the box. He lifted the items within one by one. At first sight, they might appear as simple dancing slippers, but every inch was covered with tiny images, stitched in black silk onto very fine kidskin of the same color. A butterfly. A dragon. A sailing ship. A camel. The stories of Ash's travels covered the surface.

She had started the embroidery months ago, during the winter, long before she knew when he would arrive. Long before a romance between them was more than a fireside dream.

Two weeks ago, she had enlisted Lord Arthur's help to take a pair of his slippers to give to the cobbler, who had formed her embroidered leather into the shoes he now examined closely, running his fingers over the shapes, his smile tender.

He turned that tender look on her when he found the raised heel on the second shoe. "Perfect," he said. "Ginny, I knew from other gifts you've sent me that you were a talented artist with your needle, but these are exceptional. How on earth did you make such wonderful things in the short weeks since my return?"

"I sewed them over the winter," she admitted. "A gift to acknowledge a friendship."

"And more?" he coaxed. "Did you dream of dancing with me, Ginny? For I have dreamed of dancing with you ever since your birthday ball, sixteen years ago this day. If it were not for this stupid leg, I would get up right now and show you."

"There will be other balls," Regina assured him. "Ever since you wrote to me about how your built-up heel made it possible for you to join the dancing, I have wanted to dance with you."

"There will be other balls," he agreed. "Come here and let me kiss you, Ginny, to thank you for the most beautiful dancing slippers anyone ever had."

He set them to one side and opened his arms, and Ginny moved into them.

Just then, someone knocked on the room's door. "Mr. Ashby? Regina, are you in there with Mr. Ashby? Open the door."

Regina scooted off the bed. "It's my mother!"

Chapter Twenty-Seven

"TIDY YOUR CRAVAT," Regina whispered, as she did up her buttons.

She unlocked the door, and Lady Kingsley swept inside. Wilson stammered apologies, but Regina waved him off. Her mother was a force of nature.

"Go back to your post," she told him, and closed the door. If her mother was going to make a fuss, she didn't want her servants and her son to hear.

She turned to ask her mother to explain her presence, but Lady Kingsley spoke first, to Elijah. "Do I need to ask your intentions towards my daughter, Mr. Ashby?"

"No, Mama," Regina said. "I am a grown woman, and my actions are my own business."

Lady Kingsley turned a chair around from the desk to face the bed. "You are right, Regina. I withdraw the question."

Regina's indignant response to the lecture she expected died on her tongue, and for a moment, she had nothing to replace it.

"My apologies for not rising, Lady Kingsley," Elijah said, lifting himself off the pillows enough to bow his head, and then collapsing back with a grimace.

Regina's mother frowned. "Are you unwell, Mr. Ashby?"

"Elijah was injured last night, fighting off some attackers,"

Regina explained. She resumed her seat in the chair next to Elijah's bed, so they were facing her mother together.

"Last night?" Mother asked. "Then you *were* with Regina, Mr. Ashby?" She turned a concerned gaze on Regina. "There is gossip about your activities yesterday evening, daughter. I want to know how I can help counter what is being said."

"What is being said?" Elijah asked.

"That Regina had an assignation with Mr. David Deffew in an apartment in Peach Tree Lane. That you broke in, Mr. Ashby, tied Mr. Deffew up, and threatened to shoot Mr. Deffew if he followed. Mr. Deffew claims that Regina has promised to marry him and is threatening to have you arrested for abducting her."

That perverted version of the evening's events had Regina's eyebrows twitching upward. Elijah, however, laughed. "Does Dilly truly think people will believe that?" he scoffed.

"I do not," Mother insisted. "I know Regina despises the man, and I believe her to be right in his assessment of his character. But several of Richard Deffew's friends claim to have seen her coming out of the building with you, Mr. Ashby. Richard Deffew is Mr. Deffew's nephew."

"Did those friends mention that Elijah's servant was with us, and that he and Elijah were half-carrying Geoffrey? I was there because a messenger came to tell me that Geoffrey had been injured in an accident and needed me."

"Ah!" Lady Kingsley commented. "Another abduction attempt."

"It was," Regina agreed. "An unsuccessful one, since Elijah saw me leaving here in a hackney with one of the young men that Geoffrey has been seeing. He came after me. We rescued Geoffrey, who had been drugged, and then Elijah and Fullaby fought off a group of the young men, who attacked us when we left the building."

"Rex was there too," Elijah disclosed.

Mother gave a single decisive nod. "Excellent. The pair of you have a witness that Society will accept as credible."

As opposed to Fullaby and Geoffrey, though to be fair, Geoffrey was not in a condition to be much of a witness.

"Do you happen to know whether Deffew has an apartment in that building?" Elijah asked.

Mother shook her head. "Not to my knowledge. He and his nephew live with Matthew Deffew."

Ash grinned, the flame of mischief in his eye. "Then Society might put its busy mind to wondering why he was in that building at all, let alone in the condition I saw him."

Mother raised her eyebrows and inclined her head. "The condition in which you saw him?" she repeated, making a question of it.

Elijah's grin broadened. "I should tell you that the room to which we were directed, the room in which Geoffrey was being held, was towards the far end of the passage from the stairwell. To reach it, one had to pass a door that had been damaged and loosely propped in the frame, so anyone who looked in that direction would see a man spreadeagled on the bed. He was unclothed and tied by his wrists and ankles to the bed posts."

Impressive! His statement was entirely true but left out any mention of their altercation with Deffew.

"Unclothed!" Mother repeated. "I take it you recognized this man, Mr. Ashby."

"I did," Elijah told her gravely. "It was David Deffew. One wonders how he found himself in that state, in what is, after all, a building full of bachelor apartments. A foolish jape? An assignation gone wrong? Perhaps he was waiting for the owner of the apartment?"

"One prefers not to speculate," Mother replied, dryly, "but it would be unkind not to permit other people to relish such an interesting insight into the character of the man who has been attempting to coerce my daughter into an unwanted marriage."

"I thought you might see it that way," Elijah said, and he and Mama exchanged a smile full of accord.

"May I tell your mother our news?" Elijah asked Regina.

Regina nodded.

Elijah's voice was proud when he said, "I have proposed to Regina, and she has accepted."

Mother crowed with delight. She jumped up and held out her hand to Elijah. "You love her, do you not? Anyone with eyes can see it in the way you look at her. And you desire her, too, which she deserves after all these years. I am so glad." She beamed at Regina, then turned back to shake Elijah's hand again. "Congratulations, Mr. Ashby. You are a very fortunate man."

"I am a fortunate woman," Regina commented.

Her mother bent and gave her a quick peck on the cheek, moving swiftly back to her chair as if she was afraid of Regina's reaction. "I am so glad," she repeated.

"Thank you," Elijah said. "You are the first to know, Lady Kingsley."

"But I may tell people, may I not? This is just perfect. I told Lady Bledisloe that no one with any sense would believe you would go to an assignation with David Deffew when you had a suitor like Elijah Ashby. Just wait until I let everyone know you are betrothed! That will put the last nail in the horrid man's coffin."

Regina's eyes met Elijah's, and a message passed between them. "Would you wait until I have had an opportunity to tell Geoffrey and for Elijah to tell Lord Arthur?" she asked.

"Any time after tomorrow afternoon should be fine," Elijah said.

Mother rubbed her hands together. "I am going to enjoy this. Very well, I shall start tonight, with the true story of why you were there and who with, and a few hints about Mr. Deffew's... condition, but I shall omit the news of your betrothal until you give me leave to share." She stood. "Thank you, Regina. I know I have a lot to make up for, but I am grateful you are trusting me with this."

Regina stood too. "You had your reasons, Mother. I am sorry that I refused to listen to you for so long. I love you, Mother."

Tears filled her mother's eyes. She touched Regina's hand and blinked rapidly. "I love you, too, darling. I always have. I was just too proud and too hurt to see clearly what was right for you. Gideon did well to rescue you from that horrid man."

She took a deep shuddering breath and let it out, forcing a smile. "I shall be off, then. She paused, with her hand on the door. "And Regina? Your buttons are mismatched."

With that, she left.

Regina looked down. Sure enough, she had a loop of bodice with a spare button on one side at breast level, which meant she must have an extra buttonhole at her throat. She undid them all again and turned back to Elijah.

"Now. Where were we?"

His eyes lit up and he opened his arms.

"YOUR MOTHER IS being rather magnificent," Cordelia commented.

Regina, who had been daydreaming rather than listen to her friends, replied, "Mmm?"

Margaret laughed. "You are talking to the wind, Cordelia. Regina is far away."

"The lady is entitled to be lost in thought when she is newly betrothed," Arial insisted. "The question is whether it is memories or dreams that keep her so absorbed."

Regina felt her face heat. It was both. Memories of the evening before, of the kisses and caresses—the heat, the pleasure, the closeness, the sense of something more, just out of reach. Dreams of the something more. When Ash had recovered. When they were wed and could spend private time together without scandalizing her son and the servants.

"She has left us again," Cordelia observed. Then, sharply, "Not there!"

That snapped Regina back into the present. Cordelia had already excused herself and was crossing the ballroom to correct a group of workmen on the placement of an ornamental arch.

Regina was meant to be supervising the decoration, with the help of her friends. "I am sorry," she told them. "I am a little distracted."

"As long as you are happily distracted," Cordelia said, rejoining them. "Your betrothal is much better news than this latest nonsense about Deffew."

"It is a real betrothal, is it not?" Margaret asked. "Not just a strategy because of Deffew's lies?"

"You may take her blush and her smile as your answer," Arial said. "Let alone the fact they have been smelling of April and May for weeks. No, darling, don't go away again. We want to know what really happened the night before last, and how we can help."

Cordelia cast a general's eye over the busy ballroom. "We can leave this for thirty minutes. Let us take tea in my little sitting room."

The tea tray was waiting; the urn bubbled over a spirit lamp. While Cordelia unlocked the tea caddy and measured out the leaves, Regina briefly summed up what had happened.

They listened with rapt attention and the occasional startled comment.

"AND THAT IS when Mr. Ashby was hurt." Regina concluded her story.

"How is he, Regina? Is it bad?" Arial asked.

"It is an old injury," Regina explained. "The doctor says nothing is broken, but the bones did not knit properly many years ago, so a blow in the same place causes more bruising than might otherwise be expected. Elijah is certain he will be up and around again in a few days, but the doctor said at least a week. He is staying at my place until he is well."

"And there goes another blush," Arial said.

"Your mother wants us to spend the afternoon telling everyone we meet that you and Mr. Ashby were at the apartment building to rescue Geoffrey, which we will do," Cordelia informed Regina. "It is nice to know that it is no more than the truth."

"We shall, of course, deny Mr. Deffew had any part in your adventures that evening," Arial added. She put on a kind of cooing purr to say, "No, indeed, Lady Whatever, Mrs. Paddimore did not go to that address to see Mr. Deffew, and nor did Mr. Ashby. They are betrothed, you know. Childhood sweethearts. So wonderful to see a love match. No, Mr. Deffew was the last thing on their minds, I imagine. I happen to know that Mrs. Paddimore has refused him several times."

"All perfectly true," said Margaret, approvingly.

Cordelia sipped her tea, smiling broadly. "Meanwhile, Lord Arthur and your brother William will be doing the rounds of the gentlemen's clubs with my husband and Arial's, wondering how Mr. Deffew came to be naked and tied to a bed in another gentleman's apartment. Your mother," she added, "is a masterly strategist."

"Well, ladies," Arial said, putting down her cup, "Shall we check progress in the ballroom?"

ASH SPENT MOST of the day with Geoffrey, who continued to feel responsible for Regina's abduction and Ash's injury, despite what anyone said. The young man was pleasant enough company. They played cards for penny points, argued trade politics, and shared opinions on books, poets, music, and all sorts of other things.

Regina had joined them for breakfast but had otherwise been out for most of the day.

She came in again late in the afternoon and crossed straight to the bed to kiss Ash on the cheek. "I am sorry to have neglected you today," she said. "Wilson tells me, Geoffrey, that you have been keeping Elijah company. Well done." She gave him a kiss on the cheek, too, and he blushed and ducked.

"There is no one to see except Elijah," she scolded fondly, reaching up to tousle his hair. "He does not think the worst of you for allowing your mother to show you affection. Do you, Elijah?"

"On the contrary," Ash said, honestly. "I just regret my own mother cannot be here to embarrass me in front of other people."

Both Paddimores laughed, as he had intended.

"I have returned to collect my maid and my costume," Regina explained. "I have a few more things to do at Cordelia's, and I will get dressed there. Remember, Geoffrey, you are having dinner with us at the Deerhavens before the ball."

She hesitated, frowning.

"What is troubling you, my love?" Ash asked.

Regina put her hand on her son's arm. "Geoffrey, you will keep your temper, will you not? If anyone says horrid things to you about the other night? We have been telling everyone that Elijah and I came to get you from your friend's place after you were taken ill. That's all anyone can prove. All the rest is speculation and a lot of it is lies."

"I will not stand for people insulting my mother," Geoffrey insisted.

"You will turn it away with a laugh or with scorn," Ash commanded, "rather than making a fuss that will lead people to believe there is something in the rumors."

Geoffrey, who would have argued with Regina had she said the same thing, looked helplessly at Ash. "I can see that's best, but I don't know what to say."

An impish mischief lit Ash's eyes. "For example, 'My dear

Lord Pompous, I am not surprised Mr. Deffew wishes to turn attention away from his own—shall we say activities? I would not have thought him the low kind of worm that would do so by insulting an innocent woman. I suppose she hurt his feelings by repeatedly refusing his proposal. Instead of taking his dismissal like a gentleman, he appears to have decided to find comfort in unfortunate practices and then slander an innocent woman in what I can only assume is some kind of revenge. Alas that a gentleman cannot dirty his hands with such slime. A horse whip, perhaps?' Would that do? Or something like?"

Geoffrey had brightened as he listened to Ash's drawl. "Can we practice some more," he asked.

"Just try not to be late for dinner," Regina said.

Ash and Geoffrey were still entertaining themselves with different ways of painting Dilly as the villain of the piece when Rex and William arrived. Geoffrey insisted on sharing the latest riposte. "If someone suggests to me that my mother has behaved an unseemly manner, I am going to say, 'A mother should be able to be escorted by her betrothed to the bedside of her son without villainous people telling lies about her and casting aspersions on her reputation. It is a sad reflection on Society that these calumnies are being repeated.'"

William nodded. "That's it, lad. You're not letting them get away with it, but you are being civil and dignified."

"You need to go and get changed for dinner," Ash reminded Geoffrey.

Chapter Twenty-Eight

A FTER THE YOUNG man had left the room, Elijah asked the other two, "How bad is it?"

"Our friends are all with us, of course," Rex said. "And many others are content to be convinced. However, some have made up their minds the other way, with Deffew as the victim of a designing woman."

William sighed. "This goes back before this Season, for I've had people tell me that they've known for years that there was something between Regina and Deffew. Mother suspects the Deffews and others in their circle of building up to this for a long time."

"I need to go to the ball," Ash announced.

"Regina won't like it," William warned. "She wants you to stay still with your leg up."

Ash set his jaw. "I won't like it if Regina is scorned at her own ball, and I am not at her side."

"We will need something smaller than a bed," Rex announced. "Lord Kingsley, see if your sister has a sofa long enough for my large friend here to stretch his leg out. Footman to carry it will not to be a problem. And I can have most of the seats taken out of the landau to fit the sofa in. Ash, my friend, you will go to the ball."

William nodded. "That just might work. It is no distance at all to the Deerhavens, and the streets are in good condition."

"It will work." Ash grinned. "Not a word to Regina," he warned.

"Not a word to Geoffrey, then, either," William said. "That boy has promised to never again keep a secret from his mother."

Rex went home to change for the ball and to send Ash the costume he planned to wear, the landau, and a team of footmen. William, having found a suitable sofa, left too. He needed to escort Lady Kingsley to the ball in time to be part of the reception line. The Kingsleys, mother and son, wanted everyone to know that Regina had their full support.

Ash asked one of Regina's footmen to help him with a body wash and a shave. By that time, Rex's valet had arrived with Ash's clothes. "My lord is having most of the seats removed from the landau, Mr. Ashby. It will be here in half an hour."

The worst parts were putting on a pair of breeches and being moved to the sofa, but Ash was soon fully dressed in all of his finery, including the new dancing slippers that Regina had embroidered for him. He was costumed as Oberon, King of the Fairies, to match Regina's Titania. Her maid Annie had been very helpful in providing a description of her costume so he could have one made to match it.

She would be in blue, in a shade chosen to match her eyes. The costume included a gown with a high collar and two long pointed pieces of blue brocade draping from her shoulders nearly to her hem, the insides embroidered and embellished in white, gold, and shades of blue to look like moth wings. Her crown and mask, Annie had told him, were gilt with blue stones. "My lady will look wonderful," she had enthused. Ash had no doubt of it.

Ash's costume was black, embroidered with silver. A black, floor-length robe buttoned from the neck to the waist and then open below. He wore breeches and stockings beneath, a silver crown, and wings, made the same as Regina's. Long trailing wings of black brocade with the moth-effect lining in blue and silver. Lying on the sofa would not show it off to its best advantage, but that could not be helped.

His mask was silver, too. Supported at one side by a silver holder, it was designed to be held in front of the face. He would take it with him, but he didn't plan to wear it. He wanted everyone to know who he was, and to have no doubt that he had come to support his betrothed.

Only four Paddimore footmen remained on duty in the house. Almost all the other servants were working at the ball. Rex's footmen arrived, however, shortly after Ash was ready, and were able to carry him, sofa and all, down the stairs.

The landau was not a particularly stately vehicle, and he had never thought to arrive on a sofa, of all things, but at least Ash was going to the ball.

Chapter Twenty-Nine

T HE BALL WAS not the disaster Regina had feared. Clearly most people had discounted the gossip. Not all. Several guests had sent last-minute cancellations, and others just failed to turn up. Some of those who attended were clearly looking for something scandalous to report.

Masquerade balls often did without a reception line, but under the circumstances Regina wanted to be sure that only invited guests arrived. She, William, and Cordelia had decided to forego public announcements, so that guests could have the fun of being anonymous to other guests, but they set up the reception line so that everyone had to identify themselves to their hosts.

Footmen either side of the main door checked invitations and sent a page boy up the servant stairs with a note naming the new arrivals. Guests then funneled up the main stairs where Regina, Geoffrey, William, and Regina's mother presented a united and confident family front. They were supported by the Deerhavens, as owners of the ballroom.

Those wearing masks needed to drop them briefly as they passed down the reception line, their faces unseen by those waiting behind them and to those who had already entered the ballroom.

Even after the ball started, a page would be sent into the

ballroom to fetch someone to greet new arrivals, just to confirm the person matched the name on the invitation.

The array of costumes made the scene colorful and fantastic. Kings and Queens of England and abroad, other historical and folk tale characters, mythical creatures, gods and goddesses from various pantheons, characters such as shepherdesses and highwaymen improbably clean and richly dressed.

Lord and Lady Arthur arrived in full oriental style. Lord Arthur, tall and blond, made an unlikely if resplendent Indian ruler, but Lady Arthur was every inch his princess, dazzling in a richly colored gown, dripping with gold and jewels from the ornate headdress she wore under a filmy shawl to the ankle bracelets that flashed into view as she walked.

The Stancrofts had taken advantage of the opportunity to be anonymous. Both wore full-face masks that included feathered headdresses, covering Arial's scars and Peter's golden beauty. Their costumes—Arial in blue and Peter in red—were gown and sleeves in one, so that, when they raised their arms, the fabric arched out into great wings either side of their bodies.

The Deerhavens had gone for the mythological—king and queen of winter, him all in black with a stag-horned headdress, and her in white wearing a crown made of ice-like crystals.

Some, of course, her mother among them, did not bother with costumes, but even most of those carried masks. Mother's was a confection in gold lace on a long stick, which she held up in front of her eyes from time to time as a nod to the theme of the evening.

Regina danced the first set with Deerhaven and the second with William. She did not dance the next set, instead circulating the ballroom on Geoffrey's arm to speak with her guests.

If anyone was going to rude, this would be the time. While her dearest friends were as warm or warmer than usual, she sensed a reserve in others, though no one mentioned Deffew or even hinted at his accusations. Not to Regina's face, at least, though undoubtedly, there was plenty of conversation behind her back.

Twice, they interrupted their progress around the room to go and greet a late arrival. The third time a page entered the ballroom, he went to Deerhaven, who looked around to find William. The two men left the room. "I wonder what is happening," Regina said to Geoffrey.

"Shall we go and find out?" he asked.

She nodded, and they followed the two men out. From the top of the stairs, they could hear a furious voice. "We have invitations, and these stupid fools are not letting us in."

"The invitations are for Lord Snowden and his son," Deerhaven replied. "I know Lord Snowden, and you are not he."

"I have invitations. I have a right to be here," the voice insisted.

"Lord Deerhaven," said William, "I believe these to be the Deffew brothers."

Regina peeped over the balustrade, but all she could see was the top of masked heads.

"Take off your masks and identify yourselves," Deerhaven commanded. The two intruders backed away. "Kingsley, unmask them."

The intruders backed still further, then broke and ran, one punching a footman who tried to stop him, the other evading the clutching hands of another footman. In a moment, they were out the door and gone.

"Let us return to the ballroom," Regina suggested, when Geoffrey looked as if he would give chase. He sighed and offered her his arm.

They continued their circuit of the room. William and Deerhaven reentered a while later. She would have to remember to ask them what had happened.

As the set approached a close, they reached Lord and Lady Arthur, and Geoffrey was beside himself with delight to meet the other author of the adventures he so enjoyed. "I would love to travel above all things," he told Lord Arthur.

Really? Regina had had no idea. She eavesdropped on the ensuing conversation even as she chatted with Lady Arthur and Lady Barker. Apparently, Geoffrey intended to complete his university studies and then embark on an inspection tour of all of the far-flung business interests he had inherited from Gideon. Regina wondered how long he had been nurturing such a plan.

He was growing up and away from her.

The music ended, just as a page ran up to whisper to her, "Mr. Ashby has arrived, ma'am."

She must have misheard. She turned to look, and there he was, reclining on the sofa from her private sitting room, being carried down the shallow steps into the ballroom by a phalanx of sturdy footmen.

"By all that is famous!" Geoffrey said. "Ashby knows how to make an entrance."

Those who had been heading to the dance floor had stopped. Even the orchestra had ceased tuning their instruments, staring as avidly as the guests at the adventurer and his bearers.

Ash looked around, caught Regina's eyes, and gave a command. With no dancers in the way to impeded them, the footmen marched across the center of the room, straight toward where Regina stood with her friends.

"The combination of fairy king and English gentleman is quite irresistible," commented Lady Barker. Ash had clearly had inside information, for his costume matched hers.

Lady Arthur chuckled. "Your intended is keen to claim a place at your side, I think."

Regina barely heard them. Elijah was in front of her, his hand stretched towards her. She placed her hand in his, and he lifted it to his lips for a kiss. "I could not stay away, my Titania. Not tonight."

"What of your injury? The doctor said—"

"To keep my leg up for a week." He gestured to his legs. "I am doing so, I promise. Hence the sofa." He grinned and wagged his eyebrows. "There is room enough for you if your duties as hostess allow you time to spend with the man who loves you."

He looked only at her, ignoring the onlookers who had gathered around, and who were relaying every detail of their conversation to those who could not get close. She followed his lead. What did they matter, all these social butterflies who rejoiced in the troubles of others? "I will join you for the supper dance, King Oberon. It is to be a waltz, and I do not intend to waltz with anyone but you."

He kissed her hand again, and the murmuring grew louder. Regina gave herself another moment with her hand warm and comfortable in his, and then withdrew it.

"Put the king's sofa over here by these chairs," she told the footmen. She gestured to the orchestra, and they began to play again. "Oberon, I must go and attend to my duties as a hostess, but I shall return."

On a whim, she gave him the curtsey she had learned from her mother for her presentation to the Queen, down until one knee nearly touched the ground, her gown billowing and then settling around her.

Elijah inclined his head, regal in all but the spark of mischief in his eye, the broad grin on his face. "My queen," he said.

Her own grin was as broad as she commandeered Geoffrey's arm and took him to present to a partner for the set that was now forming.

A crowd soon gathered around Elijah's sofa. Regina caught glimpses of him as she moved around the room. He seemed well entertained, and his arrival had changed the mood of the room, the slight distance Regina had sensed washed away in an air of sentimental approval.

She cornered William and demanded an explanation of the confrontation in the entry hall. William admitted that he and Deerhaven had not planned to mention it to her. "They did not get in, Regina, and they escaped into the night. Nothing to tell. No idea what they hoped to achieve. Put it out of your mind."

That was not hard, since it was time to return to Elijah. As the orchestra began a waltz, she tapped on the shoulder of one of the ladies in the crowd around his sofa. "Excuse me."

The group parted, allowing her passage, and closing behind her.

When Elijah's smile welcomed her, she forgot about them. "It is time for our dance," she told him.

"Ladies and gentlemen," he said to those around them, without taking his eyes off Regina. "I cannot at the moment waltz with my betrothed, but I would like to spend the dance with her, and—though I thank you for your company—your presence is now *de trop*."

Laughing, the crowd melted away, and just the two of them were left, with a large empty space around them.

"All the world loves a love story," Elijah told her, as she perched on the edge of the sofa, his body stretched behind her.

Regina wanted to lean back, to rest her hand on his chest, but that might be a bit much even for this suddenly supportive audience. She folded her hands in her lap to keep them out of trouble. "Thank you for coming."

"I thought you were going to scold me for not staying in my bed," he admitted.

"I am just too pleased to have you here."

He reached a hand to touch her arm. "Has it been difficult, my love?"

"Not awful," she reassured him. "In any social event, there are those who come to pick fault. None of them did so to my face, Elijah. And your arrival appears to have disarmed even them. With you at my side, I do not care. Let us give them no more of our dance."

"I agree. Let's talk about us, Ginny. When and where do you want to wed? And can it be soon?"

REGINA HAD ALWAYS beautiful. The sprite who had captured a part of Ash's heart when he was a boy and garnered more over the long years of his correspondence, now held the entire organ in her kind and capable care.

That she had given him her heart in return seemed a miracle almost beyond believing. This evening, he saw her glow with love, and knew he had been granted that miracle.

What had been added to her loveliness was not the gown in the finest silk, the exact blue of her eyes, though that was a perfect setting for the smooth pale perfection of her throat and shoulders. Nor was it the intricate styling of her hair, dressed high on her head and adorned with some of the pretty trinkets he had sent from the far-flung corners of the world.

It was her eyes that made her more stunning than ever before, or rather the look in her eyes when she smiled at him. The message of love and desire passed between them in their gaze, not needing spoken words to be received and understood.

Indeed, in the half hour of the set, they spoke little. They agreed they would wed by common license within the next few weeks. "Perhaps we could dance at our wedding breakfast," Ginny suggested.

Leaning close enough to keep his remark private, Ash commented, "The waltz, while we are still in company, and then Adam's jig, which is also dance for two, but a more private one."

"I think you are being naughty," Ginny said. "Are you?"

He wrinkled his nose at her and mimed a kiss. "I am thinking very wicked thoughts, my Ginny."

After that, they fell silent, not wishing to shout their feelings to be heard over the music nor to continue the intimacy of heads close together, lest they attract comment that would sully the moment.

A smile, a twinkle of the eye, a press of the hand. These would have to do for the moment, and they were enough for Ash, for soon they would have a lifetime in which to express their love in every possible way.

Towards the end of the set, they were jarred out of their absorption with one another by the arrival of Lady Kingsley and her son. "After this display," Lady Kingsley said, when she managed to call them back into a consciousness of their surroundings, "no one will doubt you have a love match. What better way to seal the approval of Society than to announce the betrothal?"

Ash had to approve the older woman's grasp of strategy. "I am willing to shout our betrothal from the rooftops, but the decision must be Mrs. Paddimore's," he said.

Ginny met his warm smile with one of her own. "William, will you make the announcement?" she asked. "Before supper, if you please."

Her brother bowed and went off to talk to the conductor of the orchestra as the dance came to a close.

Lady Kingsley moved to stand behind the sofa, one hand resting on Ash's shoulder. Geoffrey Paddimore came striding over. "Are they going to do it," he asked his step-grandmother.

"William is going to announce it now, dear," Lady Kingsley said. "Come and stand next to me, Geoffrey, behind your mother."

At a signal from the conductor, the pianist played a series of loud chords and William held up his hand to ask for silence. When everyone was looking in his direction, he began to speak in a booming voice, even as he walked across the floor towards Regina and Ash.

"Ladies and gentlemen, I am about to disclose something that has become an open secret to Society, and particularly to all of you here present, who have seen with your own eyes the attachment between my sister and our childhood friend, Mr. Elijah Ashby, which we have all witnessed developing since Mr. Ashby returned to England.

"As her brother, it is my privilege to announce to you all this evening that Regina Paddimore has accepted Mr. Ashby's offer of marriage." He had reached the sofa and flung out his hand with a magician's flourish. "Ladies and gentlemen, the betrothed couple!"

Chapter Thirty

THE ATTACK CAME in the half-light of dawn. The first Regina knew of it was a crash, mingled with the sound of broken glass. She was out of bed and searching for her pistol before she heard the thud of boot heels and the bang of doors being thrown back against walls. Shouting, too, some of it from Wilson, calling the footmen to defend the stairs to the upper floors.

She grabbed a shawl to wrap around her and hurried down to the next floor, just in time to encounter Geoffrey and Elijah, both carrying guns.

She put a hand on Elijah's chest and protested, "You should not be up."

Another cry rang out over the hubbub. "Fire! Mr. Wilson, they're setting fires downstairs!"

Elijah took her hand. "Ginny, do the maids sleep upstairs?"

Regina nodded.

"Go and wake them. Geoffrey and I will see what can be done to repel the invaders."

Regina obeyed, for his command was sensible. She dropped the shawl so she could move with more speed, and by the time she'd reached the attic, she had a further plan. The maids' rooms took up half the attic space, with the rest given over to storage. And Geoffrey had years ago discovered a little door in the wall in one corner of the attic that opened to a crawl space, which extended the length of the terrace houses.

Two of the smaller maids volunteered to crawl to the other end of the row and make a racket until they were heard. "Tell them what is happening. Get them to send for the constables and the fire brigade," Regina told them.

She told the rest what she had in mind to do next and offered them the chance to escape through the crawl space or at least to stay up in the attics out of the way. They all chose to come with her, bringing impromptu weapons they had ransacked from the storage space—broomsticks, cricket bats, an unaccountably sturdy trident from a costume box.

She and her impromptu army crept down the attic stairs. The hullabaloo from below grew louder as they descended. Cousin Mary peeped around the corner of her door, but otherwise the second floor was deserted. The butler and the housekeeper both had their bedrooms up here, as well as Mary and Regina. Both of them must be downstairs.

They could smell smoke as they tiptoed down another flight and then another, the noise increasing. From the sounds of it, the battle had shifted to the ground floor. Yes. Two footmen, one of them Charles, stood watch on the staircase. Beyond, in the entry hall, Regina could see shifting shapes in the dark and smoke, swinging at one another, grappling, falling back.

"What's happening?" she called down to Charles.

"We have them on the run, ma'am. The servants who were in the basement attacked them from the kitchen stairs, and Mr. Ashby and Mr. Paddimore led a sortie from up here. In a minute, we'll be able to get you all safely out of the house and focus on putting out the fire."

Even as he spoke, someone called out, "Let's get out o' 'ere, lads!"

As the miscreants broke away from the fight and ran, Regina saw Elijah, leaning against the newel post at the foot of the stairs. "Elijah? Are you...?"

He looked up and smiled. "We've expelled them, Regina, but the fire has caught the curtains in three of the rooms. We'll have to send for the fire brigade. Which one do you use?"

Geoffrey loomed out of the smoke. "They're gone from the back of the house, Ash," he reported. "Hello, Mother. We chased them off."

Elijah extended a hand to Regina. "Come. We had better get you and the others to safety."

Cousin Mary silently passed Regina her shawl. "I sent some maids through the crawl space to fetch the brigade and the constables," Regina told the men as she wrapped it around herself.

With Geoffrey on one side and Elijah on the other, she stood in the entry hall, shepherding her companion and her maids out into the street before her. She could hear the crackle of the blaze on the other side of the doors that lined one side of the entry hall.

It was her turn next. She stopped on the doorstep, stunned by the flames shooting out of the broken windows.

In that moment, someone shouted from the street, "Get down," and Elijah hit her with his body, knocking her off the doorstep. As he did, something buzzed past, several inches from her check, and hit the stone of the doorway with a clang. Then she was falling, rolled by Elijah so they landed at the bottom of the steps with him beneath her.

He rolled again, sheltering her with his body.

Another yell, this one high pitched with anguish. "You shot him! You shot my father!"

"Take him into custody," commanded someone.

Regina knew the next voice. "This one is dead, the one around the back wounded, their hired help scattered. It's over."

Elijah must have recognized Mrs. Wakefield, too, for he shifted to allow her to sit up, then hugged her to him, giving fervent thanks. "Are you hurt, my love? That was quite a fall."

"I should be asking you that question. You took the brunt of it, and you should not even be up from your bed, yet. How are you, Elijah?"

He kissed her nose. "Glad you are safe."

The ringing of bells heralded the arrival of not one but three fire carts and their fire fighters. Geoffrey marshalled the footmen and maids to cart water from a street pump, and soon the fight against the fire was in full swing.

While Elijah and Regina were watching, Mrs. Wakefield approached with a gentleman. "Mrs. Paddimore, Mr. Ashby, may I present my husband, Mr. Wakefield."

>>>><<<<

"GIVE ME UNTIL early afternoon, and I'll be able to tell you all," Mr. Wakefield had said, before he and Mrs. Wakefield had left with the constables and their prisoners.

So now they were all gathered in a parlor at the Deerhavens, where Ginny and her household had taken refuge while her townhouse was being cleaned and repaired. Ash, too, aching from head to foot, though the doctor Ginny insisted on calling said he had done no further damage beyond a few more bruises.

William Kingsley had joined them to hear what Wakefield had to say, as had Lady Kingsley. The Deerhavens and Stancrofts, too, and also Rex and Rithya.

Mr. and Mrs. Wakefield had brought with them a young man Ash recognized—the scoundrel who had watched over a drugged Geoffrey Paddimore.

Geoffrey recognized him, too, and started forward with a snarl. Mr. Wakefield put up a hand. "All things in their place, Mr. Paddimore. Muggworthy, go and wait over there. I'll let you know when I am ready for you." The youth slunk to the chair indicated.

"Please sit, Mr. and Mrs. Wakefield," Cordelia said, ever the perfect hostess. "Would you care for a cup of tea?"

Once they were all settled with a cup of tea or coffee, Ash

could wait no longer. "What brought you to Mrs. Paddimore's house in the nick of time to catch our sniper?" he asked Wakefield.

Wakefield nodded towards the young man in the corner. "Young Muggworthy. He overheard the Deffew brothers plotting to use fire and smoke to drive you, Mrs. Paddimore and Mr. Paddimore out of the Paddimore townhouse, and shoot you when you emerged. We came as soon as he told us and arrived just in time."

"It was the Deffews?" Regina asked.

"Yes, it was. Matthew Deffew shot at you and Mr. Ashby and is dead. David Deffew was posted to cover the rear door. He shot at Mr. Paddimore and missed. Mr. Paddimore shot back and did not miss. David Deffew is wounded and may or may not recover in time for his appointment with the hangman."

Regina turned wide eyes on the boy she regarded as her son. "Geoffrey! You never said."

Wakefield recovered control of the conversation. "Let me tell it in order. First, we found out that the Deffews have been lurching from one financial crisis to the next for nearly two decades. They both gambled, and they were as bad at cards and dice as they are at investments. They succeeded in living beyond their means, however, and a close look into their finances made it clear that several members of Society gave them regular gifts of money and favors.

"Blackmail?" Ash asked.

Wakefield nodded. "Mrs. Paddimore, you gave us the hidden piece of the puzzle when you told us about Major Deffew's, and later David Deffew's, attempts to blackmail your father and Mr. Gideon Paddimore. We searched Matthew Deffew's house today and found a hidden safe full of other people's private letters, diaries, and more."

"So that is why they wanted to marry you, Mother," Geoffrey marveled. "Because you are rich."

"Thank you, Geoffrey," Regina said, wryly.

Mrs. Wakefield took up the explanation. "From what I gather, the brothers thought the Paddimores owed them compensation. Mr. Gideon Paddimore responded to the repeated blackmail attempts and to the Deffews' efforts to stir gossip about him and Mrs. Paddimore by blocking any attempt they made to find investors for their schemes. Then Major Deffew was killed attempting to kidnap Mrs. Paddimore. When she returned to Society a wealthy widow, they decided the easiest way to get that money would be to persuade her into a marriage."

Wakefield explained, "Last Season, some of their schemes were working quite well, and David Deffew did not press his suit. Although he had persuaded himself you would accept him whenever he offered, he was not in a hurry to marry. But they had a bad winter. By the time you returned to London this year, they were desperately in debt. Then Mr. Ashby arrived back in England, and Mrs. Paddimore showed a preference for their despised stepbrother.

"That—and the failure of David Deffew's attempts to compromise Mrs. Paddimore—led them to seek revenge instead," Wakefield said. "Young Muggworthy, tell the company your story. Ladies and gentlemen, Mr. Muggworthy is one of a pack of young men who runs with Richard Deffew and his closest friend, a young gentleman known as Chalky, whose real name is Edmund Snowden, son of Viscount Snowden."

Muggworthy stood up when he was addressed and shuffled forward. "I am so sorry, Mrs. Paddimore, Mr. Ashby, Padders. I cannot apologize enough."

"My mother could have been killed," Geoffrey hissed.

Muggworthy stared down at his boots. "I'm sorry. I didn't know."

"You can make amends by telling the company what you were asked to do," Wakefield commanded.

"Chalky and Defter said Padders had attacked Defter for no reason. They said we were going to pretend to be his friends and then Defter would have a chance to get his own back. But

Padders wasn't like they said. Most of us thought he was a pretty decent fellow. And when we found out Defter had said rude things about his mother... But Chalky told us that Mrs. Paddimore had promised to marry Defter's uncle, and Defter was just a bit upset because she broke her promise. I didn't know what to think."

Ash could see what had happened. Uncertain of the facts or of his moral ground, in the way of bewildered young men everywhere, Muggworthy had gone along with the majority.

Muggworthy hadn't lifted his head from its intent focus on his boots. "They said they had a plan to make Mrs. Paddimore keep her word. They wanted me to go and get her, but I wouldn't. I agreed to sit with Padders, though, to make sure he didn't choke or something. Then Mr. Ashby came, and Mrs. Paddimore said that Mr. Deffew was lying, and I was so confused." He cast a quick glance around the room, clearly decided he did not have a sympathetic audience and lowered his gaze again.

"Mr. Ashby locked me in," he complained.

Wakefield interrupted. "Just to save time, I will tell you that Muggworthy had the bright idea of crawling along the ledge below the windows until he found an open window," he said.

"The first one he came to belonged to young Snowden, but it was occupied not by Viscount Snowden's promising sprig, but by David Deffew. As it happens, Muggworthy arrived just as Deffew was being rescued. Carry on, Muggworthy."

The young man gulped. "They were arguing. Mr. Deffew and Mr. David Deffew. I don't like arguing, so I stayed on the ledge. I hoped they would go away, and I could get in. I couldn't help but hear what they were saying."

He fell silent.

"And what were they saying?" Ash prompted.

"Mr. David Deffew was complaining that you were not dead. Except he called you Ash Boy. He said that you had stopped him from fu—ruining a woman to force her to marry him. He must have meant Mrs. Paddimore, because he said she would have given in to save Padders. The Paddimore pup, he said."

Ash knew dozens of expletives in seven different languages and could not think of one that would relive his feelings.

Regina commented, "You said arguing. What did the older brother say?"

"He blamed his brother for insisting on courting the lady. If Mr. David Deffew had forced the lady when she first came out of her blacks, they'd have had their hands on her money early last year. And the pup's too, after they got rid of him." He turned to look at Wakefield. "I figured it out later," he said. "They were going to kill Padders. That's what they meant, isn't it?"

"And attempted to do so this morning," Wakefield agreed. He addressed the room. "Muggworthy stayed on the ledge until they left, then crept back to his room and waited to be let out."

"After Chalky let me out," said Muggworthy, "I went home to my mother's place. I didn't want to be part of it anymore. But the more I thought about what the Deffews said, the worse I felt. So last night, I went to talk to Chalky. I was going to ask him to get his father to stop it, because Mr. Deffew usually does what Lord Snowden says, but he wouldn't listen. He said we were going to have a wild time. Then Defter arrived, and they both told me I had to go to a meeting." He lapsed into silence again.

Wakefield stood to pace the room. "Muggworthy found himself hobnobbing with a gang of miscreants Deffew had recruited in the slums and on the docks. Some of the criminals would invade the house, Deffew assured the young gentlemen. Their only job would be to run messages between those watching the front door, and those watching the back. But Muggworthy, already uncomfortable, became more so when he heard Deffew instructing David Deffew on where to stand for a clear shot."

Muggworthy spoke up. "He said they couldn't waste any more time on the widow, because she had Wakefield and Wakefield investigating. They needed to cut their losses, but he was damned—" he blushed. "I beg your pardon my lady, Ma'am. He said he wanted to make sure Mr. Ashby and Mrs. Paddimore did not win even if they had to lose."

Wakefield gave Muggworthy the first approving nod the boy had received that afternoon. "Muggworthy took the first opportunity to drop away from the group as they marched on your house, Mrs. Paddimore, and came to find me. And the rest you know."

"Mr. Wakefield said he won't let them get to me," Mr. Muggworthy explained, gazing worshipfully at Wakefield.

"Then we owe you our thanks, Mr. Muggworthy," said Regina, graciously.

Ash could not bring himself to be quite so pleasant to the youth who had kept Paddimore drugged and helpless, so he changed the subject, asking, "So the two Indians had nothing to do with it?"

Wakefield laughed. "Shall you tell them, Mrs. Wakefield, or shall I?"

"We soon found why they were watching your household, Mr. Ashby," Mrs. Wakefield explained, "and particularly you, Lord Arthur, and Lady Arthur. Once it was clear they had no connection with the Deffews, I walked up to them and asked them what they were doing."

She grinned. "Lady Arthur, your brothers have followed you here to England to make sure you are well. I have told them to call on you at your townhouse. They were a little concerned that your Maharajah might object, but I assured them Lord Arthur would be pleased to meet them."

Rithya leapt up, clapping her hands together. "Ajay and Sanjith? How wonderful! Rex, can we go home now? I want to show them my children, and my house, and my husband!" She shifted to Hindi in her excitement, then remembered her manners as Rex bowed to Lady Deerhaven. "Thank you for your hospitality," she said.

She inclined her head to the two enquiry agents. "Thank you for saving my friend Ash and my friend Regina. I am so glad no one was shooting at my husband."

The couple left, Rithya back to telling Rex, in Hindi, how excited she was that her brothers had come to see her.

Ginny stood. "Mr. Ashby needs to rest," she announced. She summoned the footmen who had carried him chair and all down from his bedchamber, and they did the trip in reverse. Ash didn't object. He was sore and tired, and besides, he couldn't wait to have Ginny to himself again.

Chapter Thirty-One

T HE NEXT DAY, Regina and Elijah were moving to separate houses. Elijah was returning to Rex's townhouse, and Regina and Geoffrey had been invited to make their home at her brother's place while her own house was being repaired and refurbished.

In fact, Geoffrey had already moved in with William and Mama, and was going to stay on after the wedding, at least until he went back up to Cambridge. Cousin Mary had gone with him. She and Mama had become great friends, and—since both treated William like a favorite grandson—William was sure to have a marvelous time.

Regina regretted she had allowed her pride and her sense of hurt to keep them apart all these years, but when she once again said that to her mother, Mama had insisted it was all her fault. "I should have reached out to you years ago, my love. But we are a family again now, so let us agree to let the past lie, and enjoy the next eight days getting to know one another again."

"It will be wonderful," Regina assured herself as she moved quietly along the deserted passage towards the bachelor bed-chambers. It was only eight days, and she was looking forward to the time with her mother.

She was not looking forward to being separated from Elijah.

Since his rescue the day before her birthday, she had seen him several times a day, often for much of the day, usually at every meal. Even here at the Deerhavens', she had spent time in his bedchamber the first two days of their stay, chaperoned by Cousin Mary or her mother.

They insisted on guarding her reputation by accompanying her everywhere even once Elijah rejoined the household, insisting he was well enough to move around on his own feet with a little help from a crutch.

And that was the rub. When he kissed her, she felt desired and desirable. Away from those drugging kisses and mesmerizing caresses, she worried about how she would compare to all those foreign lovers he had mentioned.

She had hoped for more tonight, with her kind guards both out of the way. Then Elijah insisted on going with Lord Arthur and Deerhaven to the Bow Street Magistrate's Court. Mr. Wakefield had sent to tell them that Lord Snowden had somehow managed to convince the magistrate to hear the case against Chalky and his friends in the evening and with little notice.

Left alone with Cordelia, Regina had blurted her plans for the evening, spoilt now that Elijah had gone out. To her surprise, Cordelia not only approved, but wanted to help. "You are betrothed," she pointed out. "Besides, you are a widow, and there's no need for your mother and your companion to hover over you as if you were a nervous maiden and Ashby a wicked rake."

So here Regina was, counting doors until she reached the bedchamber assigned to Elijah then unlocking the door with the key Cordelia had provided and locking it again behind her.

"Wait for him in his room," Cordelia had suggested. "And if all goes as you hope, do not worry about sneaking away in the morning. I will tell the servants assigned to that floor to stay away until he rings." She frowned a little as she thought about that. "If you take a day dress with you, you can come to the nursery when you get up, and nobody will know where you have been."

So much for being a widow, and therefore free to do as she pleased. However, Regina saw the point of not adding the gossip currently floating around the ton. She sent Annie off to bed early, told her not to come until Regina called for her, and lay down under her sheets to make the bed looked used.

Not that Annie would gossip about me. But still.

Elijah's borrowed room had little of his personality in it. The bed was neatly made. One of the chairs by the fireplace had a book on the table next to it—*A History of a Six Weeks' Tour*, by Mr. and Mrs. Shelley. Regina had read it, but preferred Elijah's travel stories.

Behind a dressing screen, a few clothing items hung on hooks or were folded into baskets. A shaving set and hairbrush stood ready on the table next to the washstand.

None of the rest was personal, from the pleasant paintings on the wall to the finely crafted decanter and glasses on the sideboard. She could have been in any well-appointed guest chamber in England.

She wondered how long he would be. Where should she wait for him? And how? In her night attire and on the bed seemed presumptuous, though she did not think he would send her away.

Perhaps she should take a chair by the fire. Not the chair with the book. She sat on the chair opposite for a few minutes, then leapt up and poured herself a finger of brandy and returned to the chair. The brandy soothed, even as its fire heated her throat.

The fire had been banked for the night, but it had been a barmy day for April, and the bedchamber caught the evening sun. She was warm enough. Warmer still as she wondered about the night to come.

If her friends were anything to go by, she would enjoy it. Not that they discussed such private matters, but she had stayed in their houses. The frequent touching, the longing looks, the disappearances in the middle of the day and early departures for bed. She would have had to be far more innocent than she was and a complete fool not to know each couple enjoyed their marriage bed.

The women, as well as the men, for a glance from their husbands sent them blushing, glowing, and looking decidedly smug. Given the kisses and caresses she had shared with Elijah, she thought she knew why.

Perhaps she should have a second brandy. No. She did not want to be the worse for drink when Elijah arrived, and she did not have much of a head for spirits. How late would he be? Perhaps she should lie down on the bed. Surely, he wouldn't mind? She could lie on the covers and remain fully clothed, so he did not feel that she was throwing herself at him.

She was throwing herself at him. Oh dear. Perhaps it was not too late to return to her room.

As if the thought had summoned him, she heard the sound of his key in the lock.

ASH WAS DISAPPOINTED.

The magistrate had accepted Snowden's excuses, evidence of good character, and pleas for clemency. "Boys of good family misled by a pair of villains," was the verdict. They'd been dismissed into their parents' custody with a sermon and a hefty fine.

The viscount had been made guardian to the orphaned Richard Deffew, which added weight to the suspicion that Deffew and Snowden had been close. However, Wakefield had been unable to prove any wrongdoing.

David Deffew had also cheated the hangman, by dying of his injuries earlier today. Snowden had used the fact in his argument for mercy, calling young Deffew alone in the world, bereft of all family.

Ash had arrived home hoping to spend time with Ginny, only to be told by Cordelia—as she walked off hand in hand with

Deerhaven in the direction of the bedchamber they shared—that Regina had gone early to bed.

As he unlocked his bedchamber door, he hoped she would be up early for breakfast, so they might steal some minutes together before the Deerhavens appeared on the scene, before their separate transport arrived to take them away.

Preoccupied as he was, he still realized instantly that someone was in his room. It took him a moment to realize who it was, the floral fragrance that said "Ginny" to him turning his state of lethal awareness into a different kind of alertness altogether.

His eyes found her in one of his fireside chairs. "Ginny, my love. Is there something I can do for you? Did you want to know what the magistrate decided?"

Ginny shrugged. "I imagine he let them off," she said, dismissively. "No. I wanted something else."

Her face turned rosy red, hinting at thoughts that were dangerous to his fragile control. *We are to marry in eight days. Where is the harm?* Was that his intellect talking, or his body? In any case, he should be sure of his assumptions before he leapt on her.

In fact, given she was a virgin, leaping had better wait for a later occasion. After he had slowly and thoroughly seduced her, to the delight of them both.

He crossed the room and sat down in the chair opposite hers. "What is it you want, Ginny? Anything at all, and if it is in my power, it is yours."

Her color deepened, and she stumbled over her words. "This is our last chance... We will be separating... I wanted..." She bit her lip.

He took pity on her confusion and leaned forward to take her hands. "I think I see where you are going with this, delight of my heart, but you will need to be specific. I don't want my own desires to push you into something for which you are not ready."

His gentleness must have abraded her nerves, for she responded tartly. "If I am not ready to lose my virginity now, Elijah, at the age of thirty-three, the situation is hardly likely to improve in the next eight days."

Ah. She was nervous and had been stewing about the marriage bed. "Do you wish me to make love to you, Ginny? I will happily comply."

Her blush, which had begun fading, "You will need to tell me what to do." she said.

"Anything that pleases you," he told her, tugging slightly on her hands as he stood, so she found herself in his arms. "The only rule is that you tell me if I do something you find unpleasant."

He started with a kiss, and her response turned it carnal and wild. She had learned fast. Only the knowledge that this was her first time let him keep a small modicum of reason, even as his fingers found the buttons that conveniently buttoned her gown down the front.

His mouth followed his fingers, while she clawed at his coat and then his cravat. He separated from her enough to shuck them both off, and then his waistcoat, which she had unbuttoned while he was shrugging his shoulders from his coat.

He pushed at her gown, and she shimmied to make it fall to the floor. He lifted her out of the pool of fabric and carried her to the bed, continuing to rain kisses over her face, neck, and breasts.

They rolled on the bed, unfastening one another's remaining garments, helping one another to remove them, pausing for ever more passionate kisses and caresses, until at last they were both naked.

Ash reared back on his heels, his arousal increasing at the desire with which she regarded him, at the sight of her before him, her lips swollen from his kisses, her nipples tight with desire. As his gaze drifted lower, she moved a hand as if to hide her gorgeous quim from his sight.

"Please," he begged. "Let me see you." He bent closer. "Let me touch you."

She reached for him, and he for her, mouths joined, hands busy, bodies pressed together. Ash devoted himself to Ginny's pleasure. Her moans, her attempts to mimic her actions, the way she arched and writhed—all frayed at his control, but never enough that he forgot the need to see her reach her climax.

As his fingers delved her moisture increased, and so did the passion of her response. She was nearly there. He covered her mouth with his and pressed his thumb repeatedly into the seat of her pleasure, tongue, and thumb in rhythm with his fingers, and she crested with a muffled cry, riding his fingers desperately, surging on and on until at last she sank into stillness, every muscle slackening.

He lifted his head to enjoy the sight of her, relaxed and sated, her eyes closed, her lips curved in a small smile. She was so beautiful. Aroused though he was, harder than he had ever been in his life, for the moment he was content just to admire the woman he loved.

After a moment, she opened her eyes. "But we didn't..." she said and lifted her head to examine the clear evidence that he hadn't.

"That comes next," he said, and she smiled and spread her legs in welcome. He fitted himself to her and slid home with barely a check, assisted by the moisture and her state of relaxation. A moment to allow her to accommodate herself and then he moved, and she with him, in the most ancient dance of all.

He tried to make it last, hoping she would reach her peak again, but he had waited so long and longed for her so much. He was going to come. It was too late to stop it. And then he realized she was with him, reaching for Heaven at the same time as him, and they arrived together, in a crescendo of sensation that left him uncertain where he ended, and she began.

He collapsed as bonelessly as she had a short time before, rolling as he did to set them side by side, still joined.

He drifted, stroking her hair with his free hand, until he felt her begin to shake. Surely, she was not crying? He moved enough to see her face. "Ginny? Are you laughing?"

She was, chortling against his chest "Adam's jig," she gasped between giggles.

Her laughter was infectious, but he didn't know why they were so amused. "The blanket hornpipe?" he suggested, and she laughed still harder.

"I have no idea why that is so funny," he admitted.

"When I was a girl, I thought I knew how I would know the man I should marry," she told him, her eyes still laughing. "I still do, I suppose. All these years, I have been waiting for the perfect gentleman to partner me in one perfect dance."

He chuckled, as he followed her thought patterns. "The mattress reel," he said, and she dissolved into giggles.

He gathered her to him, tenderly kissing her hair. "My perfect lady," he said.

"My perfect gentleman," she responded, "and my one perfect dance."

AUTHOR'S NOTE

The fairy tale of Cinderella appears to be as old as storytelling, or at least as old as poverty and abuse. The key elements are that a person (boy or girl) is born to wealth and status but is left to the care of an adult (often a stepparent) who abuses their charge and makes them work in the most menial of tasks. Through a series of events, often magical, the Cinderella character is raised up above their persecutor by marriage to a monarch.

Versions of the story abound throughout the world, and throughout time. In this book, I refer to the Charles Perrault story, *Cendrillon ou la petite pantoufle de verre*, published in 1697. It is very close to our modern version, including the pumpkin, the fairy godmother, and even the glass slippers. In fact, the name is usually translated as *Cinderella, or the little glass slipper*, though a more literal translation of "Cendrillon" would be "Little Ashes."

My hero Ash might also have had access to the version by the Brothers Grimm published in 1812, *Aschenputtel* (The Little Ash Girl). This version is much more bloody than the Perrault version. In my version, I kill my ugly stepbrothers, but at least I don't have their eyes pecked out by doves.

The Treaty of Amiens marked the end of the French Revolutionary Wars and brought about a temporary end to the hostilities between France and the United Kingdom. As noted in chapter nine, British visitors flocked to Paris.

In May 1803, the British declared war again, out of suspicion about Napoleon's economic and territorial ambitions. The official reasons given were France's imperialist actions in the West Indies, Italy, and Switzerland.

On 17 May 1803, Britain seized all French and Dutch merchant ships in or near British ports. On 22 May, Napoleon ordered the arrest of all British males between the ages of 18 and 60, trapping many traveling civilians. It wasn't until his abdication in 1814 that the last of them was permitted to go home. Ash and Rex were fortunate to have escaped in time.

From that point, Ash's and Rex's travels in Europe and the Middle East were shaped by the war. They left the Kingdom of Naples when Ferdinand, the Bourbon king, was ousted by a French invasion in 1806. They only entered the lands under the control of the Ottoman Empire after the Ottomans changed sides in 1809, with the Treaty of the Dardanelles.

The British had been gifted the colony in Ceylon by the Dutch Republic in 1794, after it was conquered by Napoleonic France. In 1815, just before Ash and Rex got there, the British forced the remaining part of the island, the Kingdom of Kandy, to accept protectorate status. At the time, the colony was one of the few sources of cinnamon in the world, and if I'd known that when I was writing, I would have allowed my travelers to invest in its production. I daresay they did, anyway.

Rex's father's attitude to educating his son in how to be a patron for commercial sex is based on historical examples. As every reader of Regency romance cannot help but be aware, behavior that would have been totally unacceptable if known was regarded as entirely appropriate in private. The unwritten code of behavior was particularly permissive for men.

In the eighteenth century, Henry Fox took his son, Charles James Fox, to Paris to lose his virginity. One young gentleman on a Grand Tour wrote home to his uncle (an Anglican minister) that Swiss brothels were not as good as London ones. Benjamin Franklin advised a young friend to choose an older mistress, because they were more discreet, better conversationalists, and presented less risk of unwanted pregnancy. "And as in the dark all Cats are grey, the Pleasure of corporal Enjoyment with an old Woman is at least equal, and frequently superior, every Knack being by Practice capable of Improvement."

Ash, on the other hand, was closer to his mother and his

model for manly behaviour was a saintly vicar. He wasn't comfortable with the licentious life of his friend. Again, this is based on historical precedent. Attitudes to sexual adventures outside of marriage varied widely, even within families.

ABOUT THE AUTHOR

Have you ever wanted something so much you were afraid to even try? That was Jude ten years ago.

For as long as she can remember, she's wanted to be a novelist. She even started dozens of stories, over the years.

But life kept getting in the way. A seriously ill child who required years of therapy; a rising mortgage that led to a full-time job; six children, her own chronic illness… the writing took a back seat.

As the years passed, the fear grew. If she didn't put her stories out there in the market, she wouldn't risk making a fool of herself. She could keep the dream alive if she never put it to the test.

Then her mother died. That great lady had waited her whole life to read a novel of Jude's, and now it would never happen.

So Jude faced her fear and changed it—told everyone she knew she was writing a novel. Now she'd make a fool of herself for certain if she didn't finish.

Her first book came out to excellent reviews in December 2014, and the rest is history. Many books, lots of positive reviews, and a few awards later, she feels foolish for not starting earlier.

Jude write historical fiction with a large helping of romance, a splash of Regency, and a twist of suspense. She then tries to figure out how to slot the story into a genre category. She's mad keen on history, enjoys what happens to people in the crucible of a passionate relationship, and loves to use a good mystery and some real danger as mechanisms to torture her characters.

Dip your toe into her world with one of her lunch-time reads collections or a novella, or dive into a novel. And let her know what you think.

Website and blog:
judeknightauthor.com

Subscribe to newsletter:
judeknightauthor.com/newsletter

Bookshop:
judeknight.selz.com

Facebook:
facebook.com/JudeKnightAuthor

Twitter:
twitter.com/JudeKnightBooks

Pinterest:
nz.pinterest.com/jknight1033

Bookbub:
bookbub.com/profile/jude-knight

Books + Main Bites:
bookandmainbites.com/JudeKnightAuthor

Amazon author page:
amazon.com/Jude-Knight/e/B00RG3SG7I

Goodreads:
goodreads.com/author/show/8603586.Jude_Knight

LinkedIn:
linkedin.com/in/jude-knight-465557166

CPSIA information can be obtained
at www.ICGtesting.com
Printed in the USA
BVHW042042130423
662312BV00011B/133